LIBER

The moment he began to fall, Emma whipped a knife out of her belt and stabbed herself in the chest without a moment's hesitation. The blade slashed deep into her flesh, sinking into the gap between her ribs. Her face tightened with pain, and she sagged toward him, blood spurting from the wound in a grisly arc. It painted both of their clothes in a red torrent. Christopher's eyes locked onto the bright and shining liquid as horror overtook him.

"Emma!" he shouted. "No!"

Time slowed to an excruciating crawl. His heart seized as he stared at the hilt of the weapon in her chest. This couldn't be happening. He wanted to cry and hide in his room and eat comfort food while someone else fixed this horrible mess, but the cavalry wouldn't be coming. There was no one but him, and that terrified him most of all.

MARVEL XAVIER'S INSTITUTE

LIBERTY & JUSTICE FOR ALL

CARRIE HARRIS

ACONYTE

FOR MARVEL PUBLISHING

VP Production & Special Projects: Jeff Youngquist
Assistant Editor, Special Projects: Caitlin O'Connell
Manager, Licensed Publishing: Jeremy West
VP, Licensed Publishing: Sven Larsen
SVP Print, Sales & Marketing: David Gabriel
Editor in Chief: C B Cebulski

Special Thanks to Jordan D White & Jacque Porte

First published by Aconyte Books in 2020
ISBN 978 1 83908 058 6
Ebook ISBN 978 1 83908 059 3

Cover art by Anastasia Bulgakova

Distributed in North America by Simon & Schuster Inc, New York, USA
Printed in the United States of America
9 8 7 6 5 4 3 2 1

ACONYTE BOOKS

An imprint of Asmodee Entertainment Ltd

Mercury House, Shipstones Business Centre

North Gate, Nottingham NG7 7FN, UK

aconytebooks.com // twitter.com/aconytebooks

For Sarah, fellow Spice Girl
and super hero fanatic.

CHAPTER 1

Loud screams jolted Christopher Muse out of a deep and dreamless sleep. He jerked upright, his heart pounding with the realization that something new and horrible threatened the students of the New Charles Xavier School. Adrenaline flooded his limbs. As an X-Men trainee, he needed to help, even though he'd much rather hide in some dark corner and let the instructors take care of it. But he couldn't abandon his fellow students when they were screeching like that. He tried to leap out of bed, got tangled in the fuzzy blanket he'd brought when he moved here from his college dorm room, and fell into a disjointed heap on the floor.

Fear washed over him as he struggled to orient himself. His limbs were still heavy with sleep, his mind groggy. The overhead lights flicked on, buzzing as they spilled their incandescent light over the small room. Christopher threw his forearm up to shield his eyes, but it did no good. The move had effectively blinded him, leaving him helpless against whomever had chosen to attack them this time.

Not for the first time, he questioned his decision to leave

college to join the new mutant school. The offer had been a no-brainer at first. The manifestation of his powers had been a bit traumatic, what with getting arrested and all, so when Cyclops and his team had shown up to help, he'd accepted gladly. He'd leaped at the chance to join the new school as a member of its inaugural class. If he was going to be completely honest, he'd never been very cool. He was the president of the board game club, favored suits and costume pieces as opposed to normal clothes, and got straight As without much effort. Joining the X-Men had seemed like his chance to finally belong after years of being the last guy picked for the team. For once, he'd been first, and he'd been proud of that.

Now he'd likely be killed by something he couldn't even see, because little spots danced in front of his eyes, and he couldn't hear it either, because of all that infernal screaming. Maybe Magik had opened up another portal to Limbo. The screaming hadn't stopped, and it sounded awfully rhythmic now that he really listened...

He flailed around, extricating himself from the blanket, and sat up. But instead of the expected portal to the netherworld, he only saw his roommate, David Bond, also known as Hijack, perched on the edge of his bed, snickering uncontrollably.

David had only joined the school a few nights earlier. At first, Christopher had looked forward to having a roommate despite the tiny space. He'd hoped for someone he could talk to, because sometimes he felt a bit out of his comfort zone. But David wasn't a "talk things out" kind of guy. He was older – maybe mid-twenties – with a neatly trimmed goatee and an impeccable sense of street style. Because he had a few years on the rest of the college-aged students, he carried himself with an air of massive superiority on an average day. Now he looked so full of himself that he might burst.

"Man, I thought you were gonna wet yourself," David crowed, rocking back and forth. "That was the funniest thing I've seen in ages!"

"What is that awful noise?" Christopher demanded.

"Don't insult my music, dude. This is Ashes on the Breeze. It's a screamo band out of Chicago. They'll be the next big thing for sure. By this time next year, there's gonna be a screamo category for all the major music awards. I'll bet you on it."

Christopher winced. "It sounds like someone's killing a small woodland animal. Please turn it down. I think my ears are bleeding."

"I listen to music every morning. It's bad enough that I had to leave my apartment to live at this dump; there's no reason I should have to give up my tunes too."

"Hey, the school isn't… that bad."

Christopher lied through his teeth, and they both knew it. He'd seen pictures of the old Xavier Institute. The mansion, with its lush green lawn and wood paneled hallways. The tennis courts. The hangar underneath the basketball hoop, where the X-Jet would emerge to take the mutants on their missions. But now Professor X was gone, and the school had split in two. Wolverine ran the Jean Grey School at the mansion, and Cyclops ran the New Charles Xavier School at this converted military installation. Some of the other students claimed that Wolverine had gotten his Adamantium skeleton here. Christopher wasn't sure about that, but someone had definitely done experiments in this building. The kind that weren't exactly on the up-and-up, if you asked him. After spending a little time in the place, he thought Cyclops got the raw end of the deal on the location front.

It certainly hadn't been the kind of school he'd expected when he'd said yes. Mysterious machinery cluttered the corners and filled the unused rooms. The whole place was grungy and dank, with a claustrophobic lack of windows. All of the doors had key card readers, half of which no longer worked. Some of the painted cinder block walls had actual bullet holes in them. He had one over his bed, and he stared at it at night. It didn't do much for his dreams.

"You know, you wouldn't be so grumpy in the morning if you didn't stay up half the night reading," David said.

"It's not my fault that I can't sleep," Christopher replied defensively. "If you don't like that, you can shove it."

The moment the words left his mouth, he knew he shouldn't have said them. After all, he and David had to live and work together as a part of a very small team. But the screamo music pounded at his head after only a few hours of rest, and the past few weeks had been so stressful. He spent every day secretly worried he might die, or be hauled off to some other dimension where he might die, or that one of his new friends might die, and he'd be powerless to stop all of these things from happening.

Because with every passing day, he'd started to wonder if he had it in him to be a member of the X-Men. They all had astonishing mutant abilities that made them useful in a fight. Wolverine had his Adamantium claws and his healing factor. Storm could summon lightning and fog and wind. Cyclops could cut through steel and rock with his powerful optic blast. He couldn't compete. After all, what could he do? Christopher was a healer. He patched up the real heroes after they killed the bad guys, and nothing more.

The pressure had grated on him more and more with each passing day, and now, with David pushing his buttons, he'd snapped. Some teammate he was, picking fights with his fellow mutants. At this rate he'd end up getting kicked out, and then where would he go? He couldn't go back to school. He'd probably end up getting arrested again the moment he showed up on campus.

"You think I should shove it, huh?" David snapped. "Maybe I will. Maybe, just maybe, I'll take that old decommissioned jet out there and shove it right down your throat. What do you think about that?"

Christopher leaped to his feet, and David flew up a second later. The two of them went chest to chest. They were pretty evenly matched in size, although David had a streetwise vibe that suggested he knew how to carry himself in a fight. For a moment, it felt like one was inevitable. Christopher avoided them whenever he could, but he'd been in enough of them that he'd square up if he had to. But then he thought about what Cyclops would say, and about what he would do after he got expelled. He couldn't go back to the university, and he wouldn't go home. He didn't know if his mom would let him in if he did. He had no other options, which meant that no matter how much David angered him, he had to hold onto his temper.

"Look." He swallowed hard, trying to calm himself. "I'm not like you, Hijack. I can't just get into a helicopter and make it do what I want, and I'm supposed to fly today. And that means that I've got to read the damned manual."

"You're right. You're not like me, kid. I'm useful."

For a moment, they stared at each other. Christopher clenched his hands so hard that his amber skin went bloodless at the knuckles. He wanted to hit David so badly. He could do it too, and then heal him afterwards. Cyclops couldn't punish him then, not without evidence, right? But he wouldn't let David make him sink so low. He might not be useful, but he still had standards.

His lower lip trembled as he said, "Low blow, man."

David let all of his breath out in a whoosh as he sat back down on his bed, running his hands through his hair. He looked ashamed.

"You're right. Damn. I'm sorry. I really shouldn't have said that. Especially after you pulled our beans out of the fire in Limbo. People would have died if you hadn't been there," he said.

Christopher shrugged.

"I'm just…" David appeared to struggle for words. "I don't like this. None of it. This place bites. The food is awful; there's no cell service, and there's nothing to do around here other than freeze in the snow and hunt caribou or some crap. But I can't go home. I'm stuck here, and it sucks, and there isn't a damned thing I can do about it."

"Me either."

David finally turned down the music on his boom box, leaving Christopher's ears ringing in the sudden quiet. The two of them sat there for a long moment, awkwardness settling over them like a blanket. Just for something to do, Christopher made his bed neatly and tidied his things. The organization of his side of the room sat in stark contrast to the chaos on David's, but he wasn't about to complain about it. Not now. As he pulled the blanket tight and tucked it in, David's voice split the silence once more.

"I would never drop a plane on you. I hope you know that," he said.

When Christopher looked at David over his shoulder, they both grinned a little.

"That's very reassuring. Thanks," said Christopher.

"Don't mention it."

"You know, you like loud music. I like quiet. There are a lot of empty rooms left in this wing. There's no reason we should have to double up if this roommate thing isn't working. No hard feelings," Christopher offered.

David took a long hard look at him and finally nodded. "Yeah, I agree. I get the whole idea behind it. Nothing wrong with trying to encourage us to make friends, but if it's causing more harm than good, it's probably better that we split up so we don't end up hating each other. I can move out, since you've been here longer."

"Thanks. I think it would be for the best. I'll help you move your things later, if you want."

"That would be cool."

David held out his hand, and after a moment, Christopher shook it.

"You know, I had you pegged all wrong," said David.

"Yeah?"

"When we first met, I took one look at the suit and the goggles, and I thought you were gonna be some kind of weirdo. But you turned out to be a pretty cool cat."

Christopher glanced at the closet, where his suit and tie hung at the ready. A set of steampunk goggles dangled from the hanger, the light glinting off the coppery metal. He'd gotten plenty of flak over the years for his style, and he'd become tired of explaining the reasoning behind it, so he just shrugged.

"You're pretty cool yourself." His teeth flashed in a grin he tried valiantly to suppress. "Although I can't say much for your taste in music."

Before he could even attempt to dodge, a pillow flew across the room, hitting him in the face.

A short time later, Christopher walked down the hallway towards the showers. He wore his fluffy robe, a thin towel hung over his shoulders. A small plastic bag held his clothes and a bottle of shampoo sat tucked in the crook of his elbow. Back at college, he'd had a full caddy of shower supplies, but here, he didn't even have shower shoes. At least if he caught some kind of foot fungus, he could cure it himself.

How sad was it that the best use for his mutant powers was to cure fungal infections caused by the dingy tile? At the end of the day, Hijack had been right. He could control cop cars and jets, and what could Christopher do? Keep your feet from peeling. He had to admit what he'd been slowly beginning to suspect: he didn't belong here. He would never be a true X-Man. The best he could hope for was to be the one who stayed behind in the jet or at the school, waiting to mop up after the real heroes did the difficult work. It was still an important task, but deep down inside he wished he could have gotten a different mutation. Super speed, maybe, or the strength to punch through a wall. Something useful.

Sighing, Christopher trudged into the boys' showers. He carefully hung his suit and goggles from the rusty hook outside the stall, brushing a bit of dust off one sleeve. From a young age, his mother had dressed him up, no matter what the weather. It might be 90 degrees out, and he'd be in shirtsleeves playing basketball. But she'd insisted that the dress clothes might save him one day. She'd said a Black dreadlocked boy in a backwards ball cap might be a hoodlum, but one in a suit could be anything else. He thought people would see what they wanted to, but he'd followed her instructions anyway, and now he felt naked in regular clothes. The suit and the goggles were all a part of his armor against the world, and he needed them more than ever now.

He stepped into the shower, trying to ignore the unidentifiable stains in the corners. When he turned on the water, it came out ice cold, making him yelp. He just couldn't catch a break. He could only hope that the day would get better, because otherwise, he had no idea what he would do. He didn't want to drop out, but he wondered if he would have a choice.

CHAPTER 2

Eva Bell dimly became aware of someone screaming, but it was way too early to do anything about it. She put her head under her pillow and tried to drift back off to sleep instead. Luck wasn't on her side. The screaming continued for a good fifteen minutes, accompanied by a pounding backbeat. Someone in the dorms was playing their music at full volume. When she'd left Australia and moved to the States to join the New Xavier School, she hadn't expected the change to come with quite so much noise.

She sat up blearily, rubbing the sleep from her eyes, and pounded on the wall. The music continued on unabated. She considered marching next door to tell them to knock it off, but that would require putting on pants, and she wasn't quite ready to take such a drastic step. Eva had never been much of a morning person, and she'd been having trouble sleeping. Nightmares. These days, waking up usually took her a good hour and somewhere around three cups of strong coffee.

So she leaned back against the wall, and the cinder blocks

vibrated underneath her head with the force of the rhythmic screaming that emitted from Christopher and David's room. It had been so quiet up until the past couple of days when David had moved in. Now all hell had broken loose. Hopefully not literally, but Eva wasn't willing to place bets on that.

For a moment, she considered the possibility that the noise might not be music. It could be a portal to Hell, or something even worse than that, but she didn't think so. If it had been, she figured that someone would have called for help by now. The school had been massively disorganized when they'd arrived, but things had become much better. They'd established a class schedule and bought toothpaste and everything. The thought of toothpaste made her realize how slimy her mouth felt, and she picked up her watch to check the time.

She was so late for class that it wasn't even funny. A striped coverlet was neatly stretched over the other bed in the room, its occupant nowhere to be found. Her new roomie, a young, time-traveling Jean Grey, had already left for the day without bothering to wake her. Had she even slept? Eva didn't know whether to be worried or annoyed.

She jumped out of bed and pulled on her pants, hurrying toward the door. Although there wasn't enough time for a shower, she had to get cleaned up. She couldn't go to class looking like she'd styled her hair with a hand mixer. This room didn't have a mirror, but she didn't need one to know that her hair stuck out in seven different directions simultaneously. She'd faced enough mornings to know what her head looked like after a night of tossing and turning.

With little time to spare before her first class, she flung open the door and ran down the hallway toward the bathrooms. Inside the girls' bathroom, she found Jean standing at the sinks, the handle of a toothbrush jutting out from between her lips. As always, the sight of her roommate short-circuited Eva's brain for a split second.

She'd grown up idolizing Jean, watching her on TV and reading about her in the papers. She'd had a Jean Grey poster on her bedroom wall, in a super hero display that also featured the Avengers and members of the Fantastic Four. Her dad hadn't liked it; he'd been worried about her so-called mutant sympathies, but she hadn't understood the difference. Why was Captain America one of the good guys but mutants were automatically bad? That made no sense. The source of someone's power didn't inevitably doom them to a life of evil things. Your choices made you good or bad, from the strongest person to the weakest. That was what made Captain America so amazing. He'd always made good choices, even when he'd been so terribly weak. She'd always been his biggest fan.

As she thought of all this, she realized she was staring at Jean like an idiot. Again. Jean gazed right back, the toothbrush frozen in its place. Eva flushed, her cheeks going scarlet with embarrassment.

"I'm sorry," she said. "I'll stop doing this eventually."

Jean took out the toothbrush. "It's OK. This is as weird for you as it is for me," she replied.

Eva could believe it. The Jean that stood before her was in her mid-teens, a bit younger than Eva herself. She was pretty too, with long red hair and a pale cameo of a face. A light smattering of freckles covered her nose, to Eva's surprise. Poster-Jean hadn't had any. It thrilled Eva to know that she knew things about Jean Grey that no one else ever would, like the fact that she had freckles and talked in her sleep.

Jean had traveled forward through time along with a few other mutants, including a younger Cyclops and Angel, only to be stranded in the present after an altercation with evil mutants from the future. The older Cyclops had been working on a way to help them, but in the meantime they'd enrolled as students in the school. That had to be awkward. Eva didn't think she could enroll in a school run by her future husband, in a future where she'd died and most people wouldn't even speak her name. Jean seemed to be managing, but she hadn't exactly opened up about her emotions either, and Eva had been too intimidated to ask.

Instead, she'd been trying to play it cool. Emphasis on trying. She usually had no problem with people, but she'd had Jean up on a pedestal for so long that it was hard to remember to chill. She forced herself to approach the sink calmly, like it was perfectly normal to brush one's teeth with the likes of Jean Grey.

"I bet," said Eva, loading up her toothbrush. "I freeze time, and even I think it's weird."

Jean snorted. "Yeah."

"You doing OK?"

"Peachy keen."

It didn't take a sharp eye for falsehoods to know that Jean was lying through her teeth, and her exasperation made Eva forget her nerves for a moment.

"No, really," she said. "I know we barely know each other,

and I don't want to pry into your private stuff, but who else do you have to talk to? You've got young Scott, I guess. But he's got his own problems to deal with. He's got to go face-to-face with his future self, which must be creepy. I'd just stare the entire time, right? So, you can't really unload on him. And it sounds like Angel is new. He doesn't quite have the… uh…" Eva trailed off and then stuck her toothbrush in her mouth, because otherwise she'd end up sticking her foot in it.

Jean's eyes met hers in the mirror. "It's OK," she said softly. "You can say it."

Eva looked down at the sink. "Baggage. You've got baggage to deal with in this time period, and it's not even your fault. It comes from decisions you haven't even made yet. If you need a mate to help you deal with that, I'm here, OK?"

It took a moment for Jean to respond, and Eva wondered if maybe she'd gone too far. It was one thing to try and treat the time-traveling psychic like a normal person, but another thing entirely to accuse her of having excess baggage.

Then Jean said, "You know, that would be really nice. You want to grab breakfast together?"

"I'd love to, but I'm late for my first class. I don't even have time to shower. I've got to stick my head in the sink and run."

Eva turned the faucet on full blast and shoved her head under it. She gave her face a rinse while she was at it. When she came up for air, Jean handed her a towel. Good thing too, because she'd forgotten to grab one.

"Thanks," she said, examining herself in the mirror.

She wouldn't win any style awards, but for a day of

training she'd do just fine. Her short black hair stuck out in wild, chaotic spikes. One strip at the front had begun to bleach out, growing whiter and whiter for some reason she didn't understand. It had started at about the same time when she'd first exhibited her mutant abilities. Hopefully she wouldn't go completely white-haired, although she could probably pull the look off if she had to.

Jean watched her stare at herself with a look of bemusement. Eva snickered, her cheeks flushing bright red.

"Yesterday, I spent half of the day with toothpaste on my face. Did anyone tell me? No, of course they didn't. So now I'm paranoid. You would be too, in my shoes."

"I would," Jean said with mock seriousness. "Can't be taken seriously as an X-Man with toothpaste on your face."

"See? You get me. Anyway, I'll catch you later. We'll hang out, OK?"

Rushing, Eva swept up all of her bathroom supplies and managed to knock half of them off the vanity. Her hairbrush went skittering into the toilet stall, her toothbrush came to rest against her foot, and her toothpaste was nowhere to be seen.

"You have got to be kidding me!" she exclaimed. "This is positively ace. Why is it that things like this only happen when you're late?"

Jean snagged the hairbrush and offered it with an expression of sympathy. "Here. I'm not sure I'd use it on my head, though. That tile is gross."

"No kidding."

Eva stared at it for a moment before using two fingers to put it on the vanity, trying to minimize her contact with it.

Then she leaned down to look for her toothpaste. For the first three days at the school, she hadn't had luxuries like toothpaste. It had felt like her teeth were growing fur, which sounded like a neat new mutant power but most certainly wasn't. She'd fought for this toothpaste, and she wasn't about to give up on it so easily. Who knew when she might get another tube? She didn't take such things for granted any more.

She didn't see it anywhere near the toilets or in the showers. It wasn't in the corners under the towel racks or the ill-fitting recess underneath the door. That left one place– under the vanity. Under the row of sinks, a set of heavy cabinets held a lone roll of paper towels that looked like it had been immersed in some mystery liquid at some point in the distant past and an ancient ant trap. The cabinets ended approximately six inches from the floor, leaving a gap where the toothpaste could have slid. She reached in and flailed around blindly, unable to see what she was doing and hoping to luck out.

"Here," said Jean. "Let me."

Jean stared at the gap between the cabinet and the floor for a long time. So long that Eva started to get restless. The morning session teacher would be so mad. None of the students had been late yet, and Eva didn't know what the penalty would be. She didn't want to be the example for everyone else. How embarrassing.

"I've got it," Jean said, her jaw clenched with effort.

Slowly, Jean's telekinesis edged the toothpaste out from underneath the vanity. She relaxed, smiling in pleased self-satisfaction.

"Thank you!" Relieved, Eva threw her arms around Jean. After a shocked moment, Jean hugged her back, and any last vestiges of hero worship Eva had harbored slowly faded away. "I owe you."

"You don't owe me anything."

"Oh, but I do." Eva looked at her thoughtfully. "Maybe I can help you get back home. My powers have to do with time manipulation, you know. I'll work on them as hard as I can."

Jean shrugged. "You really think you could help?"

"I think it's worth trying for a friend."

The corner of Jean's mouth twitched, but she didn't argue with the terminology. Instead, she said, "Well, as your friend, I ought to remind you that you're so late that you just stuck your head in the sink. You should probably get to class, don't you think?"

"Crap. You're right." Eva grabbed her things and rushed out, her hair still dripping. "Thanks!"

CHAPTER 3

Eva raced through the empty halls, hoping against hope that Magneto wasn't teaching this morning's class. He began every session promptly at nine, and if she was going to be completely honest, he scared the living daylights out of her. Sure, he'd changed. After the dramatic events of M-Day, when a vast majority of the mutant population had died, and the remaining mutants had lost most, if not all, of their abilities, Magneto had joined the X-Men, leaving behind the Brotherhood of Mutants and their terrorist ways. With so few mutants left and anti-mutant sentiment growing to a fever-pitch, they had to band together for protection, and he had a deep survival instinct.

But something in his glittering eyes still gave her the creeps. As she got to know them, most mutants felt like regular people behind the impressive facades, but not him. She wouldn't dream of chatting with him the way she had with Jean. He just wasn't the kind of person you could treat with casual familiarity, no matter how much he'd changed.

He also wouldn't tolerate lateness, so when she charged

into the Danger Room for morning class, her knees went weak with relief when she didn't see him. Actually, she'd lucked out, because none of the instructors had arrived yet. Instead, the rest of the students milled around the large chamber. She saw Christopher Muse in his crisp suit and dreadlocks, deep in conversation with David Bond. A few feet away, the Stepford triplets stood, their heads bowed and their arms linked together, locking out the rest of the world. Fabio Medina sucked down a sports drink as Benjamin Deeds told him a joke. After the punchline, Fabio roared with laughter and clapped Benjamin on the back, sending the much smaller boy staggering.

Eva slid to a stop and looked at them. Every time she saw their class, she marveled at its small size. It seemed like there ought to be more of them, but they didn't even fill a quarter of the seats around the big circular table at the center of the room. They were so wildly different, though, with such a vast array of personalities and powers. Maybe that's what made it feel like their group contained multitudes. That, and the fact that Fabio shot about a billion gold balls out of his body when he got nervous. Eva wouldn't admit it out loud because she didn't want to embarrass the guy, but secretly, she found it hilarious. They went "poink!"

Now Fabio approached her, holding out a plastic bottle. "You want some, Eva?" he asked. "They say it's orange flavored."

"Thanks," she replied. "I got up too late for breakfast, so I'll bite."

He tossed her the bottle, an easy underhand that she caught with her left and twirled just to show off.

"Nice!" he said appreciatively.

"I played girls' softball six years running," she said, striking a melodramatic pose to show that she didn't take herself too seriously. "I was going to play in uni, but it turns out that I can control time, so my plans changed."

Fabio chuckled. "I know how that feels. What position did you play?"

"Shortstop. And if you make a crack about my height, I'll peg you with this bottle."

He held up his hands disarmingly, a grin stretching his lips. "I wouldn't dream of it."

"If you'll all take a seat please."

Emma Frost's icy contralto pierced the room. Eva hadn't even seen her enter, but she sat at the table as if she'd been there all along, poised and contained. People used to call her the White Queen, and the nickname suited her. Her pale hair, icy blue eyes, and perfect blonde bob gave her a cold, beautiful perfection. But at some point in the past, something must have changed, because she'd abandoned her old all-white getup for a black one. Funny how she'd dressed in white when she worked for the bad guys and now that she'd switched sides, she'd switched colors too. Maybe she'd gotten them backwards, and no one had ever had the guts to correct her. Eva certainly didn't. Instead, she took her spot at the table, where the seats had been bolted to the floor at equal intervals.

She sat between Fabio and Christopher. She hadn't been here long enough to make friends unless you counted Jean. Oh, she was nice to everyone, but it took her a while to really trust people. There were exceptions, of course. It had only taken her a few days to break the ice with Jean, but her difficult situation had bypassed Eva's defenses.

All of the time travelers had been assigned to a different group this morning, but Eva reminded herself that she needed to talk to one of the instructors about helping to send them home at the first possible opportunity. But for now, she needed to concentrate or risk getting lost. Classes here tended to move quickly, and even fifteen minutes' worth of woolgathering could spell serious danger. They'd all learned that the hard way over the past couple of weeks.

"Before we start class today, I'd like to talk a bit," Emma said. She looked around at the semi-circle of rapt students. "I think you all deserve some updates on what's going on as well as some feedback on how you're doing, so these updates will become a regular thing in the mornings. I advise you to show up on time from here on out." Her gaze paused on Eva, and a ghost of a smile flitted over her face before she moved on. Eva's cheeks flared. Somehow she'd been busted, and the subtle rebuke felt worse than whatever Magneto would have done to her. Christopher reached over and squeezed her arm, a gentle and reassuring pressure. It shouldn't have made her feel better, but for some reason, it did.

"I'm not going to blow sunshine up your skirts," Emma continued. "The last couple of weeks have been rough. We've thrown some difficult challenges at you. Some of them were well beyond your pay grade. I want to be clear: there is no shame in failing them. We didn't intend for you to succeed. We simply wanted you to see what you were getting into early on, rather than playing it easy on you and letting you think there would be no actual danger. The danger is real. If you stay, you will face it. We don't intend to sugarcoat that fact for a minute."

As she spoke, Eva wanted to cheer. She'd begun to regret coming to this school, with its grimy hallways and awful food. For a while, all she'd done was follow the instructors around while they picked up more students. She wanted desperately to learn how to be an X-Man, and at times, she'd felt like it might never happen. The fact that classes were finally moving forward delighted her, but a glance around the table suggested that her classmates didn't feel the same. Fabio had broken out in a cold sweat. Eva began to wonder if he might faint. If he fell in her direction, she wasn't sure if she had enough strength to catch him. She caught Christopher's eye and tried to communicate her worry to him, but there was no way of knowing whether the message got through or not. He smiled at her reassuringly, but that could mean anything.

Emma continued on. "We could have done a better job of explaining that from day one. Quite frankly, we could have done a better job at a lot of things. We'd been talking about starting a school, but we hadn't even begun any legwork when we found the first of you. We've been playing catch up ever since. Although I probably don't need to tell you that."

A faint smile played on her face, but it faded when one of the Stepford sisters – Eva still had trouble telling them apart – said, "No, you definitely don't. We spent the first two nights sharing a bed."

"And a blanket," added another.

The three of them glared at Emma. Eva didn't know what

their problem was. Given Emma's reputation, she thought the White Queen had been unexpectedly nice. Then again, the triplets didn't seem to like anyone. Now all three of them shifted their glares to her. She knew they had psychic abilities, but that didn't give them the right to snoop on her thoughts and hold them against her. It just wasn't in good taste to use your abilities on your fellow mutants. That would be like her freezing them when they were adjusting their bra straps and then waiting until someone else was in the room to pop the bubble. Did they want her to do that? She thought the question at them hard and was rewarded with nonplussed looks in response.

"Is there a problem?" Emma asked, looking from the Stepfords to Eva and back again.

Eva wondered if the X-Men teams of the past ever had ridiculous squabbles like this. Did Wolverine and Nightcrawler ever fight over missing snack food? Or did Storm and Rogue ever start tossing lightning bolts at each other because they were tired and grouchy? During infamous battles against the Brotherhood and the Hellfire Club, did Professor X ever have to tell the X-Men to quit squabbling like toddlers, or they'd be grounded? The more Eva thought about it, the more amused she got. She snickered under her breath.

"Care to share with the rest of the class?" asked Emma.

Eva glanced around, a little embarrassed. "Well," she said, screwing up her courage, "I was thinking about some of our screw-ups, and then I was thinking about some of the other X-Men. You know, the good ones. And I was imagining them doing some of the dumb stuff we've done."

"What, like imagining Wolverine shooting gold balls everywhere?" asked Fabio eagerly.

"Not exactly," replied Eva. "Although that sure is a mental picture."

"I think I get what you're saying," interjected Christopher. "Imagine Wolverine and Cyclops and Emma getting teleported to Limbo and having a complete freak out like we did until the Stepfords psyched us up. You'd never expect them to pee their pants like we nearly did, but they had to be new sometime."

Eva flushed as she thought of it. They'd all been transported to Limbo, and instead of greeting the challenge with excitement, they'd all panicked. Even her. Only the psychic powers of the Stepfords had saved them from imprisonment and damnation. If she was going to be a famous superhero one day, she'd have to get over that.

"You had it inside you all along," said one of the triplets.

"We just helped you along a little," added another.

"Honestly," said Benjamin. "We need to get you guys nametags or something, because it's driving me nuts not being able to tell you apart."

They all smiled at him in unison, and he blanched. Eva didn't blame him. Honestly, it was more than a little creepy.

"Um... so yeah. I was just thinking about that," said Eva. "I'm sorry to interrupt."

To her surprise, Emma didn't seem upset about it at all. Instead, she seemed amused. "You're more right than you know, Eva. We made so many mistakes, but they tend to get left out of the stories. Heroism and villainy sells. The more extreme, the better. And once people think they know you, it's hard to change their minds."

"Kind of like how most people feel about mutants," said Benjamin sadly.

They all fell silent. None of them wanted to touch that topic. After all, what could any of them say about anti-mutant sentiments that hadn't been said already? M-Day had come and gone, wiping most of them from the planet, and it had fixed nothing, because the existence of mutants had never been the problem. The problem had always been in the darkness and hatred that grew in people's hearts, and no words would ever change it.

"We should get started," Emma said finally, breaking the heavy silence. "We're going to try something a little different this morning. We're going to do a little team building. Because again, I'm not going to lie to you. Your teamwork is embarrassing. I've never been the best of team players myself. If I think you're bad at it, then you must genuinely be awful. If you're ever going to go out into the field on your own, you've got to get better, because honestly, you're not even close to ready."

Eva and Christopher met each other's eyes, wincing. Eva didn't know what bothered her more, the implication that the students were miles away from seeing any real action or that Emma Frost had a better grasp of teamwork than they did. Emma had never been a team player. Not at the Hellfire Club and certainly not with the X-Men. She had a reputation for it.

"Here's the thing," Emma was saying, "for a long time, I thought I didn't need anyone. When Professor X offered to let me join the X-Men, I turned it down, because I thought that teamwork equaled weakness." She paused, looked down at the table in front of her. "But now I know that I have that backwards. Which is why we're going to work on it. You're stronger together, but only if you can work together. You need to develop trust, and that comes with practice. Are you with me so far?"

She glanced around the table. Everyone nodded.

"We're starting with trust falls," she added.

The students collectively relaxed.

"Is that all?" David asked. "That'll be a snap."

Emma bared her teeth in a chilly grin. "I'm sure you think so," she responded.

Like the rest of the group, Christopher had expected trust falls to be a breeze. He'd thought they were beneath him. After all, he was an X-Man now, or at least a trainee. He didn't think that Shadowcat or Colossus had spent an afternoon falling backwards into their teammates' arms. Kitty would have phased right through them, and Colossus? Well, he would have crushed them into kibble. So he hadn't exactly been thrilled with the activity. He'd put his all into it, because he'd always been that kind of student. He'd always found most classwork to be stupid, but you had to play the game to succeed, so he played it with panache.

It turned out that the lesson had been tougher than he'd anticipated. He kept wanting to catch himself. It wasn't that he didn't trust Eva and Fabio. They weren't the kind of jerkwads to dump him on the ground and guffaw like they'd just pulled a fast one. But he could catch himself, so why shouldn't he?

He asked the question as Emma made a circuit around the room, monitoring their progress. In response, her teeth flashed in a pleased grin that made him instantly nervous. If the White Queen was delighted, she had something up her sleeve.

"That's a good question," she said. Then she raised her voice. "Everybody circle up. Christopher wants to know why he should trust his teammates to catch him when he's perfectly capable of catching himself."

"That's easy," said one of the Stepfords.

Emma shook her finger at them. "Easy for you, maybe. But you three are unique in how well you work together, and you ought to know that by now." They sighed and nodded. "They need to see it for themselves. Besides, could you coordinate as easily with Eva? Or Christopher?" The Stepfords blanched, and Emma nodded. "That's what I thought."

She turned back to the rest of the class and nodded thoughtfully.

"Let's experiment. Christopher, we're going to put you up on the table. You'll fall backwards, and we're going to line everyone up to catch you. I want everyone in on this. It's a long way to fall, and Cyclops will be ticked if we end the session with a head injury," said Emma, completely serious.

They did as she instructed. Christopher climbed up on the table, already regretting his question. Part of him said that a trust fall exercise couldn't possibly be that bad. The other part said that with the White Queen on the other end, a sharpened pencil could be a lethal weapon. They'd learned that last week, so he really shouldn't be making any assumptions of safety.

But he was committed now, and he really wanted to know. Why should he trust his teammates to catch him when he could easily do it himself? If this exercise would show him, he needed to trust Emma Frost enough to volunteer. Maybe that more than anything was the test. If they were really going to become X-Men, they had to be all in, even when they didn't quite know what was going on. Even when they were kind of scared.

He crossed his arms over his chest and clenched his muscles, preparing to fall backwards into the waiting arms of his classmates. Emma climbed up onto the table, standing just a few inches away. Did she plan to push him? Of course, it made sense to be caught when you got shoved over. He wouldn't be able to catch himself. If this was the big lesson that she intended to teach, he would be very disappointed.

"Go!"

The moment he began to fall, Emma whipped a knife out of her belt and stabbed herself in the chest without a moment's hesitation. The blade slashed deep into her flesh, sinking into the gap between her ribs. Her face tightened with pain, and she sagged toward him, blood spurting from the wound in a grisly arc. It painted both of their clothes in a red torrent. Christopher's eyes locked onto the bright and shining liquid as horror overtook him.

"Emma!" he shouted. "No!"

Time slowed to an excruciating crawl. His heart seized as he stared at the hilt of the weapon in her chest. This couldn't be happening. He wanted to cry and hide in his room and eat comfort food while someone else fixed this horrible mess, but the cavalry wouldn't be coming. There was no one but him, and that terrified him most of all.

Eva and Fabio both screamed.

As he fell backwards, he snatched at her desperately. If he didn't heal her right away, she'd be gone. The school's remote location made emergency medical help a non-starter. Every second counted.

He nearly missed her. She collapsed in slow stages, more slowly than he expected, and he almost missed her as he fell backwards off the table. His blood-smeared grip nearly slipped off her. But then he held her tight with one arm, and he pulled the knife free, put his hand over the wound, and his senses slipped over her like a net.

When he'd first arrived here, Cyclops had asked him to describe what using his powers had felt like, and he hadn't known what to say. The first word that came to mind was that it felt intimate. He was lost in the universe of Emma Frost: every atom of her moving in perfect concert. But he could also see the vast and horrible injury she'd inflicted upon herself. He matched her heartbeat to his, brought her breathing in line with his, and sped up the healing process to repair the damage to her heart. Finally, she began breathing on her own again, and he could release her.

He realized then that his teammates held him tight in a cradle of their arms as he embraced the blood-spattered White Queen. While he had tended to her injuries, they'd caught him. They set him reverently on the ground as he inhaled great gulps of air like he'd just run a marathon. His heart raced so fast that he could feel his pulse throbbing at his temples. Normally, his powers didn't tax him so, but the panic and adrenaline overtook him at last. He couldn't believe that had happened. How could Emma have done such a rash thing just to prove a point about teamwork? The lesson didn't match the risk. It didn't even come close.

A metallic clatter drew his attention – the bloody knife, clattering to the tile.

The noise roused Emma. She opened her eyes and smiled in evident self-satisfaction. Then she stood up, calmly retrieving her blade and wiping it clean with a cloth she pulled out of her pocket.

"That's why you need your team to catch you sometimes," she said calmly. "Because sometimes there's a job that only you can do. If you're falling and you take the time to catch yourself, the job doesn't get done. If you don't catch yourself, you die doing the job. The only way to get it done and get out alive is teamwork. You get me?"

"You… that…" Fabio said, gaping.

"Do you have a problem with my teaching, Fabio?" she asked, her expression inviting.

He blanched. "No. No, ma'am."

She turned her pale gaze onto Christopher. "And what about you?"

He didn't know what to think, but he wasn't going to pick an argument with someone who was crazy enough to stab herself. Who knew what else she was capable of? He shook his head, clamping his lips shut.

"Fine. I think that's enough for the morning," Emma said. She looked vaguely disappointed. "Simulation over."

The room flickered and the blood vanished as if it had

never been there. The knife flickered out of existence. The students looked around, shocked and confused. David kept repeating a very bad word under his breath. Christopher stared mutely at his hands as if unable to believe what he saw. No blood. His hands and clothes had been covered with it, but now it was gone. The rip in Emma's clothes where the knife had gone in had vanished.

The whole thing had been a simulation.

He should have known all along. They'd been training in the Danger Room on a regular basis. The room projected very convincing holograms to allow the students to safely engage in combat training. Most of their lectures were held in a series of monotonous grey-painted classrooms in a separate wing. Moving this one to the Danger Room should have clued him in, but he just hadn't thought about it. After all, the instructors had always told the students before they entered a simulation. He'd felt the heat of the blood as it washed over his hands, and it had never once occurred to him that it might be fake.

He felt like an idiot.

Emma put her hand on Christopher's shoulder. When he looked up at her with wet eyes, she returned his stricken expression with what seemed like a genuine smile. He had no clue what she was smiling about. He should have seen through the ruse, and he hadn't.

"I'm sorry to have tricked you, and doubly so to have frightened you," she said in her low voice. "But the lesson isn't as effective if you know it isn't real, and there are two important things to be learned here. Trusting your teammates is important, of course, and I'm glad that you did. If you hadn't trusted them to save you, and I truly had been in danger, it would have put me at additional risk."

"That's what I thought," he cut in, his voice hoarse. "In the middle of it."

"You did well." Her gaze swept the room. "And that brings me to the next point. Out of everyone on the team, you all need to trust your healer, and you need them to trust themselves. They might not be the flashiest one on the squad, but when your blood's spurting out between your fingers, they're the only ones standing between you and the reaper. I know you've had your doubts, Triage, but you belong here. And now we all know it."

The students all stood, silent and thoughtful, and digested this. She flashed them all a pleased smile and sauntered out the door with the air of a cat with canary feathers in its mouth.

"Crikey. Did that really just happen?" Eva asked in a shaky voice.

"I'm pretty sure we're on one of those prank shows. Somebody with a camera's going to jump out at us any minute now," suggested Benjamin.

"I sure hope not," said Christopher. "It won't do wonders for my reputation if I puke on camera."

He staggered out of the room towards the bathrooms, wondering what the heck he'd gotten himself into.

CHAPTER 4

During the lull between classes, Eva decided to follow up on her offer to Jean. The question was: who to approach? The whole stabbing situation with Emma had freaked her out quite a bit, and Cyclops had all of the time-displaced students in the infirmary, running them through the physical and mutant ability testing for new students. She wanted to avoid Magneto if at all possible. That left Illyana, also called Magik, who she finally located in the cafeteria.

Magik looked a lot like Emma Frost, blonde-haired and blue-eyed, but with longer, straighter hair. Like the White Queen, she also favored skintight black clothes, but when she got angry, instead of turning into a giant walking diamond, she pulled a sword out of thin air that was almost as tall as she was and stabbed things with it.

Although given recent events, Eva didn't want to think about stabbing anything. She'd reached her daily quota.

Eva sat down on one of the stools and waited for Illyana to notice her. The sorceress rummaged through the cabinets, grumbling to herself, but finally she realized she wasn't alone. She stood up and dusted off her palms, looking Eva over with a critical eye.

"Something happened," she said in her heavy Russian accent.

"It shows on my face, huh?" asked Eva.

"I would not advise playing cards."

Eva told her everything. Illyana wouldn't flip out on her. After all, she went to Limbo all the time. Eva had been there only once, and it wasn't exactly on her list of top ten vacation destinations. Dormammu, an evil sorcerer, had trapped their entire team there, and she'd had trouble falling asleep at night ever since. Every time she closed her eyes, she thought of the implacable onslaught of the Mindless Ones and their cold, clammy hands, the sorcerer's mocking laughter, or the fiery, barren expanse of Limbo stretching further than her eyes could see. If she never had to return to that awful place or see Dormammu again, she'd be happy. Returning there repeatedly – on purpose, no less – took guts. They'd been lucky to escape with their lives.

"So that's what happened. Should I be worried?" she concluded.

"Worried?" asked Illyana. "About what?"

"About Emma."

"Oh." Illyana waved her hand. "I wouldn't be concerned. Injuries suffered in the Danger Room do not carry over into the physical world. Once, I came out with a headache, but I believe that was due to the shrieking."

"But it was awful! We all thought she'd stabbed herself in the heart. That's not normal!"

Eva started to shake. She'd held it together pretty well

after that first shocked scream. After all, she'd seen death over the past few weeks. She'd been on a few easy recruiting missions recently chasing down minor criminals, and sometimes innocents had gotten caught in the crossfire. Their instructors had taught them to be careful about friendly fire, but bad guys never seemed to care who they hit, so Eva had seen a few things that shook her, but nothing as extreme as what Emma had done. She could have died. Couldn't she have given Christopher an inspirational poster with a kitten on it and called it a day?

Illyana poured her a glass of water and slid it toward her. Woodenly, Eva sipped at it. Water sloshed over the edge as her hand trembled uncontrollably.

"I understand what you are saying. It was not so long ago that I was in your shoes. I was new once too, and many things were overwhelming." Illyana looked down at the table, sighing. "What Emma did is in many ways awful. It was a hard thing to see. But there is no lasting damage, yes? Your life goes on unchanged?"

"Except for the nightmares," Eva muttered. "I'll probably dream about it. I dream about Limbo a lot too."

"Ah. I am sorry about that. Dormammu is trapped there, and he's eager to find a way out. He sees his magical skill as a road to power over the planes of existence, and it blinds him to what is truly important. That, I think, is what frightens me: the possibility that someone might live blinded to all but their own desires."

Eva shuddered. Although she hadn't thought it through completely, Illyana was exactly right. The evil sorcerer had scared her for many reasons, but most of all, what had stuck with her was the aura of bottomless hunger that hung around him. She knew without a doubt that he would stop at nothing in his quest for power. She had faced that and lived. She might bear the scars, but she could still go on.

"Limbo bent us, but it didn't break us," she offered.

"Exactly." Illyana agreed. "Every fear we face teaches us a lesson. Today, Christopher learned how strong he is. When the chip is down, as you say, he now knows he has the courage to save a life under great pressure. He has never done this before, and now he knows without a doubt that he can. Doubt is a powerful thing. One day, the self-confidence he acquired from Emma's stunt may save someone's life. Now he believes in his abilities in a new way, and so do the rest of you."

Eva thought about that for a moment, staring into her glass. She'd never doubted Christopher's abilities, but she had to admit that they weren't exactly flashy. After spending years idolizing the likes of Captain America, it was hard to be impressed by a healer. But maybe she should be.

"I reckon you're right. But I'm still glad it wasn't real," she said, sagging with relief.

Illyana smiled. "The Danger Room takes some getting used to. Don't get too comfortable. I have seen students who started thinking that everything was a simulation and got their butt handed to them on a platter because they quit trying. They thought that since the damage didn't carry into the real world, they didn't have to give their best effort all the time. So, their instructors met them in the real world and wiped the carpets with them. Don't make the same mistake, yes?" She paused, looking at Eva's face. Eva tried not to snicker, but Magik's occasionally mangled slang cracked her up. "That is the right phrase, yes? Wiped the carpets?"

"I know what you meant," Eva replied, her lips twitching.

"Good enough." Illyana paused. "I had better move. I was hoping to sneak a snack before lunch, and I don't want to get caught." She grinned.

"Oh! I almost forgot. Before you go, can I ask you a quick question?"

Illyana quirked an eyebrow and gestured for her to get on with it.

"I feel awful for Jean, and all of the other time-travelers too. Being stuck here must be difficult for them," said Eva.

"It has been awkward."

"No kidding." Eva snorted. "So I thought I'd offer to help. I'm the only mutant here who manipulates time, after all. Maybe with my time bubbles and your magic, we could…" She fumbled for specifics. "You know. Send them back somehow. You know more about these things than I do. Obviously, I'd need more training."

Instead of laughing off the idea, Illyana tilted her head and gave it genuine consideration. Eva could have hugged her. It would have been easy for Magik to dismiss her as new and inexperienced, but she chose to take the suggestion seriously instead.

"It isn't a bad concept," Illyana finally admitted. "Although its success will depend on the limits of your abilities."

"How do we find out what those limits are, and does it involve any stabbing?" asked Eva.

Illyana's teeth flashed as she grinned. "Probably not, although I make no promises."

"I cannot believe I'm joking about this already."

"The mind is a flexible thing. You are already recovering. When you return to class, you will see." Illyana paused. "Speaking of class, I believe that you are late."

Eva looked around for a clock, swearing.

"That is OK. I am teaching, so you're off the hook." She grinned again. "Find me a snack and join us in the Danger Room. We will discuss this more later."

The cafeteria had been stocked mostly with pre-packed food, yet another sign of the last-minute preparations that had been involved in the school's establishment. Eva scanned the cabinets with a sense of disappointment. She hadn't realized it was possible to get sick of junk food, but she was well on her way. She didn't feel the slightest temptation to snag something extra for herself. It was just all so boring.

She didn't know what Illyana liked, so she ended up bringing a variety of convenience store delicacies – an apple, a granola bar, and a little bag of chips. When she opened the door, David clicked his tongue and said, "Late again?"

Illyana froze him with a stern glance before crossing the room toward Eva, her slinking stride like a lion on the hunt, and plucking the chips from her hands.

"Thank you for fetching these for me, Eva," she purred. "Please take a seat, and we'll get started."

Eva did. The group had shrunk since the morning session. To her intense relief, Christopher sat in his usual spot, looking none the worse for wear. He even smiled at her as she sat down. Fabio, David, and Benjamin also remained in their places. The Stepfords had gone to another class, and Eva didn't particularly miss them.

"We're going to do a combat session in the Danger Room for the rest of the morning," Illyana said with a wide grin. "I hear that you passed one earlier thanks to Christopher's excellent grace under pressure, so I expect you to do well." Christopher's cheeks went crimson, and Eva clapped him on the shoulder. "You must defend yourself against all attacks. If all members of your team survive, you pass the test. Simple, yes?"

Eva's heart sped up, fueled by nervous excitement. She'd given up her entire life to learn from the best, and it felt like the instructors were finally ready to teach. But on the other hand, she already had enough nightmare fuel for the next year. She knew Emma's trick with the knife would haunt her for a long time, as would her experience in Limbo. She still wanted to be an X-Man; she'd wanted to be a hero all her life. But coming to this school hadn't been at all what she'd anticipated, and sometimes she wondered if she'd made the right decision. If she really had what it took.

"Piece of cake, with Chrissy-boy here on our team," said David, reaching out to ruffle his hair. "As we saw earlier, he can heal anything. So we've got this in the bag."

Christopher ducked out from underneath his hand.

"Please don't call me that. Not unless you want me to call you Davey-boy," he said.

"I'd like to see you try it," said David, jokingly.

"Dang," said Christopher, ignoring him. "If I would have known we were fighting in the Danger Room, I would have brought my staff. Is it too late to run back to my room for it?"

"Yes. Make do without it."

Illyana left the room, leaving no space for argument. The conference room fell away, to be replaced with a busy city street. Scents assailed Eva's senses, overpowering after the long weeks spent in the unending monotony of the school grounds. The hallways all smelled the same: old and cold, with an underlying layer of mildew that never fully abated no matter how much they cleaned. Now, exhaust and smog hung in the air, a cloying fume that threatened to choke the air from her lungs. But underneath it she could catch the sweet scent of the oranges from the fruit vendor on the corner. A woman who walked past them as they stood dumbfounded on the sidewalk wore a pretty floral perfume.

"I smell tacos!" David declared, pointing. "I'll be right back."

"Tacos?" Fabio's expression lit up. "I'd kill for just one meal that didn't include a squishy sandwich."

Eva looked in the direction that David had indicated. A taco truck sat halfway down the block, its gaily striped awnings shielding its patrons from the bright midday sun. Chalkboard signs advertised a long list of daily specials. Her stomach rumbled. After weeks of peanut butter and jelly sandwiches and bags of potato chips, she would have killed for a bite even though she knew it wasn't real.

Fabio nearly stepped out in front of a bus in his eagerness to get his hands on one. She yanked him back with both hands just in time, and the driver laid on the horn with both hands and then saluted them with his middle finger for good measure. But Fabio just grinned.

"Guess I should watch where I'm going, huh?" he said. "I'll be right back."

"That's a bad idea," said Christopher, his face pinched with worry. "One, you don't have any money."

"I do," said David, beginning to search in his pockets. "I always carry my wallet."

"Two," Christopher continued without waiting for him to finish. "That taco truck isn't real. This is the Danger Room, remember? We're here to fight. There are probably big... bad guys. Of some sort. Waiting to punch us."

"Yeah, and you heard Magik, right? All we got to do is survive it." David ran his hand through his hair and straightened his shirt. "Look, we've been cooped up in that school for weeks, eating the same boring food in the same boring room. This is our first opportunity to live a little. I'm gonna go with Fabio to scope out that truck and talk to some honeys. You in or not?"

"This is a bad idea," said Christopher.

"You probably can't even eat those tacos," added Eva, scowling in disapproval.

"Well, I'm gonna try," declared Fabio.

"You in, Benjamin, or are you hanging here with these killjoys?" asked David.

"Uh..." Benjamin said, looking between the two groups with the stricken expression of someone who really wants to be anywhere but there.

"Feel free to join us if you want," said Fabio. "Those tacos are calling my name, and man do they sound good."

"But..." said Eva.

She wanted to stop them, but short of grabbing onto

them, she didn't see how. Idiots. Their immaturity made her want to scream in frustration. But she could do nothing but exchange an exasperated glance with Christopher as Fabio and David dashed across the street. They didn't even use the crosswalk, which in this traffic was like holding up a sign saying you'd really like to be run over by a car, please. It nearly happened, too. Multiple times.

When they finally hit the sidewalk on the opposite side of the street, she heaved a sigh of relief. The feeling lasted all of about half a second. A big black van with SWAT painted on the side came screeching around the corner and squealed to a stop right in front of Eva, Christopher, and Benjamin, blocking their view of their teammates.

Benjamin said, "What the…?"

Then the rear doors opened, and SWAT officers spilled out. They wore head-to-toe black body armor and black helmets that gave them what Eva thought of as the evil motorcycle rider look. White letters spelled out SWAT on their chests, just in case their affiliation wasn't entirely clear. Each officer carried a lethal-looking assault rifle in black gloved hands. The weapons loomed menacingly in Eva's mind. She'd never even seen a gun in real life before about a month ago, and now they seemed to be everywhere. She'd become desensitized enough that she no longer flinched every time she heard gunfire, but the sight of drawn guns still shook her badly. She couldn't help but wonder how fast the bullet would travel after being fired from one of those things, and how much pain the Danger Room would allow her to feel.

Although she knew the cops were only holograms, and

Triage would heal any injuries they received anyway, her heartbeat still sped up. Adrenaline flooded her veins. The urge to run and hide made her feel physically ill. The thought of being shot terrified her. Even worse, someday she would have to face down armed assailants in real life. For the first time, she began to wonder if she had it in her or if she would fold at the first sign of true danger.

Two of the guns swung around to point at her, and her heart began pounding so hard that she felt it in her ears. All rational thought went out the window. She completely forgot about the fact that this was a simulation, because every cell in her body screamed that she was in terrible danger.

"If you move, we will shoot you, mutant," said the one on the left, her voice distorted by the speaker on her helmet.

Eva swallowed, her throat dry. She held her hands out to her sides in an attempt to look nonthreatening. "This is a mistake," she said.

One of the officers poked her in the sternum with the gun, pushing her backwards, isolating her from the others.

"You can't do that!" Christopher exclaimed. "She has rights!"

For a tense moment, it seemed like everything would explode into violence.

"Hey, guys," David called out, casually interrupting them before chaos could break out. He leaned on a lamppost on the opposite sidewalk, Fabio at his side. A few of the cops whirled to train guns on them while the others continued to aim at Eva and Christopher. But David didn't even blink. Eva had no idea how he could be so chill. Maybe he also had unflappable calm as a super-power? He gave them a cocky grin and said, "You didn't forget to put that transport vehicle in park, did you?"

After a shocked moment, all eyes went to the armored vehicle, which sat idling at the curb. Nothing happened. For a moment, Eva considered making a run for it while the cops were distracted. The tips of the assault rifles wavered a bit as their owners watched the van nervously, but then they steadied as it failed to move. Eva's heart sank. She'd lost her chance to escape, although she probably would have ended up getting shot anyway. Everything seemed so hopeless. Then the van's engine roared to life and it lurched into gear and began spinning wildly. Everyone scattered as the vehicle careened out of control. Tires screeched as it barreled toward Benjamin, who tripped as he scrambled to get away. Eva barely managed to yank him out of the way. They toppled to the pavement, the thick tire passing inches from his head. His face went white.

The van tore past them, swerving through a lane of traffic before it collided with a pickup truck. It pushed the pickup out of the way and continued on, mowing through a sports car before it impacted on a fire hydrant, sending a spray of water shooting into the air.

"You nearly killed me!" shrieked Benjamin.

"How was I supposed to know they didn't straighten the wheel out before they got out of the vehicle? You always straighten the wheel out!" David shouted back.

POCK POCK POCK!

The dry pop of gunfire drowned out the remainder of the argument. Everyone on the street screamed, running for cover. David and Fabio dove to the ground as bullets pounded the pavement around them. They had nowhere to go, no cover to seek. If someone didn't do something, they'd die.

Eva tried to psych herself up. She had to help them. But she couldn't make herself move. She didn't want to die. She wanted to go home.

"Help!" shouted Fabio. "Please! Dios mio!"

The plea firmed her resolve despite her terror. She stood up and whipped her hands out, freezing the officers and their van in a pale blue, gleaming time bubble. Bubbling took a certain amount of mental strain, although she'd been practicing so much that it had started to get easier. It felt like she was trying to balance a shaky stack of plates in place with her mind. Once the plates had stabilized, she could release them, but for a moment she had to concentrate with every fiber of her being. The more complicated the subject, the harder it was to bubble it. Bigger bubbles would be like trying to balance huge towers of plates. Moving targets would be like trying to balance them while walking. Bubbling during a fight sometimes felt like trying to balance plates while riding a unicycle on a tightrope. She just couldn't carry the mental load, which was why she usually tried to catch all of the bad guys in a single bubble. Had she gotten them all this time?

As she looked around, a bullet caught her in the shoulder, spinning her around in a wild loop and throwing her to the ground. Strangely, it didn't hurt as badly as she'd expected. Her arm felt like lead though, and the impact site burned. She toppled onto the pavement, her eyes wide with shock.

Apparently, she'd missed at least one of them, and he had good aim.

Benjamin threw up noisily on the ground right next to her head.

She clutched her shoulder and rolled onto her back, avoiding the puke. They were dangerously exposed out in the middle of the street and desperately in need of cover, but she couldn't make herself move. Her shoulder had begun to throb, and although it didn't hurt as badly as it should, it still didn't feel good. She had no desire to take another bullet. As she hesitated, Fabio emitted a barrage of heavy gold balls from his body at random, knocking some of the shooters – and David – to the ground. He'd lost control completely. He flailed his hands, looking panicked as the balls kept on coming, taking out windows and setting off car alarms.

"No! Stop!" he yelled.

POINK! POINK! POINK!

"AAAH! What'd you do that for?" yelled David, rolling on the ground and holding his head. "That hurt!"

Benjamin retched again.

Eva didn't know what to do, and things weren't looking good.

CHAPTER 5

In the midst of all this chaos, Christopher crept belly down on the dirty street toward Eva and Benjamin. The occasional stray bullet pinged off the concrete nearby, but so far, he'd escaped miraculously unscathed. He could do nothing about the car or the shooters. He had no idea how to get them out of this mess. But he could do one thing: his job. He could make sure Eva didn't die.

To his shame, he'd frozen at first. The moment the cops had arrived, years of conditioning had taken over, and he did as his ma had taught him when he was young. He took his hands out of his pockets and kept them visible, stood still and waited for instructions, and kept his expression open and polite regardless of the weapons trained on him.

"They'll be looking for an excuse to see you as a thug, Christopher," she'd said. "So don't you give them one."

So he'd stood there, trying to show the cops how unthreatening he was, and they'd started shooting anyway. He'd watched it in shock and horror, a cry stuck in his throat, knowing all the while that he needed to help – in fact, it was his job to help – but he was too afraid to do it. Because he'd grown up knowing that he couldn't afford to give anyone the excuse to put a bullet in him, and now he had even more reason to be cautious, because he was a young Black mutant in America.

Eva's injury had finally thawed him. Here was something he could do. Some way he could help. He wasn't much of a fighter, and he hadn't brought his staff with him anyway. So he'd dropped to the ground and made his way toward her, thankful to have something to do that made him forget his fear of becoming a target himself.

He finally got to her, tugging her toward him as gently as possible. But before he could heal her, he felt the cold muzzle of a gun press against his temple. His entire body went rigid with fear.

"Hand her over, mutant," said the SWAT officer who stood above him.

To his immense shame, he almost did it. But if he did, what did that say about him? His Ma had said he'd amount to nothing, like his pop, and he'd wanted to prove her wrong. Turning Eva in to save his own skin would only prove her right, and he was stronger than that. After all, he'd saved Emma Frost earlier.

The thought of her reminded him – this wasn't real! The cops, the guns, all of them were Danger Room simulations. The bullet might hurt, but it wouldn't kill him.

"If you want her, you'll have to go through me," he said, closing his eyes.

Illyana's voice came from thin air. "End program."

The room faded away in slow stages, taking the SWAT

officers, their guns, and the busted van along with it. Eva's bullet wound faded away along with their surroundings. As the simulation ended, Fabio moaned.

"Wait!" he exclaimed. "I never got my taco!"

After the Danger Room, the students filed into the dining hall to find Magneto standing over a tray full of wrinkled paper lunch bags. Christopher felt too numb to even consider eating, given everything that had just happened, but he didn't have the energy to protest. Fabio didn't share his reluctance. He picked up a bag and peered eagerly inside. His face fell.

"Turkey sandwiches again?" he asked. "Man, after taunting us with tacos, that's harsh."

Magneto's eyebrows crept toward his hairline, salted with iron gray. Although age lined his face, he still looked like he could spit nails. Literally. Christopher had only seen him in action a couple of times. He didn't often accompany the students on their training missions, and as a result, none of the students were very comfortable with him. Fabio shrank before his disapproving gaze, and his hand closed over the lunch bag.

"I mean, it'll be fine," he mumbled.

"There are more important things in play than the contents of your sandwich, Mr. Medina," said Magneto. "You would do well to remember it."

"Yes, sir."

Fabio's eyes went to the ground and stayed there. He took his lunch and found a spot at a table. David joined him a moment later, clapping him on the shoulder. The other boy's face instantly lightened, and they began to joke around.

"Man, we should have gotten those tacos, and let the others handle the cops," said David. "They would have been fine."

"You think?" Fabio looked down at his squashed, sorry excuse for a sandwich. He took a bite and chewed sadly. "They sure sound good right now, even if they weren't real."

"They were real to us, man. That's good enough for me."

Benjamin sat down, his elfin features eager underneath his fluffy hair. "So they were like Schrödinger's tacos?" David and Fabio turned identical blank looks in his direction. "You know, real and not real at the same time?" Still no reaction. "Well, I thought it was funny." He tore into his sandwich.

Christopher debated joining them but quickly decided against it. Although he and David had made peace after their argument that morning, they just didn't mesh. He didn't see how anyone could joke about the morning's training. It had been terrifying and sobering in turn, not funny at all. Besides, the morning's excitement had given him a rare headache. Strange how he could heal others but didn't know how to help himself. So he found a spot at an empty table and hoped the relative quiet might help.

He opened his lunch bag, pulled out his food, and groaned. Slices of green, glistening pickles covered the sandwich, their juice soaking the bread. He hated pickles. There were few things in the world that he hated more than pickles. Sighing, he tried to soak up the juice with his napkin, but the bread already looked like a lost cause.

Eva pulled out the chair opposite him and took a seat. He

nodded a hello and continued blotting his sandwich as she watched with a curious tilt to her head.

"You don't like pickles," she said, finally understanding.

"I hate them," he responded, exhaustion saturating his voice.

"Allow me." She took his sandwich from him, opened her own, and divided them both in half. She put the two pickle-free halves together and slid them toward him, keeping the remainder for herself. "There you go, mate. Problem solved."

It was such a little thing, but he could have cried. Exhaustion, probably. Lack of sleep exacerbated by stress could make anyone a little overemotional. He wanted to curl up in a corner and take a nap, but that wasn't going to happen. Oh, no. He had a class. He'd finally passed enough flight simulator modules to take his first solo flight in the X-Copter. He'd be lucky if he didn't kill somebody.

He took a bite of his sandwich. Once he got some food into him, he'd feel better. Hopefully.

"Thanks," he said, indicating the sandwich. "I'm famished."

"Hey, I owe you one. You healed me, didn't you?"

"Didn't get a chance. Illyana ended the simulation too soon. But I would have," he said. "You almost passed that simulation singlehandedly. Between the two of us, I think we could pass it if we had another chance."

"No doubt." Eva nodded, holding her fist up for him to bump. "We make a pretty good team. We'd have it in the bag." They bumped fists, and then she continued. "We should team up for the copter flight this afternoon. You're cleared to fly too, right? Cyclops said we have to pick partners, and I don't want to team up with somebody who isn't going to take it seriously." She scowled in the direction of David and Fabio's table.

"Yeah, cool. OK," he said. His headache faded as the joy of being asked took him over. It felt good, especially after such a crappy day. He waggled his eyebrows at her in a ridiculous manner. "You sure you're not just trying to get me alone for a couple of hours?"

"Not in the slightest," she said, deadpan.

"OK. Just joking."

A heavy hand fell on his shoulder, making them both jump. Christopher looked up to see Magneto standing over him. The mutant leader's face cracked into an unaccustomed and somewhat terrifying smile. He looked less pleased and more like he might take a bite out of someone.

"I hear you had an eventful morning, Triage," he said.

"Oh. Uh..." Christopher gulped, fighting the wave of nerves that threatened to overcome him. Yes, Magneto might be intimidating, but they were on the same side. "Yeah. But it wasn't real."

Magneto squeezed, and it took every ounce of willpower Christopher possessed not to cry out.

"Ah, but I know full well that the Danger Room feels real in the moment. And still, you went to the aid of a fellow mutant. Well done, my boy. Very well done. I shall have to keep my eye on you..."

With that, Magneto released him, patting him on the shoulder like an approving uncle and wandering off to check on the other tables. Christopher pulled a can of apple juice out of his lunch bag and opened it with a hand that didn't shake, possibly because it was entirely numb.

"That wasn't frightening at all," said Eva in a quiet little voice.

"Nope. Definitely not terrifying."

"So we're flying together?"

"Yeah. Can't wait. The sooner we get out of this cafeteria and away from him, the better."

Their eyes met over the table in a moment of complete understanding.

CHAPTER 6

After lunch, all Christopher wanted to do was find some quiet place and sleep. The food had calmed his shaking, but his heartbeat still pounded in his ears. He needed rest, preferably without any screamo music. He didn't care what David said; he thought it was awful. Hopefully they could move him to another room before lights out.

He considered sneaking back to bed for a quick nap but rejected the idea. It just wasn't his style. At college, a lot of his friends had skipped classes to hang out on the quad, enjoying the sunshine and playing games for hours on end, but he couldn't afford to lose his scholarship. The hard work ended up paying off anyway. At the end of the semester, while his friends had panic attacks and sent desperate emails to their professors trying to salvage their grades from the garbage heap, he rested easy on a soft carpet of straight As and excused finals.

He hadn't skipped then, and he wasn't about to start now. Not when the material really mattered. If he forgot the difference between cubism and surrealism, which they'd covered at lengths in Art History, it wouldn't really matter. But here, the things they learned might literally make a difference between life and death. As a result, David and Fabio's preoccupation with the tacos bothered him more and more as he continued to mull it over. How could they think about snack foods when lives were on the line? How did he see it when they didn't?

At least Eva seemed to get the importance of their training. He had to admit he'd written her off when they'd first met. She looked like a goth pixie with her striped hair and short black skirts, and for some reason, when he heard her Australian accent, he inexplicably thought of surfboards. He'd thought she'd end up being a slacker, but he had been very wrong. He'd heard Illyana and Cyclops talking in the hallway on the way to lunch; she'd offered to train extra in order to help send the time-displaced mutants back to where they came from. It was a big offer, and he respected her for it.

She'd also helped him with his pickle dilemma, which qualified her for sainthood in his book.

To his surprise, he found himself looking forward to their flight that afternoon. He did, however, find a quiet corner of the lunchroom to rest for a few minutes after he finished his food.

When Eva shook him by the shoulder, he startled.

"Come on," she said. "I let you sleep as long as I could, but they're starting."

He sat up, rubbing his eyes.

"Thanks. Guess I needed that more than I realized. How long was I out?" he asked.

"Only about twenty minutes. I would have let you go longer if I could, but…" She shrugged. "I told Cyclops you were in the bathroom. If you don't come to class soon, I think he'll send a rescue mission to the toilets."

"Thanks."

He rubbed his hand over his dreadlocks, trying to shake the cobwebs from his mind as she led him toward the hangar. The halls were silent. Tomblike. Their footfalls echoed as they rushed to class, and the only other movement in the hallway was the repeated flashing of the security panels at the doors. Although they'd tried, none of the instructors could figure out how to turn them off. Illyana had destroyed one of them with her Soulsword, but Cyclops had told her to knock it off before she'd got any further.

"We're flying in groups," Eva explained breathlessly as they neared the hangar doors. "You and I are first. Jean and young Scott are working in the simulator while we fly. Then when we come back, Fabio and David go out, while Benjamin and Angel do the simulator. The Stepfords are going to do their flight tomorrow."

"Sounds like a plan." Christopher flashed her a thumbs-up. "Now that I've had a nap, I'm feeling pretty good."

Cyclops stepped into the hallway and stared them down. Although they couldn't see his eyes from beneath the red-tinged ruby-quartz glasses, Christopher felt pinned by the instructor's knowing, laser-like gaze.

"Nap?" said Cyclops. "I thought he was in the bathroom."

"I… fell asleep on the toilet. That's what took me so long," Christopher lied transparently.

Cyclops stared at him for a moment, clearly not believing the lie for a moment. But he let it go anyway.

"Right. If you two would join us, we can get started."

"Yes, sir," said Eva. "Sorry, sir."

She scurried into the room, looking chastised, and Christopher followed. He liked the hangar. The tall ceilings made the space feel less cramped in comparison to the rest of the facility, and it smelled like clean metal and cold air. In here, he couldn't detect the faint tang of mold that pervaded the lower levels. The X-Copter sat in the first bay, gleaming and perfect, ready and waiting for their flight. In the second one, a broken-down X-Jet sat amidst a pile of parts. Cyclops and Hijack had been tinkering with it nonstop, trying to get it working again. But apparently it needed a variety of parts that weren't just available at the corner store, if they'd had a corner store to go to. Which they didn't, since the school was located in the middle of a frozen wasteland and didn't have any nearby corners.

Next to the X-Copter stood Jean Grey and the younger Scott Summers. Christopher had found that being in a room with both versions of Cyclops was very distracting. He couldn't resist the urge to keep comparing them. Young Scott had a fresh-faced appearance. His jaw was firm and strong, his bearing straight and proud. He looked ready for whatever life threw at him. The older version bore a few more scars, and the dark hair had a hint of gray at the temples, but he was still the kind of man who could lead armies. Christopher had followed him. He wanted to learn from the best, and he firmly believed that Cyclops was it. Learning from him made sticking around this dump worth it.

Cyclops cleared his throat and looked them over, making sure he had their full attention before beginning.

"OK, let's get started. We're going to review the pre-flight inspection. You might be tempted to skip this. I know a lot of X-Men who felt the same." A ghost of a smile flitted over his face. "They'd tell me things like, 'But Kurt can teleport us out if the engine cuts out over the ocean,' and 'But Ororo can keep us aloft with wind currents if the propellers fail,' but that's rubbish. You do the inspection. Every time. Because doing it every time creates habits, and the one time you forget to will be the one time you need it. You got me?"

His gaze raked over them once again, the overhead lights flashing off the red glint of his visor. They all nodded, and he nodded back.

"Good. Once we're done, we'll be splitting into teams. Eva and Christopher are flying, and Jean and... uh... Scott..." His hand rubbed at his face, rasping against unseen stubble. "That's awkward. You'll work on the simulator."

Christopher raised his hand. "Can I ask a question?"

"You don't have to raise your hand, Christopher. Just ask."

"OK." He put his hand down. "When you get a pilot's license, you have to put in hours and hours of training before you can fly solo. Is this legal?"

"How do you know? Is your dad a pilot or something?" Jean asked, with what sounded like genuine curiosity.

"I used to be addicted to this flight simulator video game, and I wanted to be a pilot for a while. It was just one of those kid things."

"Oh." She smiled. "That's cute."

"It's a good question, though," said Cyclops. "And I'm going to answer it honestly. Will you have a legal right to land at an airport? No. We're not flying out of those. We're not using air traffic controllers. We're bypassing a lot of government regulations here, because we're needed. People are dying, and I think that makes cutting a few corners justified. But I understand if you're not comfortable with that. I also understand that your training kicked up a notch this afternoon, so I want to make this clear, and I'll make sure that every student hears this. If at any point you feel that this place isn't for you, I'll take you home. But you need to know that the minute you go back, I can guarantee that S.H.I.E.L.D. will be breathing down your necks. You're a mutant now, whether you like it or not, and I'm sorry to say that this means that your life will never be exactly the same as it used to be. But it's still yours to do with as you like."

He paused, looking around at them. Christopher met his gaze, nodding in appreciation for his honesty. Then Cyclops turned to Jean and the younger version of himself. "I … wish I could make the same offer to the two of you. But we're working on that."

Jean's luminous green eyes gazed into his. "It's OK."

They stared at each other for a long moment. Christopher felt incredibly awkward, and he was fairly sure that he wasn't the only one. Young Scott shifted uncomfortably, clearing his throat. The tension felt somehow incestuous and strange. When the older Cyclops looked at Jean, he saw the wife he'd lost. But she hadn't lived through any of that, and the whole convoluted mess made Christopher incredibly uncomfortable.

"That sounds good," he said loudly. "Thanks for explaining it."

Cyclops blinked, coming back to himself with visible effort. "Right. So let's go through all of the elements of a thorough inspection, and then we'll get you up in the air. Your task will be to take the X-Copter to a specific set of coordinates, record what's on the ground, and then return back. You don't need to land the copter, especially since as Christopher here has pointed out, we don't have the authority to do that. So we only do so when there are lives in danger. Are you with me so far?"

He paused, waiting for their nods.

"Good. Now, this is an older model of the X-Copter, so you'll notice some differences from the most current model. I know we've gone through them in class, but let's review and make sure we've got them all down pat before I let you fly it…"

He led them around the massive, gleaming body of the armored helicopter, pointing out its many attributes and features. Although Christopher had spent hours memorizing all of this, he wrote it all down again. After all, this knowledge could mean the difference between life and death, and he needed to be ready.

CHAPTER 7

For the third time, Eva adjusted her headset, squirming in her seat with barely restrained excitement. She'd always loved to fly. Some kids had looked forward to vacations spent on beaches or on ski slopes, but she'd always had an irrational love of planes and airports. She even liked the uncomfortable seats and tray tables and the little bags of peanuts. She couldn't believe she was in the cockpit of a state-of-the-art stealth helicopter now. It fired missiles, for heaven's sake.

Cyclops had pointed out during the pre-flight briefing that said missiles had been removed for the purposes of their first solo flight, but still. It had the capability, so it counted.

Christopher sat in the pilot's seat next to her. His poised stillness sat in stark contrast to her hyperactive fidgeting. She didn't understand how he could be so calm, like he flew million-dollar machines every day. If they crashed, she wondered if Cyclops would make them pay for it. Once, she'd dropped an entire tray of dishes during a summer job at a cafe, and she'd had to work overtime to cover the cost. She wondered idly how many hours of dishwashing would pay for a helicopter, and if she'd be dead of old age before she finished.

"You ready?" Christopher asked, cutting off her nervous woolgathering.

"I think so."

"Call it in, then." Before she could protest, he flapped his hands at her. "I know how psyched you are. You should do it."

"OK," she replied, absurdly pleased. "Thanks."

She adjusted the headset again – four times now – and opened the private channel to the communications tower where Cyclops would monitor their progress and respond to their radio transmissions. They used a private channel, which he'd assured them would be undetectable by outsiders.

Eva adjusted the mic in front of her lips and said, "Comm Tower, this is Copter X. Preparing for liftoff."

The speakers hissed in her ears for a moment, and then Cyclops replied: "Acknowledged, Copter X. This is Comm Tower. Liftoff imminent. Hangar bay area clear."

Her eyes went to the checklist that Christopher had set out between the control panels. His neat printing provided a simple reminder of the steps they needed to follow, and although they'd both drilled this process in the simulator until it had become boring, moving it to a real helicopter had made it alien and nerve-racking again. She worried that the novelty might make one of them miss something, and the list helped alleviate that fear.

With each item they checked off the list, Eva grew increasingly more confident. Based on his widening grin, Christopher felt the same way. He flipped the switch to start the rotor, and it hummed to life above them. The cabin lifted imperceptibly as the helicopter hovered on the verge of takeoff. Eva's stomach did a slow flip, and she whooped aloud with delight, forgetting that her comm channel remained open. Christopher snickered as she covered the mic with an expression of abject horror, her cheeks suffusing with red.

"Comm Tower, this is Copter X, and I'm a moron," she said finally.

When Cyclops responded, it sounded like he was trying not to laugh, and that just made her feel more humiliated.

"Copter X, this is Comm Tower. Don't worry about it," he said. "Looks like you're ready for liftoff?"

"Yes, sir," said Christopher, when it became obvious that Eva was too stricken with embarrassment to respond. "Prepared for liftoff."

"Copter X, you are officially cleared for liftoff." Cyclops's smile came clearly through on the radio. "Remember to keep your mic on at all times. It's the only way to reach us. Have a good flight and come back safe."

"Thank you, Comm Tower," said Christopher. "We will. Copter X out."

He toggled off his mic and took the yoke. They'd agreed that he would take the lead on takeoff, but Eva would stick the landing. They'd work together on programming the in-flight navigation and telemetry. Otherwise, the flight should be a piece of cake. The autopilot would do most of the work once they got up in the air.

The X-Copter rose with minimal bobbles out of the hangar and over the frozen woods that surrounded the school grounds. Cold winds buffeted the aircraft, but its top-of-the-line stabilizers protected them from much more than a gentle rocking sensation. More than anything, they felt a strong forward push as the copter tilted forward, rocketing through the air at terrific speeds, scattering startled birds and frightening small woodland creatures. They would remain at low altitudes to avoid crossing into protected airspace for the duration of their trip, which Eva thought would make for a beautiful and exhilarating ride. She'd worried that the sound would hurt her ears, but with her headset on, she found it quite bearable.

"Hey," Christopher said, the headset transmitting his voice to Eva without the need to shout, "you want to program in those coordinates?"

Eva nodded, her cheeks still flushed. "Let's get it done before I die of embarrassment."

"If you hadn't shouted, I would have," he said kindly. "I felt like my stomach was going to climb out my esophagus."

"That's very... graphic. But thanks. Gimme the coordinates."

He read off the numbers as she typed them into the navigational computer. They triple checked them, neither of them wanting to get their ultimate destination incorrect. The newer nav computers would calculate the location based on the latitude and longitude provided, but these older models lacked that functionality. They only calculated the travel time – about two hours. They would just have to wait and see. It would be some significant building or location. If they ended up circling a tree in the middle of a random field somewhere, they'd know they had transposed a number somewhere.

Once they'd programmed the nav computer, they had little to do but watch the scenery go by. According to the compass, they were heading roughly south-west, which could indicate a variety of potential destinations. For a while, she tried to guess, but she kept getting distracted by the gorgeous views. After spending so many days pent up in the awful confines of the cinder block monstrosity of the school, getting out was a relief that she decided to allow herself to enjoy.

The enjoyment lasted for about an hour before boredom set in. They passed over some small towns, and abruptly the scenery became much less interesting. Cars and houses and the occasional swimming pool still closed for the season. Spring had just begun to rear its head, but in Canada the snow still clung to the lawns and the shady spots.

"I hate snow," muttered Christopher.

"You can say that again," replied Eva.

"Do they have snow in Australia?"

"In some parts, yeah. Not so much where I'm from, which is fine by me. I miss it, though. Home." She swallowed against the sudden lump in her throat. It hurt to talk about home. That made her think about her mom. They'd butted heads when Eva had been younger, but now her mom was her best friend. After spending so much time dreaming of being somewhere else, Eva thought it was awfully ironic that she'd been overwhelmed with homesickness ever since she'd got here. She hurriedly changed the subject before she became overemotional. "Does it snow a lot where you're from?"

"Michigan? Yeah. It snows and then the snow ices over. The inside of your nose freezes when you go outside. I don't recommend it," said Christopher.

"My feet have been damp ever since we got here. I had no idea this was a thing. My boots claim to be waterproof, but they were lying. By the time summer comes along, I expect my toes will have shriveled up into prunes," Eva declared.

"That's … I'm sorry?" said Christopher.

"You should be," Eva declared.

They grinned at each other.

The nav system beeped, and Eva twisted in her seat to check it.

"We're a little over a half hour out," she announced.

"Great. I wouldn't want to be late for dinner," Christopher said. "I hear we're having sandwiches."

Eva groaned.

"You think they'd notice if we landed and got something to eat?" he continued, looking out the windows. "I think we're closing in on Chicago."

She peered out her side. They flew over the deep, gray waters of what she assumed was one of the Great Lakes. A bustling metropolis hugged the distant shore. Although she wasn't one of those people who could easily identify major cities by their skylines, she assumed that Christopher was right. Based on their approximate location and the size of the city, this would most likely be Chicago. The thought of deep-dish pizza and hot dogs made her mouth water.

"It sure is tempting," she admitted.

"I bet they even have tacos."

She was looking for something to throw at him that wasn't bolted down when the comms crackled to life once again. But instead of Cyclops, they heard an unexpected and unfamiliar voice. The speaker was male and difficult to hear due to the static crackling in the speakers.

"You in the X-Copter! Who's up there?" he said.

Christopher and Eva exchanged a look.

"Who is this?" Christopher finally asked.

"Sabretooth. Who is this?" came the none-too-patient response.

Sabretooth!? Eva could barely believe her ears. Like a lot of kids, she'd grown up half terrified of Sabretooth, the mutant terrorist who bombed human buildings and gutted people who stood in the way of what he wanted. That's what the stories said, anyway. Although Cyclops had shown them over the past few weeks how many of the stories about mutants were exaggerated by people who feared what they didn't understand, so now she took them with a grain of salt.

Christopher seemed to feel the same, because he answered with obvious caution in his voice. "This is Triage," he said.

"One…" A hiss of static cut through the transmission. "… damned trainees."

"We're on a–"

"No time, kid. Tell whoever's in charge…" More static. Eva swore, fiddling with the dials, but it did no good. "Status is critical. We need pickup immediately."

"Where?" Christopher demanded. "Tell us where."

"Grace Museum. We've got…" HISS. CRACKLE. HISS. "Send the cavalry."

The comms went silent.

"Sabretooth?" Christopher said. "Sabretooth!? It's just us, man. The other X-Men aren't here; it's just us!"

But there was no answer. They'd lost their connection. Sabretooth was gone.

CHAPTER 8

The X-Copter rocketed towards the Chicago shore as Eva desperately punched buttons, trying to get Sabretooth back on the comms. If only someone at the school had taught her how, but her training had fallen short once again.

Unfortunately, Christopher offered no help. He sat there, mumbling, "This is not happening. This is seriously not happening," over and over until she thought she might snap.

Finally, she said, "If you don't stop that, I'm going to slap you right across the face."

He blinked. "Please don't. That would hurt."

"Precisely. Now will you help me out here? I'm trying to find Sabretooth again."

The prospect of having something concrete to do knocked the remaining panic out of Christopher's eyes. He nodded. The two of them worked through the comms channels with rapid efficiency, but unfortunately they came to the same conclusion: they had no way to reach Sabretooth again without going to the Grace Museum as he'd requested.

"What do you want to do?" Eva asked.

Christopher stared at her like she'd suddenly sprouted horns. "I'm going to pretend you didn't ask that. It's a no-brainer, Eva. Sabretooth wants the real X-Men, so we deliver them. We radio back to Cyclops. We'll swing back and cart them out here to take care of Sabretooth and whatever mess he's gotten himself into. Because, trust me, if it's too much for him to handle, it's definitely out of our department."

"I thought we were real X-Men," she said, not unkindly.

"In training, sure. But trainees do stupid things like get distracted by tacos, and then people die. We need to go by the book here."

Eva understood his logic, but so far the training they'd been offered had fallen short. The horrific experience with Dormammu in Limbo had more than proven that the entire team needed guidance they weren't getting. Eva didn't think it was intentional neglect. Cyclops and the rest of the instructors were trying to fight a war and found a school at the same time, and they were simply spread too thin. Meanwhile, it felt like the world was burning down around her. Maybe she just had to take the plunge and learn by doing. The idea both frightened and excited her by turns.

Besides, if they called Cyclops, what would he do? She wasn't sure he would even believe them if they told him about the distress call. If he decided to believe them, he'd have to cancel class to come all the way here and help. She didn't see the sense in doing that when she and Christopher were perfectly capable of picking Sabretooth up and flying him back to the school. How hard could it be? She just had to make Christopher see things her way.

"I hope you know that I respect you," she said. "But I disagree."

"Oh yeah?" he asked.

"We can do this. All we have to do is land the chopper, pick up Sabretooth, and get back into the air. Hauling Cyclops or any of the other instructors all the way out here to do something we're fully capable of handling ourselves is silly."

"So why don't we radio in and tell him that?"

"Do you really think he'd listen? He's overprotective. I've got to be honest, Christopher. Sometimes I feel like we're spinning our wheels at that school. They've made a lot of improvements, but half the time I feel like we'll never learn how to be real X-Men if we don't figure it out ourselves."

"Yeah," he said reluctantly. "I know what you mean. But he'd be really ticked off if we went off on a mission without saying anything."

"Not when he realizes what we did," she said. "This could be an opportunity to broker peace between the X-Men and one of their most long-standing enemies. He'll be grateful, don't you think?"

"Maybe…?"

"Besides, what could go wrong? All we have to do is pick Sabretooth up and leave."

Christopher shifted his goggles on his forehead, a gesture she had begun to recognize as a nervous habit. "I'm not sure about that," he said. "I'm getting pretty good with the healing thing, but I still need a lot of work with the staff, and I didn't even bring one. In a fight, I'm practically useless. I know you're pretty good with your time bubbles, but we're talking about something that's got Sabretooth's panties in a bunch!" His voice dropped to an awed whisper. "It would probably kick our butts."

"What do you think I am, nuts? We don't engage. We tell Cyclops that we're hearing a rattling noise, and we're going to touch down to check it out before we head back. The Grace is right near the harbor. We find somewhere to drop off and then set the X-Copter to stealth mode. If we park it on the water, nobody'll even know it's there. We head to the Grace, grab Sabretooth and head straight back to the chopper. That way, we don't have to fight."

"And you think Sabretooth will go along with this? He hasn't always been buddy-buddy with the X-Men. Maybe this is a trap."

"Before M-Day, I would have agreed with you, but now? We can't afford to fight, like Magneto said. There aren't enough of us left."

Christopher considered this. "I guess. Based on everything I've read, Sabretooth is a survivor. He won't jeopardize his own skin if he doesn't have to. So if we did pick him up, we'd have to make sure he needs us to get out of here. Hide the chopper so he can't ditch us and take it. Keep the ignition codes to ourselves. That kind of thing."

"So you'll do it then?" she asked.

The navigation system beeped at them again before he could respond. They had arrived at their destination.

The Grace Museum of Natural History. It sat on the shoreline, a large and imposing building fronted with pillars and a massive staircase, flanked by an ornamental garden. Rows of lights at the entrance gleamed, driving away the midday gloom. Banners hung over the museum entrance flapped in the wind, advertising the newest exhibit on the Evolution of Mutants.

The two of them looked at each other as the helicopter drew closer. Christopher's brows knitted in thought.

"Do you think Cyclops knew that Sabretooth would be here?" he asked. "Or about that exhibit?"

"If he did, he would have said something. Unless this is part of the test," answered Eva.

"We aren't still in the Danger Room." Christopher reached up and very deliberately pinched himself as if trying to shake himself out of it. "If we are, I want out."

"I think that only works for dreams. I'm fairly sure this is all real."

He nodded. "You want to radio Cyclops about the rattling sound, or should I?"

She squealed aloud. "So you'll do it?" Before he could answer, she shot across the control panel and gave him a kiss on the cheek. "You are the absolute best! I mean it. You're a total rock star."

He smiled a little, wiping his cheek. "Just remember that later if something attacks us and I scream like a little kid, OK?"

"Yeah, sure. I'll radio Cyclops. You figure out somewhere for us to land that isn't full of people, OK?"

He gave her a cheesy thumbs-up and a wide grin that seemed to be an attempt to convince them both that he was incredibly excited about the prospect of rescuing one of the X-Men's longstanding and most powerful enemies. Instead, it made him look borderline psychotic. Eva burst into giggles and sprayed the control board with spittle, which only made her laugh harder as she tried to wipe it clean with her sleeve.

"Stop! Stop! With our luck, you'll accidentally deploy the missiles and take out the Chicago skyline," said Christopher, deadpan.

"Impossible. Cyclops deactivated the missiles, remember?" she replied. "Speaking of which, I'm calling him now. Shut up."

He made a show of clapping a hand over his mouth and nodded. Eva cleared her throat and turned on her mic before she realized she had no idea what she was going to say.

"Uh… Copter X to Comm Tower, come in Comm Tower."

After a brief pause, Cyclops responded, "Copter X, this is Comm Tower. What's your status?"

"Comm Tower, we've reached our destination and we're ready to turn around, but we've started to notice a noise from outside. We think there might be something hanging from the…" Christopher started waving his hands at her, pointing down at their feet and mouthing words she couldn't catch. "From… uh…"

"We'll be right there," Cyclops said. "I'll grab Illyana, and she can get me there in minutes. Helicopter problems are no joke, Eva."

"There's no need, sir," said Christopher in a firm voice, shocking her. "There's something wrapped around the skid. No damage to the engine or the rotors or anything dangerous. I just don't want to risk any additional damage with it flailing around, especially since it looks like we've got a storm coming in. I didn't want you to worry when you saw us make an unscheduled stop."

"Oh." The worry in Cyclops's voice eased significantly. "That makes much more sense."

"Sorry, sir. I keep losing track of the terminology," said Eva sheepishly.

"You'll get the hang of it," he replied. "Do you have a safe place to land?"

"We have a few options. It shouldn't take too long. And we have enough fuel to make the trip twice over, so adding an unanticipated stop shouldn't be a problem."

"Thanks for letting us know. Looking forward to hearing about the trip. Comm Tower out."

There was a click as Cyclops signed off.

"Well, I guess that does it," Christopher said. "We're on our own."

"Thanks for trusting me. If we get into trouble over this, I'll take full responsibility."

"Heck no, you won't," he said with an indignation that surprised her. Somehow, at that moment, it seemed like a much older person sat behind the eyes of the young body in the black tailored suit and trench coat. He couldn't have been any older than she was – maybe early twenties at the most – but he seemed full of a world-weary resignation at that moment. "This is my choice, Eva. We do this together or not at all."

"OK," she said. "We're a team then."

"That's right."

"Why did you do it, though? You know why I'm here. I want to know why you agreed to come. If it was just because

I asked you to, be warned that I'm going to punch you in the throat."

"You'll try." He grinned, but it quickly faded. "I keep thinking about that moment in the Danger Room when I thought Emma was dying. I was so scared I nearly wet myself, but I just did the job anyway. My dad was a Marine, you know. He had his problems, and we were never as close as I wanted, but one of the things he said that I never understood until today was that being brave has nothing to do with not being afraid. He told me he was always terrified before he went on a mission. But he did it anyway, because somebody had to. After that thing in the Danger Room, I think maybe I'm finally starting to get it. That's why I covered for you. I'm scared as all get out, but I'm going to go anyway. We'll get Sabretooth, and we'll probably never be allowed to fly the X-Copter ever again, but it'll be worth it."

"Yeah," she said. "Maybe after all this is over, you can tell your dad about it too."

He shrugged. "I'd have to tell his headstone. He's been gone for years. Heart attack." She reached toward him to offer some comfort, but he reached toward the control panel before she could touch him. "If we're going to do this, we should get on the ground before we run out of time."

"Yeah. OK."

It only took a few moments to set up the autopilot and cloaking device. Within minutes, they were ready to disembark into the growing storm. Eva unstrapped her safety harness and stood, feeling the craft rock beneath her.

"You ready for this?" she asked Christopher.

"Nope. You?"

"Not in the slightest."

"Let's go then," he said, unfastening his own harness. "On the count of three… one… two… three!"

In tandem, they both jumped into the rain-spattered afternoon air. It hit Eva's cheeks with a sudden wet smack, pushing the breath from her lungs. She pushed away from the rocking body of the chopper and hung a few feet above the ground for what felt like an impossible amount of time even though it must have only been a second or two – as if one of her time bubbles had popped into miraculous existence around her, preserving this perfect moment. She would have whooped aloud again if she'd had the breath. She felt like a real super hero for the very first time. Like she might someday wear the X and truly deserve it. If only her mom could see her now.

Then she landed, rolling into it as she'd learned in training. The move didn't work quite as well as she'd hoped. Her teeth clacked shut on the tip of her tongue, drawing blood, and her left knee hadn't liked the maneuver at all. But at the end of the day, she'd jumped out of a moving helicopter without getting badly hurt, so she considered the operation a success.

She stood on the sandy Chicago beach, near the very edge of the swimming area, just as they'd planned. Her overcoat had opened as she soared through the air, and freezing rain pelted her bare legs, stinging them. Cyclops had given them the long black coats "just in case," which had seemed like overkill on a task that required them to fly around in a big circle, but now Eva was grateful for it. The coats not only kept the rain off, but, as an added bonus, if anyone decided to start shooting, they would protect them. They were made of some fancy polymer something-or-other that worked like Kevlar. They also had X-Men insignia sewn on the inner pockets just in case.

A few feet away, Christopher straightened his tie and dusted off his trench coat, acting for all the world like he was preparing for a job interview instead of heading off on a mission to rescue a fellow mutant. He paused and grinned at her.

"That was so cool," he said.

"Right," she answered.

He paused and looked over her shoulder for a moment before his face screwed up into an expression of concern.

"Uh… Eva?" he asked. "Weren't you supposed to cloak the X-Copter before we got to the shore?"

She followed his gaze to find a group of determined tourists in rain slickers and ugly plastic visors with the Chicago skyline printed on the brim, snapping pictures of the helicopter as it hung in the air.

"I thought you were supposed to do it," she hissed, patting at the many pockets of her overcoat. "Didn't you bring the remote?"

He threw up his hands, acting as if he was carrying this entire mission while she hung like dead weight on his shoulders.

"I never even had the remote. See if you can find it while I deal with this," he said, squaring his shoulders and marching toward the tourists with a determined expression. As he approached, he waved them down, drawing their attention away from the aircraft that still hovered a short distance above them.

"Hello!" he said, smiling widely. "It's so good to see you. Where are you from?"

Eva watched, torn between wanting to smack him and shake his hand in congratulatory admiration as he made small talk with the Petersons from Topeka. Then he invited them to a new circus show at the convention center, complete with acrobatic tricks performed from a real live helicopter just like this one, the likes of which had never been seen on stage before!

"Unfortunately," he said, "I've just given away the last of our flyers to someone else, so I'm completely out. But if you call the convention center and mention the circus with the helicopter, they'll be able to sell you tickets. It's not like there's more than one!"

They all laughed.

"I hope they'll let you go inside now, young man," said Mrs Peterson, patting him on the shoulder with maternal concern. "It's awfully cold outside to make you stand out here all day. You'll catch pneumonia, and that'll be the end of your days of jumping out of helicopters."

"Oh, now that we've given out all of those flyers, we'll be heading home," he said reassuringly. "You should get inside too. This wind is wicked!"

"They don't call it the Windy City for nothing!" said Mr Peterson, his hearty belly laugh suggesting that he thought this was the deepest of wit.

"You are very right, sir," replied Christopher.

He made his goodbyes and sent them on their way. Luckily, the inclement weather meant that the beach and waterfront were otherwise largely deserted, leaving no one else to witness the spectacle of the helicopter still hanging in the air above the rocking waves. Christopher glowered at it.

"Still no luck finding the remote?" he asked. "It's up in the cockpit still, isn't it?"

Eva, who had checked every pocket over her overcoat three times for good measure while he entertained the Petersons, shook her head sadly. "I definitely don't have it."

"Then we have to find a way to get back up there. Otherwise we are completely and totally screwed," he said, looking up at the hovering chopper with a bleak expression.

"Why don't you check your pockets?" she suggested.

"I don't have it."

"But you should check…"

"Look, I said I don't have it. I told you to take it, remember? Maybe if you stand on my shoulders, you could reach the skids."

"Christopher, I'm not getting on your shoulders until you check your damned pockets, and that's final."

For a moment, they stared each other down in the pattering rain. She folded her arms as if to underscore her immovability on this issue. He clenched his jaw. Although this was the American Midwest and Eva was fairly sure that tumbleweeds weren't endemic to the area, she wouldn't have been surprised if one had blown between them at that moment. It had the feel of a showdown.

With apparent effort, Christopher unclenched his mouth enough to speak.

"Fine," he said. "I'll look, just to get on with this. But only because time's wasting, and Sabretooth said it was urgent."

He put his hands into his exterior pockets and turned them inside out. "But then, can we get on with it already?" He put his hands into his interior pockets, and the color bled from his face.

"Well?" prompted Eva archly.

Wordlessly, Christopher pulled out the remote. Eva didn't comment. If she had, she might have said something she'd regret. He could have checked his pockets, found the remote, and they could have been halfway to the Grace by now. But instead, they'd wasted valuable minutes bickering like toddlers because he'd made up his mind that he was right, and he wouldn't listen to logic.

Honestly, if she'd known he was going to act like a five year-old, she might have rethought her eagerness to take on this mission. But she couldn't back out now. Sabretooth needed her. This sat high on a list of sentences she'd never thought she would need to use, but here she was.

Christopher pushed a few buttons, and the helicopter settled into the water and flickered from view. If she hadn't been so angry, she would have been more impressed, but the needless drama had sucked all of the enjoyment out of the situation. All of a sudden, she felt like she was back at the school with the likes of David and Fabio. They were all great guys, honestly, but she wanted to get things done without all of the drama. She didn't want to be distracted by tacos or egos or any of that. She wanted a chance to help the folks she'd idolized ever since she was a little girl, like Captain America and Jean Grey and Cyclops. Perhaps Sabretooth hadn't been on that list, but she wasn't about to turn down the chance to make a difference, starting with him.

Fine then. She would just have to lead. Christopher would follow, whether he liked it or not. After all, like he'd said himself, he wasn't much use in a fight.

"All set now?" she asked coolly.

He nodded, slipping the remote back into his pocket. She almost made a snide remark about not forgetting that it was there but caught herself just in time.

"Follow me," she ordered instead, and then she turned on her heel, marching toward the Grace Museum with determination. She didn't look back to see if he followed.

She would continue on regardless.

CHAPTER 9

The rain settled into a steady drizzle as Christopher followed Eva up the winding path that led toward the Grace Museum of Natural History. As a native Midwesterner, he'd been to Chicago a few times, and he'd visited the Grace once as a sixth grader. He'd been on the tail end of his dinosaur obsession and psyched to see the extensive collection of skeletons that the Grace was known for. Back then, Bob, the world's largest complete T-Rex, hadn't been on display yet, but they'd had a bunch of others that he'd been eager to see. Unfortunately, Dad's PTSD had flared up, and they'd cut their trip to the Grace short. He'd lost his interest in dinosaurs after that.

He honestly didn't know what had gotten into him earlier, and he mulled it over as they walked in silence. He'd felt like an idiot when he reached into his pocket and felt the smooth surface of the remote. Why hadn't he just checked for it in the first place? Out of all the things to dig in his heels over, he couldn't have picked a more stupid one. Eva had good reason to be annoyed with him, and the most ridiculous part of all was that he had no idea why he'd done it. Sure, the stress had got to him. Not only were they walking into unknown dangers by the side of Sabretooth himself, but they would likely get in trouble with Cyclops too. Adding that on top of the double Danger Room experiences of the morning would be a lot for anyone to handle. So he understood why he'd lashed out, but he didn't quite get why he'd chosen that particular hill to die on. It was an idiotic hill to choose, but now that he stood on it, he didn't know how to get off.

Eva didn't exactly give him the opportunity to make peace, either. She stomped through the puddles like they'd done something to offend her. He stood at least a half a foot taller than she did, but he still struggled to keep up with her rapid pace. Her annoyance drove her quickly toward her goal. Maybe she'd feel more like talking once they rescued Sabretooth from whatever had messed with him. Whatever it was, it would be dangerous, and he needed to get his head in the game.

The Grace Museum stood on the grounds of Grace Park, right off the shore of Lake Michigan. The park stretched over a number of city blocks, packing all of the green spaces into one small area: an amphitheater, baseball diamonds, wooded picnic spots, lakes, soccer fields, and so on and so forth until just about every popular outdoor sport had been covered. The museum sat at the very end of the park along with the city aquarium, and waving banners along the park pathways advertised park concerts as well as aquarium exhibits and the museum's mutant exhibit.

As they hurried through the park, they only saw the most diehard joggers with the whip-thin bodies of marathon runners who went out every day regardless of the weather. Otherwise, the paths remained largely deserted, and the snack bars and food stands shuttered. There would be no open taco trucks. Christopher almost joked about that, but one look at Eva's stiff back convinced him that it wouldn't be a good idea just yet.

As they drew closer to the museum, red and blue flashing lights lit up the trunks of the trees. Something had happened, and Christopher would bet the remote he held in his pocket that it had something to do with Sabretooth. He slowed without intending to, and Eva pulled out in front of him without reducing speed.

"Wait," he called to her. He had to call again before she turned around, her face still shuttered and closed off with annoyance. "Something's wrong. We shouldn't just barge in there at top speed."

"Skulking in there like criminals isn't exactly going to make us inconspicuous either," she pointed out.

"No, but we should have a plan."

"We do have a plan. Go to the Grace and meet Sabretooth. Since we weren't able to get the details on his exact location, we've got to walk around and look for him. Unless you've developed x-ray vision in the past few hours and forgot to tell me?" She paused as if waiting for an answer. "No? Then I think we'll continue on."

With that, she marched on down the path. After a moment of frozen shock, Christopher followed on her heels. Up until this moment, he'd been feeling more than a bit sheepish and wanting to make amends, but now he wanted to scream. Yes, he'd been an idiot, but he'd admitted it, hadn't he? He was fairly sure that he had. Besides, people made mistakes, and they were both under a lot of pressure. She could have given him a break but had chosen to bite his head off instead. This definitely wasn't the kind of positive camaraderie that Emma Frost had been trying to foster. Quite the opposite, in fact.

He scurried to catch up to her. How could she run so quickly with those short stubby legs of hers? She had to have some latent super speed ability, or maybe he was just a klutz. He'd always been the last one picked in gym classes and for sports teams, and now here he was, following her blindly into battle to help Sabretooth, of all people. He felt good about their plans, but the thought of meeting the mercenary still made him nervous.

"I'm not so sure this is a good idea," he called.

By this time, Eva had almost reached the main courtyard, which was full of police vehicles with their lights flashing in wild concert. She whirled around furiously with her hand held up to her mouth.

"Sssssssh!" she hissed.

Then she turned back around and kept on going. Apparently, if it was a trap, she intended to walk right into it. He didn't know what to do about that. If Sabretooth decided to carry her off, he couldn't do a damned thing about it. He looked around wildly for something to use for a staff, but the city park didn't have many stave-like pieces of wood just sitting around, waiting for people to pick them up and use them as weapons. Go figure. If she insisted on charging into dangerous situations without evaluating them first, he would do his job, just like he did in the

Danger Room earlier. He would wait until she inevitably got hurt, and then he'd go and rescue her again. Apparently, she counted on it.

He hung back as she rushed into the wide-open area in front of the museum, waiting to see what would happen. She skirted two police cars and continued on toward the building. Uniformed officers in dark rain slickers and hats with plastic covers stood by the cars, chatting idly. None of them took any notice of her. He edged closer. The park had been largely deserted, but now he could see a fairly steady stream of people walking to and from the parking lot on the far side of the aquarium building, and a big cluster of them standing outside the museum itself, close to the building to protect themselves from the steady drizzle.

He tried to calm himself, but his pulse raced despite his best efforts. He'd never been able to relax in the presence of a uniform. What if they were walking into some locked down area where the cops would haul them in for questioning? Supposedly they couldn't do that to American citizens, but he'd learned the hard way that those rules didn't apply to mutants. If Cyclops hadn't shown up, he might still be rotting away in that jail cell in Michigan. Besides, the rules had never applied to him, not in the same ways they did to everyone else. He just wanted a fair chance, and sometimes he wanted to scream because it felt like every time he turned around, it hovered just out of his reach.

Reluctantly, he followed Eva as she approached the building. She scanned the crowd, looking for Sabretooth, although he probably wouldn't be there. He'd be too conspicuous, unless he'd gotten a makeover since the last time Christopher had seen his picture. Still, it made sense to look just in case. He joined her, surreptitiously scanning the trees to see if Sabretooth waited for them there, but if so, the dull grey afternoon light made it impossible to tell.

Unease grew in his belly. If this wasn't a trap, something must have happened here. From the looks of things, it must have been bad.

"I don't see him," said Eva. "Let's look around a little."

"Sounds like a plan."

"Yeah, I've been waiting for my sister for about a half hour," said the girl standing next to Christopher. She looked to be around twenty or so, with a heavily made-up face, a tight, glittery shirt, and tiny skirt more suitable for clubbing than museums. Her eyelashes looked too heavy for her lids to hold up. She gave him an appraising look and sidled a little closer. "It's tough to find anybody in this mess. The museum guards took a bunch of people out the emergency exits, so there's no telling which one she's at. Who are you waiting for, handsome?"

He almost ignored her, because right now, the last thing he felt was handsome. But then he realized that this was an opportunity to gather some vital information, and so he gave her a friendly smile. Most of his friends got tongue-tied in the presence of pretty girls, but strangely, he'd never had a problem with that. They were just people, like everybody else.

"Her brother. My sister. They're here on a date," he said.

"How nice for them," replied the girl, giving him a coy look from beneath those heavy lashes. "My name's Candy. What's yours?"

"I'm Christopher."

"And I'm over this already. We've got to get moving, Christopher," said Eva, trying to pull him away. "Remember, we're on a time crunch?"

"Gimme a minute," he said, gently extricating himself. "What happened here, Candy? I got pretty worried when I saw all the cops."

Finally! Eva must have realized he was digging for information instead of randomly flirting, because she let him talk without being constantly yanked on. That was a relief. Candy had started to look like she might smack Eva, and a fight would draw too much attention. Although he'd put his money on Eva in a knockout brawl any day. Candy looked like the kind of girl who would talk big and then cry like a baby the minute anybody stood up to her. Eva might have been annoying the crap out of him over the past half hour or so, but he had to admit that she was tough as nails.

"Oh my god," said Candy, grabbing his arm with both hands, as if the news she had to impart was so shocking that she needed to hold onto him with both hands to steady herself while she told him. "So my friend and I were at the Grace while my sister and her friends went to the aquarium, and you won't believe what happened. My friend and I went to that Evolution of Mutants exhibit, and while we were there? A bunch of giant robots came out of literally nowhere and started shooting up the place!"

Sentinels again. It seemed like ever since Christopher had become a mutant, he saw Sentinels everywhere he went. The mutant-hunting robots seemed to multiply like cockroaches, only they were scarier and had fewer legs. Out of all of the developments since he'd become a mutant, they were one of his least favorite, and that said something.

"Literally nowhere, huh?" said Eva. "Impressive."

"That's what I said," said Candy, her eyes flashing.

"I bet that was frightening," Christopher said, drawing her attention back to him. He smiled again, trying to soothe the anger back out of her. "What did you do?"

"It was just like in the movies! My friend ran, and a piece of debris hit her on the head."

Candy sounded more thrilled about this than anyone had a right to be.

"That's awful," said Christopher.

"Oh, she's fine. They took her to the hospital in an ambulance, but she just needed a couple of stitches, and the EMT was really hot. She'll be OK."

"OK," said Christopher. "So what happened then?"

Candy blinked. "Nothing, really. The robots shot some things, and they fought this hairy, nasty guy. One of those dirty little muties. I hope they got him." She shuddered. "The world would be a safer place."

The smile faded from Christopher's face. He didn't know what to say. He had no problem with a little harmless flirting, but he couldn't exchange compliments with someone who would wish him dead if she knew what he really was. He would still heal her if she needed help – he truly would. If a flying piece of debris hit her on the head right now, he'd save her, knowing that she thought of him as a "dirty little mutie." But he couldn't flirt with her. He couldn't force out the words.

"You OK?" Candy asked. "You look kinda pale."

Eva stepped in, saving him from replying.

"Do you know where the robots went after that?" she asked.

Candy sniffed disdainfully. "Why are you still here?" she asked. "Can't you go find your brother and let us talk in peace?"

Eva gave her a cold little smile in return. "No. Do you know where the robots went after that?" she repeated in a clipped cadence that made it clear that her patience had begun to wear thin.

"I assume that the police blew them up or something. How should I know? I'm not the robot keeper around here."

"Of course not. You are clearly a person of grace and class," said Eva. "Now, if you'll excuse us. We need to go."

Christopher nodded gratefully. He wanted nothing more than to be as far away from this horrible person as possible. He'd rather whisper sweet nothings to a venomous snake than Candy.

That might be a bit melodramatic, but he meant every word. He'd spent a night in jail because of people like her. He'd managed to stay out of trouble his entire life, and go figure – healing someone had earned him his first humiliating night behind bars. One of the guards had spat at him. He'd always known that he needed to be cautious – after all, he wasn't stupid. But he'd always felt like he would be safe so long as he behaved himself. That illusion had been shattered, and all because of prejudiced people like Candy. He hated her. He didn't want to, but he did, and he couldn't wait to be rid of her.

"No," said Candy. "We're having a conversation!"

She grabbed onto his arm, yanking on him like he was a

toy she'd claimed. She hadn't even asked him if he wanted to stay and chat. Instead, she'd just claimed him, like he had no say in the matter. Even if he hadn't been a dirty mutant, he wouldn't have wanted to be with someone so rude and inconsiderate. Who ordered people around like that? It made his earlier spat with Eva seem inconsequential by comparison. Yes, they'd both been silly, but neither of them would ever stoop so low.

Based on the disgust on her face, Eva shared his low opinion of Candy. She looked ready to throw down. Even though he really wanted to give Candy a piece of his mind, it wouldn't be a good idea to cause a scene with all of these police around.

"As much as I'd like to stay and chat, I've got to find my sister," he said, trying to pry her fingers off.

Candy pouted. "But I'm bored, and I'm tired of just standing here by myself. Why don't you take me with you?"

"I… can't," he said.

"Why not?" she demanded.

He had no idea, and an expression of triumph grew on her face as she realized he had no excuse to bar her from accompanying them. She clapped her hands, bouncing in excitement.

"You can't come up with a good reason, can you?" she demanded.

"You have to stay here and wait for your sister," interjected Eva. "Remember?"

Candy waved a hand. "Oh, screw her. I don't really like her anyway. And I do like him." She clung back onto Christopher's arm but then scowled at his goggles. "Except for those things you're wearing on your head. They're totally dumb. Take them off."

"If you touch those goggles, Christopher, I'll beat you up," said Eva. Based on her stern expression, she meant every word too. "You like them. They stay."

After a moment, he smiled at her. "Yeah. Sorry about the remote thing. I can't remember if I said that or not."

She shrugged. "Sorry I was a jackwagon."

"No big."

Candy looked between the two of them, scowling. "Hey, guys? I have no idea what you're talking about. It's rude to leave people out of the conversation, you know."

"I know." Christopher looked down at her and sighed. "By the way? I'm one of those dirty muties."

She guffawed right in his face. "Yeah, right." Then she paused, searching his expression. "I mean, you're kidding, right?"

He shook his head soberly.

She turned to Eva, her dislike of the other girl forgotten in her need for reassurance. "He's totally joking, isn't he?"

Eva shook her head. "Nope. I am too. You should probably get away from us. It might be catching."

She blew right into Candy's face. Candy took an involuntary step back before her lips firmed in determination.

"You're just trying to get rid of me. I know. I've seen this before," she said.

"I bet you have," muttered Eva.

Christopher smothered a grin. Normally, he didn't support that kind of snide remark, but Candy took awfulness to an entirely new level. He hadn't thought that it was possible to be so self-absorbed. Then again, maybe it wasn't a complete accident that everyone had forgotten about her and left her here alone, either.

Candy folded her arms. "It isn't going to work. I don't believe you."

Wordlessly, Eva stepped close to Candy, tilting her body to shield them from view. Then she opened her trench coat to reveal the yellow X-Men symbol stitched onto the inside pocket. Candy took one look and shrieked, running away from them as fast as her platform shoes would carry her.

CHAPTER 10

In the wake of Candy's hasty retreat down the museum front steps, Eva refastened the buttons on her coat as quickly as she could, snickering. Christopher shook his head.

"What a horrible person," he said.

"You have an incredible gift for understatement," she responded.

"You know, I thought it was stupid that he made us wear these coats, but now I take it all back."

"Agreed," she said. "Let's go. Time's ticking away, and we've wasted a lot."

"Yeah. We're going to be in a heck of a lot of trouble if we don't get back to the chopper soon," he agreed. "Cyclops is going to realize that something is up if he hasn't already."

They turned in tandem and found themselves face to face with a pair of museum guards who were doing their best to look menacing and official despite the fact that they were only one step up from mall cops. The grey-haired one on the left looked like an angry grandpa who liked to watch NASCAR. The one on the right was Latina and might as well have had the words "tough cookie" tattooed on her forehead. She just had that look about her.

"Hey there," said the gray-haired one, pretending to be casual. "Everything OK?"

Christopher tensed, although he tried to tell himself that everything would be fine. All he had to do was follow the rules, toe the line, convince the rent-a-cops he wasn't a threat. But he worried anyway, because he knew it didn't matter if he followed the rules or if he had the best of intentions. What mattered more was what others saw when they looked at him. Whether or not they feared his skin, or his mutations, or both.

The female guard, whose name badge read "Alvarez", said, "What are your names?" Her tone was none too polite.

"Why do you want to know?" asked Eva, her chin jutting out in defiance.

Christopher's stomach sank to his knees. She didn't get it. Of course she didn't get it. She was a cute white girl from Australia. She had no idea how much danger she was putting them – and especially him – in by antagonizing the authorities.

"Chill," he muttered.

She glanced back at him, and he shook his head minutely, trying to warn her off. She returned a confused look but subsided.

In the meantime, Alvarez had edged closer, her hand resting on the butt of her Taser as if to reassure herself. The weapon loomed in Christopher's vision like a threat. Perhaps that's exactly what she'd intended.

"Names?" she barked.

"I'm Christopher Muse, ma'am. This is Eva Bell," Christopher said. "I don't have my wallet and ID with me, though. I didn't expect to come downtown today, I'm afraid."

"And let me guess. You don't have yours either." Alvarez looked knowingly at Eva.

To Christopher's relief, Eva seemed to be picking up on the fact that she should be following his lead. She simply held up her empty hands and said, "No, ma'am," when he'd half expected her to make a smart remark.

The officers shifted, exchanging glances. Christopher didn't like any of this. Being an X-Man should have made him feel powerful. He had mutations that allowed him to do what normal humans could only dream of! But instead, he felt just as vulnerable and frightened as he had before.

"What happened with that girl?" asked the second guard, whose badge read "Louth".

"What girl?" Christopher responded.

"The one who just ran out of here screaming," Alvarez said, watching him closely.

"Candy's just dramatic," said Christopher.

"She wasn't, like, horror movie screaming," Eva added.

"Candy? So you know her?" asked Louth.

"Not very well, sir. She keeps asking me out, but I'm not that interested." Christopher shrugged, trying to will them to see him as just another college kid. Let them write him off as immature, as silly, as dumb even, if only they didn't peg him as a bad seed. Because they were looking to pin blame for whatever had happened here on someone. He knew that. Fear that it would be him made him babble. "She just won't take no for an answer, and it's starting to get on my nerves. Anyway, she wouldn't leave for the longest time. She was hanging all over me, and then she realized what time it was, and she was like, 'Oh, my god, my mom is gonna kill me!' and she shrieked, and she ran off."

The guards exchanged a look, and for a moment, Christopher thought that would be it. They'd be free to leave. But then Alvarez said, "What are you wearing on your head?"

"They're just goggles. Decorative goggles." Christopher shrugged. "They don't do anything. I just like how they look is all."

"Let me see them," she said, holding her hand out.

It wasn't a request. He looked at Eva, stricken with worry all over again, and she squeezed his hand in encouragement but there wasn't much else she could do. He took off the goggles and handed them over. He'd got them at a science fiction convention because he thought they were cool, and he wore them every day. He just liked how they looked, and as an added bonus, they kept his hair out of his eyes. Alvarez inspected them thoroughly and nodded.

"No power supply," she said, handing them back.

Did they think he'd controlled the robots through his goggles? It seemed like an odd combo. If he was going to attack a museum with some robots, he'd want a joystick or something, but maybe that was just him. It should offend him that they'd checked, and he would be offended later, when he was finally safe, but for the moment, he could only feel a desperate need to get out of here before something awful happened.

"Open the coat," said Alvarez.

Christopher wanted so badly to refuse. After all, they were just rent-a-cops. They had no right to treat Eva and him like this. Besides, if he opened his coat, they'd see the badge on the inside pocket. It wouldn't go well, but refusing them wouldn't either. They'd argue with him, and that would attract the attention of the cops scattered around the courtyard. Either way, there would be trouble. There was no way to win, and dread settled into the pit of his stomach with finality.

He unbuttoned the coat and held it open, resigned. The wind caught the fabric, pulling it from his sweaty hands. The bright yellow X and circle emblem of the X-Men flashed in and out of view.

Louth took an involuntary step backwards, his face gone pale with fear. Alvarez swore, her hand tightening on her weapon. Eva watched it all with wide eyes, waiting for Christopher's lead. With quiet pride, he straightened his goggles.

"Are you one of those mutants?" asked Lough.

They locked eyes for a moment. The bottomless fear in Lough's eyes echoed Christopher's, but the gulf between them couldn't have been wider. If only Christopher could bridge it, but he didn't know how.

"Yes," he responded simply.

Alvarez spat on the ground as if trying to clear something disgusting from her mouth.

"We're just trying to find our friends, like we said. We didn't do anything wrong," said Eva.

To Christopher's surprise, Lough seemed to consider this. "How do we know you have nothing to do with what happened here earlier? Those robots?"

Eva shrugged. "From what I heard, the robots were shooting at a mutant, not the other way around. Besides, do you see any robots here right now? I don't."

Lough looked from Eva to Christopher and back again. He rubbed at his jaw thoughtfully, his fingers rasping over the stubble.

"You may have a point," he conceded.

"Are you kidding me?" Alvarez interjected, not moving her gaze from Christopher and Eva. "Mutants killed my big brother. After college, he got a job with the government. We always knew he was destined for big things. He was the quarterback of the football team. Always got straight As. The prom king. So we weren't surprised when the feds wanted him. His first month, he got assigned to an air security detail. His chopper picked up Magneto after a big battle. It exploded. Only the mutant survived." She bared her teeth in a bitter smile. "I wonder what happened. That's some coincidence, isn't it?"

"Magneto isn't here, though. These are kids," said Lough.

"They're abominations. You're not letting them go, Lough. Not on my watch," she declared, pulling her Taser and pointing it at Eva.

Christopher felt sick with fear. Now things would go very badly. Even if they didn't get tased, the guards would turn them over to the cops for sure. He didn't want to go to jail again. The idea terrified him. He had to do something, but he didn't know what.

Before anyone could move a muscle, a tawny shape hurtled out of the sky, landing on Alvarez with a snarl and pinning her to the ground. It was an enormous man, with slabs of muscle on a frame built for quick movement. He twisted to look at the mutants, his face framed by wild, golden hair and thick muttonchops. Impossibly long fangs jutted from his mouth, which curled in a feral grin. He wore a long trench coat, the collar flipped up to hide his face.

It was Sabretooth.

CHAPTER 11

For a moment, no one moved. The guards stared in shock at the mutant that had just dropped out of the sky. Sabretooth stared at the X-Men symbol still visible inside Christopher's unbuttoned coat, a satisfied smirk on his face. Eva and Christopher stared at Sabretooth like he was Santa Claus and had just landed his sleigh in front of the museum.

"There you are," he said. "Been looking for you."

"Oh. Hi," Eva replied, overcome with shock.

Before the stunned police officers could react, he grabbed onto Eva with one hand and Christopher with the other. Tensing, he gathered strength in his massive legs and sprang up the tall pillars that ran the length of the museum. Rain and air whooshed past Eva's face, and she couldn't decide whether she was exhilarated or terrified by their rapid ascent. He landed easily, as if he carried people onto tall buildings every day, setting them down onto the puddle-strewn stone parapet with a thud.

Eva craned her head to look up at the infamous Sabretooth. He loomed over her, blotting out the dim outline of the sun.

His hazel eyes glittered despite the dull afternoon as he took them both in with a dismissive raking glance. He didn't seem hurt. After all, he hadn't had much problem leaping on and off buildings. Speaking of which, she glanced over the edge to see if the cops had mounted their pursuit yet and immediately wished she hadn't. Vertigo gripped her, setting her head to spinning, and she had to grab onto something to keep from toppling over.

That something turned out to be Sabretooth's arm. It felt quite sturdy. She'd felt weaker tree trunks.

"Don't like heights, eh?" he said, the corner of his mouth quirking up in amusement. "If you fall over, I'm not going down to fetch you again, missy. It's been a long day."

"I won't fall," she said. "I was checking to see if the cops were on their way up here yet."

"We've got a couple minutes. They have a lot of stairs to climb, and they'll want to put on their big boy pants first." He bared his teeth. It might have been a smile, but she wasn't entirely sure. "I'm scary."

"You must be Sabretooth."

"And you must be the newbies. It's about time you got here. What did you do, crawl?"

"We ran into a few problems en route. Nothing we couldn't handle."

Eva tried to project an adult kind of confidence, but something about Sabretooth made her feel childlike. Maybe because his thigh appeared to have the approximate circumference of her waistline? Regardless of the reason, she didn't like how it felt. The whole purpose of breaking the rules and haring off on this mission had been to prove that she deserved to take the training wheels off, and she did not like this feeling of instant regression one bit.

"Who's babysitting you today? I hope it's Logan. He owes me twenty bucks," said Sabretooth, prowling restlessly around the museum rooftop.

Christopher finally unfroze. He'd been staring at Sabretooth with his mouth open ever since they'd touched down on the roof, and now he closed his jaw with a click. It looked like someone had finally remembered to un-pause him with some cosmic remote control.

"No," he said. "Wolverine's not here. It's–"

"Who is it then?" Sabretooth interrupted. "Cyclops? He's got a stick up the butt, but I'll take it."

"It's just the two of us. We're on a training exercise with the X-Copter. We tried to tell you, but the transmission cut out," said Eva.

Sabretooth stopped mid-step. Now it looked like he'd been paused too. His head swiveled in slow motion to pin her with his eyes. Then he stalked toward her on quiet catlike feet, stopping inches away.

"You're pulling my chain," he said. "That's brave of you, missy. But I'm not in the mood for it today."

If this had been one of the hero storybooks that she'd read to pieces as a kid, this would have been the part where she gave a stirring speech. She would make Sabretooth realize the error of his ways, and they'd treat each other with mutual respect or maybe even team up to vanquish the true villain. Although now that she'd met Sabretooth in person, she thought that his likely response to such a speech would be mocking laughter or maybe a quick punch to the throat. So she kept it simple instead. To be honest, the lost opportunity disappointed her a little.

"You said it was urgent, and we couldn't reach you again, so we came," she said.

He sighed the deep, heavy sigh of a man who cannot believe how bad his luck has become. Then he ran a hand through his hair, his claws snagging on the tangled strands.

At the far end of the roof sat an emergency exit, illuminated with a red glowing sign. A heavy chain wrapped around the bar, fastening it to a jutting pipe some distance away. As Sabretooth pondered his karma, the door began to shudder as someone tried unsuccessfully to open it from the other side. After a brief pause, a deep, repetitive pounding noise began to reverberate across the roof as they tried to beat the door open instead.

"Oh, great!" said Christopher, his voice high and nervous. "We're trapped."

Sabretooth's lips curled, exposing his teeth. His back hunched, losing its upright, civilized posture as he contemplated the door, waiting for their pursuers to break through. His tawny eyes lit with a feral light from within. Eva didn't know what to do. If he lost control, she didn't know how to stop him. She could bubble him, but that would only delay the inevitable.

"Why did you radio us?" she blurted, stalling for time. "Obviously, you're fine."

He blinked, looking at her, and some of the wildness fled his eyes. He licked his lips.

"I'm not alone out here," he admitted. "What do you do?"

"Huh?" she asked.

"Your power. Mutant abilities. Mumbo jumbo. What do you do?" he snapped.

"Oh. Time bubbles."

"What the heck is a time bubble?"

"It's a bubble that freezes time inside it?"

She didn't know why it was a question, but it came out that way. Sabretooth didn't even seem to notice. He just grunted and turned to Christopher.

"What about you, Dreadlocks? What's your schtick?" he asked.

"I'm Christopher," he said. "I heal people."

Sabretooth froze. "You any good?"

"I guess so," replied Christopher modestly.

Eva wasn't going to stand for that. Christopher needed to quit selling himself short, and besides, Sabretooth wanted to write them both off as useless. Downplaying their skills wouldn't help. He hadn't shown much interest in her bubbles, but Christopher's healing had piqued his interest. Maybe Sabretooth's companion hadn't accompanied him to pick them up because they'd been badly injured.

"He's too modest," she interjected. "Emma Frost stabbed herself in the heart today, and he kept her alive."

"Emma stabbed herself?" Sabretooth asked with obvious incredulity.

"It was only in the Danger Room. None of it was real. She did it to teach me a lesson," Christopher explained. "A very bloody lesson."

After a moment's consideration, Sabretooth nodded. "I can see it. She's a little crazy."

"I won't argue with you," said Christopher in even tones.

Sabretooth grinned, visibly relaxing. He clapped Christopher on the back, making him stagger. The door boomed again, and Sabretooth hissed, the loud noise causing him visible pain. The chain rattled, and the pipe shook loosely. One of them would give out before much longer.

"I could use you, kid. We ought to get out of here before those gun-crazy idiots make themselves more annoying than they already are. Honestly, who taught them how to break through a darned door?" Sabretooth said.

As if on cue, the door burst open, the chain whipping loose and flying at them as if possessed. Sabretooth snatched it out of the air as SWAT officers in their black riot gear poured out of the doorway, assault rifles held at the ready. He swung the long length of heavy metal around in a wide arc and whipped it back at them, catching four of them with its lethal weight and knocking them to the ground before they could react.

Eva wasted no time. Sabretooth's wild aggression gave her confidence despite her fear. She bubbled three of the SWAT officers in front and watched as the men behind them ran into the bubble, smacking their helmets against its surface at full speed and bouncing off it painfully. Sabretooth spared her an admiring glance and a nod that said he'd noticed the move, and she couldn't help but grin.

Then the telltale RAT-A-TAT-TAT of gunfire pierced the air, and Christopher yelped in fear. Shaking uncontrollably, Eva began to look around wildly for cover when he yanked her behind him, shielding her with his body. Sabretooth roared, an animal sound of pure fury. Then he grabbed her, making her feel a little like a package being passed around from person to person. She would have protested, but then he grabbed Christopher too, and he leaped off the building.

Treetops rushed at them with frightening speed, and although Sabretooth had probably done this a million times before, Eva felt certain that she was about to break both of her legs. Her heart leaped up into her throat, and then strangely, a wild exhilaration filled her. It didn't drive away the fear, but it rode alongside it, and she whooped aloud in delight and terror. Sabretooth laughed in her ear, and Christopher shouted, "You're both nuts!"

They landed with a bone-jarring jolt. Sabretooth rolled into the impact, holding each of them tucked under an arm, but regardless of these significant efforts, Eva felt like her body was a giant bell that had just been rung. When he released her, it took her a moment to get her bearings. When she finally did, she realized that the gentle PIFF PIFF PIFF that surrounded her had nothing to do with the rain falling on the concrete. Those were bullets.

It scared her, of course, but by this time her system was so overloaded with adrenaline that it barely registered. She couldn't get any more frightened, nor more ready to run or fight or flee. She would do whatever she had to do, and then she would cry for about five years.

"Run!" shouted Christopher.

Sabretooth had already begun to move toward the tree line, looking back at them with an expression that spoke volumes, if those volumes contained long irate paragraphs complaining about stupid people who stood around twiddling their thumbs while SWAT teams tried to blow holes in them with semi-automatic weapons. Eva and Christopher scrambled to catch up, and the three of them took temporary refuge in the bushes at the back of the museum. For the moment, they couldn't see any cops, but they all knew this wouldn't last for more than a few seconds.

Eva and Christopher both gasped for breath, but Sabretooth remained fresh as a daisy. He looked them over critically. Eva straightened, trying to look like her legs weren't wobbling, but they'd turned to jelly underneath her. Sweat trickled down her temple. His keen eyes had to have picked up on it, but thankfully he turned away without calling her out.

"Here's the plan," he said, drawing a quick map in the dirt at their feet with a claw. "We're heading for a parking garage. We'll go around the museum and down this path to the right. Take this fork here. You'll see the garage on your left. You got it?" They both nodded. "You two stick to the trees and stay safe, no matter what happens. I'll stay out in the open and draw their fire. You can use those fancy bubbles of yours to freeze anybody who gets too close if you really want."

"You need me to heal you if you get shot?" asked Christopher eagerly. "I can do that."

Sabretooth laughed. "Kid, I eat bullets for breakfast."

Nonplussed, Christopher shook his head. "Well, then, remind me never to eat your cooking, because that sounds disgusting."

Sabretooth rose from his haunches. "You know, I was wrong about the two of you. I'm glad I didn't kill you after all." He sauntered down the path, trusting them to follow.

In his wake, Eva and Christopher exchanged a long, worried glance.

"He was kidding, right?" she asked.

"I honestly have no idea," he responded.

CHAPTER 12

Over the past few weeks, the students of the New Xavier School had done a lot of hiking. Although there was really nothing to see but snowy woods and different snowy woods, the fresh air refreshed them after spending hours cooped up underground. As a result, Eva and Christopher had both become better at moving around in the underbrush without sounding like stampeding buffalo. Now, Illyana said they sounded more like stampeding goats. Eva thought that had to be an improvement. After all, goats were less than half the size of buffalo, right? They had to be quieter by default.

The two of them stampeded like goats through the bushes and trees, trying to stay hidden from view as they followed Sabretooth toward the parking garage. The museum grounds swarmed with cops now, many more than before. For some reason, a mutant who leaped onto buildings seemed to have alarmed the police more than the violent robots had, because their presence had tripled. Eva saw mounted officers through the trees, and in the distance she heard helicopters. She worried about how they'd respond to the X-Copter once they saw it, but she didn't think the cops had enough speed to keep up once they got into the air. All they had to do was heal Sabretooth's mystery friend, get back to the chopper, and get the heck out of Dodge.

Sabretooth sauntered down the path, whistling and filing his claws on a piece of bark he'd pulled off some tree. It made a rasping sound that set Eva's teeth on edge. His plan seemed to be to make as much noise as possible to distract the cops from the students' presence in the undergrowth a few yards away.

It worked. A pair of police officers stepped onto the path before him without a second look into the patch of trees that hid the students from view. The sight of Sabretooth in all his enormous, whistling glory had short-circuited their training and made them reckless. One of them shot the dirt right at his feet and yelled, "Freeze, sucker!"

Sabretooth dropped the bark and tilted his head to look at them. He seemed unfazed by the bullet that had nearly taken off his toes. In fact, he seemed positively delighted by the cops' aggression, eager to let himself off the chain. Eva couldn't decide whether this ought to worry or impress her.

"Shoot at me again, and I'll shove that gun up your butt sideways," said Sabretooth, grinning.

The cops froze as he grabbed their service revolvers and crushed them, one in each massive fist. Then he gave them each a little nudge on the shoulder. They stumbled, faces pasty with fear.

"This is the part where you run away," he said.

They did. Sabretooth let them go without a second look. He resumed his whistling but left the bark behind as he continued on down the path. Eva and Christopher exchanged wide-eyed glances, and Eva started to wonder if they'd gotten in over their heads. But they continued to follow a few yards in his wake, keeping to the trees as much as possible.

Further down the path, a four-member SWAT team stepped out to confront him. This time, Sabretooth took a moment to crack his knuckles. The officers spread out in a wide circle that he couldn't possibly cover, but he still surveyed them with obvious delight, eager to throw down. One stepped toward him with a shock stick in his hand, hoping to subdue him with an intense blast of high voltage electricity. Sabretooth dashed forwards, teeth bared. As he did, the other SWAT officers moved in behind him, hoping to overwhelm him with numbers.

Eva knew this was her moment. She bubbled, hoping to freeze the three cops who were trying to flank him, but she only caught two, suspending them in a glistening moment in time, their sticks raised moments before they struck. The third sidestepped at precisely the wrong moment and saw her. He drew his gun and took aim.

"No! Eva!"

Christopher shoved her back, his lips pressed firm with determination despite his bloodless face as he protected her with his body once again, his arms held out wide.

But Sabretooth dispatched his attacker with swift efficiency and leaped towards them, taking the bullet himself. Red blood sprayed the air, and he snarled in anger and pain.

The gunman sighted on her again, and she stumbled

backwards, wishing for Captain America's bravery or Wolverine's anger or someone's anything, because she didn't feel ready for this. This fight wasn't anything like the Danger Room, and she didn't like it at all.

But Sabretooth launched himself forward a second time, hitting the hapless gunman just as he pulled the trigger, sending the shot wide. The gunman screamed as Sabretooth's claws descended on him. The mutant mercenary rose from the lifeless body, his tension slowly draining as he realized that they'd neutralized all of their attackers. He reached toward the bloody hole in his trench and bared his teeth but otherwise seemed none the worse for wear.

The two remaining attackers still stood with their batons raised in Eva's bubble, ready to strike.

"Too bad you can't turn them so they hit each other when you pop that thing," he said.

Eva stepped out onto the path. "Do you need healing?" she asked, worried.

Sabretooth's eyes flashed. "Get your butt back in those trees. The bullet went through. It's already closing."

"Don't talk to me like that," she snapped, all of the stress and fear finally overtaking her. "I'm just trying to be a decent person."

"Fine. Get your butt back into the trees, please."

He didn't sound any kinder the second time, but she left the path anyway. She didn't want to get into an altercation with him. He'd been kind enough to them so far, but he clearly had a short fuse. She didn't want to get on his bad side. She had the feeling that that would be a very poor idea.

"Look, missy, I don't matter," Sabretooth muttered. "You help keep Dreadlocks here safe until we get to the garage, OK?"

"Fine," she said. It came out snippier than she'd wanted, but adrenaline still coursed through her.

"Thanks," he snapped back, so quickly that she thought she might have imagined it. Then he continued on toward the garage as if nothing had happened. If not for the spatters of blood and the bodies they left in their wake, she might have thought she'd imagined the entire thing.

CHAPTER 13

Sabretooth led them into a large parking structure. It smelled like rain, old food, and motor oil, a pervasive stench that seemed to have permanently soaked into the concrete. He wrinkled his nose but otherwise didn't comment. Christopher thought that with his enhanced senses the reek must be overwhelming. He'd spent a lot of time wishing for more useful mutant abilities, but he hadn't stopped to consider the drawbacks before now.

He was still learning how to use his abilities, after all, and Sabretooth was a mercenary. He could only hope that he had what it took to get the job done so they could get out of here. To his immense surprise, he couldn't wait to return to that moldy dump of a school so he could listen to David and Fabio complain about tacos. He actually found himself looking forward to it.

Inside the parking structure, a door with chipped red paint led into an echoing stairwell. Sabretooth led them down the twisting flights of stairs into progressive levels of sub-basements. Red. Green. Yellow. Christopher began to wonder if this place might run out of rainbow colors and if Sabretooth's friend might be hiding on the puce level. But he stopped at the yellow door instead.

On the other side sat a few sports cars and a rusty minivan that looked like it hadn't been moved in about ten years. Somewhere on the levels above them, a car alarm bleeped incessantly. Something moved in the darkness. Sabretooth stiffened but quickly relaxed as a small rodent emerged into the light, carrying a chip bag across the pavement with happy industriousness.

"This way," he muttered, gesturing for them to follow.

Christopher and Eva remained shoulder to shoulder as he led them through the warren of mostly empty parking stalls. As they walked, Christopher checked his pocket to feel the comforting presence of the X-Copter remote. After everything that Sabretooth had done to keep them safe, he'd begun to trust the surly mutant, but if something did go wrong, he could call the chopper. The thought reassured him.

Sabretooth stopped at a door designated "Office" with a dingy placard.

"In here," he said.

At one point, the door had been held closed with a heavy padlock, but as he entered the room, Christopher noticed that the metal panels that had secured the door had been pulled loose as if by some great force. The panels were thick and reinforced, built for inner city nightlife and minimal supervision, but they had offered no obstacle to Sabretooth. Christopher could imagine him blasting through the door with a single well-placed kick, the metal screaming as it tore.

He touched the jagged edge of the ripped steel, blew out an impressed breath, and followed the others inside.

The office space left much to be desired. A desk ran along one wall, choked with papers, used coffee cups, and a desktop computer with a cracked screen. A pinup calendar hung on the wall above the desk. Someone with a sense of humor had drawn a bikini and mustache on the model using a black marker. The storage area at the back was cluttered with detritus and junk. A single fluorescent light hummed and flickered, doing its best to chase away the gloom but still leaving the corners shadowed. In the far corner, behind a metal storage rack stocked with jumper cables and warning signs, something on the floor shifted in pain.

A sense of wrongness punched Christopher in the gut, twisting his insides. He had the sudden urge to grab Eva, use the remote, and take off in the X-Copter without looking back. He would have thought that by this time he would have stopped being so frightened, or at least developed some kind of tolerance to it, but if anything, this wave of fear was stronger than anything he'd ever felt before. He felt physically ill. His stomach snarled audibly.

"You OK?" Eva asked.

"Yeah," he responded shakily.

She looked less than convinced, and he didn't blame her. He didn't know what had gotten into him. At some point, he'd have to get used to being in danger if he was going to be an X-Man, but his nerves seemed to be getting worse instead of better, and he didn't know why. Rather than embarrass himself, he offered up a convenient excuse.

"I'm feeling a little off," he confessed. "Healing burns

through a lot of calories, and I guess I must be low. I've got the shakes."

He held up his hand to demonstrate. It was only half the truth, but it would do for now. Maybe he'd confess to Eva later, but he'd put his head in Sabretooth's mouth before he'd confide in him.

Sabretooth looked from the shadowed figure to Christopher and back again. "Can you hold on another minute?" he asked the figure on the ground. "This kid is a healer. I ought to feed him before he keels over. I don't want him punking out in the middle of fixing you up."

"I can wait..."

The response was faint, masculine. Jagged with pain. Sabretooth's face contorted with some overwhelming emotion that Christopher couldn't place. Fear? Worry? Desperation? Maybe all of them at once. But Sabretooth closed his eyes for a moment and calmed himself with visible effort, only opening them again when he was under control.

"There's a drink machine back here," he said to Christopher. "You should get some sugar in you before you pass out. You'll need it to help him." He indicated the figure in the corner.

"That sounds great," Christopher admitted. "But I don't have any change."

"No problem."

Sabretooth walked over to the machine, an older model with a faded-out display panel. He put his ear to it, listened for a moment, and then delivered a single, brutal punch. The panel exploded in a shower of sparks and a feeble electronic whine. He reached into the guts of the machine and pulled out a cold can, condensation dripping from its sides.

"Here you go, kid. Have some soda," he said.

"I'm from the Midwest. It's pop. That's a hill I'll die on," said Christopher.

He took the can and chugged the entire contents, then let out an enormous burp right in Sabretooth's face. He felt mortified, but Sabretooth only laughed.

Christopher felt a bit more human – or mutant, to be more accurate – as the sugar hit his bloodstream. He looked toward the darkened corner.

"OK, so what's going on here?" he asked. "Can we get some light so I can see what I'm working with?"

"It hurts my eyes," said the man in the corner.

"Oh, quit being such a big baby," said Sabretooth, pushing the storage rack over without any apparent effort at all.

Without the storage rack in the way, the light illuminated the damaged figure of a man on the floor. Christopher thought he looked vaguely familiar but couldn't place the face. He had slicked-back brown hair and piercing blue eyes, currently crinkled in pain. He wore a strange jumpsuit made out of a copper-colored material that looked like it belonged in a science fiction movie. Two holes had been blasted through it, one on his chest and one high on the meat of his thigh. The skin beneath had been cooked to cinders.

Whoever this guy was, he had one heck of a pain tolerance. Christopher couldn't believe he wasn't screaming. Probably shock. He'd been waiting all this time for someone to help him. At that moment, Christopher felt ashamed. Someone was hurt, but he'd gotten used to mutants getting injured. Somehow that had become commonplace, and Christopher hadn't treated it as seriously as he should have, and was just drinking pop while this man was suffering. He would never make the same mistake again.

"My name is Christopher," he said, dropping to his knees next to the injured man. "I'm here to help you."

The man grunted. "Are you a doctor?"

Christopher shook his head. What did this guy think he was going to do, perform a skin graft in the middle of this dusty office?

"I'm a mutant. A healer. I'll get you fixed up right away," he said.

"No mutants."

The guy feebly tried to push his hands away, and Christopher looked up at Sabretooth with a question in his eyes. He'd never once run into someone who didn't want to be healed. Maybe they might fear him after he'd done it, but refusing his help just to prove a point seemed unthinkable to him, especially considering how much pain this guy had to be in.

"This is Graydon Creed," said Sabretooth, as if that would explain everything.

"Oh, crap," Eva murmured.

As distracted and exhausted as he was after all of the chaos the day had held so far, it took Christopher a moment to place the name. Now he knew where he'd recognized the face.

Graydon Creed had made a run at the presidency a few years back and seemed like he might actually win the prize.

His campaign had been built on hate and fear, most of which had solidly been directed at mutants. People flocked to his messages of us versus them and his promises of safety and a return to the good old days of yore. His ma had voted Creed and even put a bumper sticker on their old station wagon. Even before Christopher had discovered he was a mutant, it made him feel ashamed and uncomfortable, like when he'd discovered that one of his elementary school friends had family members in the Klan.

Then Graydon had been assassinated at one of his rallies, and everyone had assumed that the mutants had gotten to him. Although clearly, the assassination had been a ruse, because the politician was up and walking, if a little charred. Christopher had never been so close to a famous person before, and especially not one who campaigned against his right to exist. It distracted him from his task. He studied Graydon's face outright.

"What?" asked Creed.

Questions ran through Christopher's head, but he couldn't bring himself to ask them. He didn't think he'd like the answers.

"I always wondered how your teeth got so white," he said instead.

"Cosmetic dentistry," spat the injured man.

"Huh. Go figure."

Christopher reached for him again, and for the second time, Creed batted him away. Without quite thinking about it, Christopher smacked Graydon's hand, fixing him with a stern glare.

"Listen here," he said. "I don't care whether you were

almost the president or not. I don't care whether you're Sabretooth's friend or not. Right now, you're my patient, and it's my job to keep you alive, and you're going to quit acting like a spoiled brat and let me do my job. My dad was a Marine, and once he got wounded in enemy territory, and the people who lived there offered to treat his wounds, and do you think he smacked them like a toddler? Heck no, he didn't. He gave them some extra food and helped them keep watch that night for the patrols. Because that's what you do when you're not a complete nincompoop."

After a shocked pause, Graydon's ultra-white teeth flashed at him. "Did you just call me a nincompoop?"

"Yes, I did." His attack of confidence began to fade away as quickly as it had come. "Because you were being one. Weren't you?"

"He sure was," said Eva. "Can you get on with it? This office smells like old hamburger, and it's making me feel ill."

"Tell me about it," said Sabretooth. He tapped his nose. "Enhanced senses aren't always a field of daisies, missy."

"What happened, anyway? The cops were less than forthcoming," she said.

He shrugged. "Not much of a story. We were at the Grace when the Sentinels showed up. Seems like the darned things are everywhere these days. They must multiply like rabbits. Anyway, I told Graydon to stay under cover, but somebody doesn't know how to follow simple instructions. He got hit. So after I took out the Sentinels, I found somewhere nearby to stash him. He was in shock, and I didn't want to cart him around too much and risk hurting him more. Plus, I knew it was just a matter of time before more Sentinels showed up."

"I keep meaning to ask somebody," Eva piped up. "What's up with the Sentinels? I mean, what's their beef?"

"Bolivar Trask designed them to hunt mutants. No beef involved. It's just what they do, so get used to it." Sabretooth's eyes narrowed. "Just how new are you?"

"We've been at the school about a month or so."

Sabretooth hit his head on the wall. It left a mark and knocked the calendar down.

"Come on, Summers, can't you at least send me newbies with some seasoning?" he said, looking up at the ceiling.

"I don't think he can hear you," Eva scoffed. "Besides, it's not like we're incompetent. We fought our way out of Limbo."

"Yeah?"

Flashbacks flooded Christopher at the mention of Limbo, distracting him once again. It had been the first time he'd realized that joining the X-Men could truly kill him, and he'd folded like a paper airplane. Dormammu's magic had been overwhelmingly powerful, and he'd outmaneuvered Illyana, pulling her into Limbo and forcing her to take her demonic Darkchilde form. Anyone who could dominate Illyana – on her home turf, no less – was someone that Christopher didn't want to mess with. He'd made a mental note to avoid Dormammu at all costs.

"It was the scariest thing I've ever done," Eva admitted. "I dream about it most nights. Do the nightmares go away after you've been at this for a while?"

"I don't dream," Sabretooth replied, his clipped tone making it obvious that he lied, and equally obvious that it would be fatal to point that out.

"Could you two pipe down?" Christopher asked, rubbing the bridge of his nose and trying to block them out. "I'm trying to concentrate here."

"My apologies, Christopher," Eva said.

"Yeah, sorry, kid."

Sabretooth sounded legitimately chastised, and the two of them fell into blessed silence. Christopher turned his attention back to Graydon. To his surprise, the politician seemed almost patient. Given that he was sitting there with two holes burned into him by giant robots, Christopher thought that he ought to be writhing in pain. He must have nerves of steel.

"I'm sorry this took so long," he said. "I didn't mean to leave you hurting."

Graydon seemed nonplussed by the genuine regret in his voice, but he scraped up an attitude anyway. "Don't worry about it," he said. "It's not like I wanted your help anyway."

Christopher ignored the dig and reached for the politician, ready to wrestle him into submission if possible. But this time, Graydon just closed his eyes as if he couldn't bear to watch. At least he'd stopped fighting.

"Can you help him?" asked Sabretooth, clearly worried.

Christopher nodded in reassurance, even though he hadn't yet taken a look. Hopefully he wouldn't have to take it back. He closed his eyes and aligned his energy with Graydon's. Immediately, he knew that something was wrong, something bigger than the holes burnt into the man's flesh. Christopher could sense most people as vague human shapes. He could feel the life force within them at first, and then as he went deeper, he could focus in on particular elements that felt out of harmony. He could connect with them, using his own body to feel their wounds and sicknesses. Perhaps, as he trained, he'd be able to do more.

The moment that he connected with Graydon, he sensed something he'd never seen before: Graydon's life energy wasn't confined to his body. He wasn't a faded outline of light like a sick person or a vibrant corona of energy like a powerful mutant. Instead, the energy poured into him as if from some giant funnel nearby. He'd never seen anything like it.

Once again, his stomach did slow flip flops. This felt unnatural. The energy flowing into Graydon felt wrong somehow. He didn't want to touch it, but he had an obligation to. If he shrank away from this because he feared what he didn't understand, he'd be no better than Graydon Creed and his followers. They feared people like him just because of how he'd been born. He could give his life to do the right thing, but that wouldn't matter. Not to them. They'd only see a dirty little mutie, just like Candy had.

He had to prove them wrong. He clenched his teeth together and reached into the twisted flow of energy.

It felt as bad as he'd expected. It was like taking a big bite of your favorite food only to find that every ingredient in it had spoiled, and someone had added live bugs to it while you weren't looking. His entire body shuddered, and dimly he heard Eva calling his name, but he couldn't respond. He would finish this healing. Perhaps if he did, he might purify the energy and fix whatever was happening to the poor man. Maybe Graydon would see then that his hate was unjustified.

His body wanted nothing to do with Graydon's, but he made it cooperate. He forced their heartbeats together through sheer will. He made their breath slow in tandem. He stimulated the politician's sluggish systems, jolting them into reluctant action and finally into overdrive, knitting new muscle and skin to replace the burnt areas.

Once the healing started, it felt better. Christopher still sensed the sick taint that surrounded them, but it didn't threaten to overwhelm him any longer. He poured himself into the healing, feeling the wounds fade away, and prepared to withdraw. But he couldn't. He was stuck somehow, energy pouring out of him and into Graydon. Normally, when the injury was gone, he just stopped. But he couldn't get out this time. Something held him there, and he panicked as his senses began to fade. He couldn't see beyond his body or Graydon's. He couldn't see…

He fell on his back on the floor, the connection suddenly broken. It took him a moment to realize what had happened. Graydon had shoved him away. For a moment, he could do nothing. He just lay there, grateful to be back in his own body where he belonged, even though his stomach roiled uncontrollably with fear and nausea.

"I told you to stop," said the politician, retreating away from him, his eyes wide with fear.

"Hey." Sabretooth nudged him with a foot. "He saved your life."

"He tainted me," said Graydon, turning on him. "Or he would have, if I wasn't already tainted by association."

Christopher heard none of this. The rank, oily life energy surrounded him still. It filled his eyes and plugged his nose.

It curdled his stomach. It wasn't life, not really. It felt like unlife, if such a thing existed. He didn't understand it, but he definitely didn't like it.

Unable to contain his roiling stomach any longer, he whirled around and vomited pop all over Graydon's slippered feet.

"Sorry," he said miserably.

Graydon shuddered. "And this is why we don't spend time with mutants," he said, sliding his feet out of his befouled slippers. "We inevitably find ourselves slogging through the worst mankind has to offer. Because mutantkind is not equal to us."

Sabretooth dumped a used napkin on his lap and smacked the back of his head. "Stuff it, Graydon," he said. "The kid just healed you and made himself sick in the process, and now you're pulling this human-superiority crap? Show a little tact."

"Seems to me that if we were as bad as you seem to think, he wouldn't have gone to all that trouble to save your bacon," Eva added. She pulled a shaky Christopher up to stand. "You feeling a little better now, pal?" He nodded. "Let's get you cleaned up, and then we can figure out how to get the lot of us back to the X-Copter, huh?"

"Yeah," he said, glancing at Graydon. He thought about confessing what he'd seen, but it would probably only start an argument that he didn't feel up to having at the moment. He would wait until the right time. A short wait couldn't hurt that much, right? "That would be a good idea."

CHAPTER 14

Eva couldn't wait to get back to the New Xavier School. She'd eat a million bland sandwiches. She'd look forward to her daily sessions with Emma Frost, although she still suspected that Emma had a few screws loose. From here on out, she would accept her student status without complaint if only it meant that she could escape Graydon Creed. In the short time she'd known him, she'd quickly come to realize that his attitude stank worse than the puke on his shoes.

"I need something to wear," he declared. "These clothes smell, and they'll attract too much attention out in public."

"Well, help look for something," she responded reasonably. "You're not broken."

He glared at her. She glared back. Sabretooth broke the detente by smacking Graydon on the back of the head, and in response, Graydon glared at him too. It failed to have the desired effect. Sabretooth didn't even change expression.

"If you want something else to wear, you'll help look for it," Sabretooth snarled.

Muttering all the while, Graydon helped sift through the

junk in the office, looking for clothing that didn't have holes burnt through it, or soda and stomach acids splashed all over it. They all pitched in, looking through boxes and piles of useless crap.

"What about this?"

Eva pulled out an oil-splattered yellow jumpsuit that looked like it hadn't been laundered in about three years. It was so crusty that it stood up on its own. Graydon grimaced.

"I can't go out in public in that," he said.

"You're not trying to make an impression," said Sabretooth. "Either stick with the aluminum foil suit, or wear this one. You pick. Anybody got shoes?"

"How about these?"

Christopher emerged out from underneath a shelf, his goggles and dreadlocks covered with dust and spider webs, holding a pair of work boots that had seen better days. Someone – probably the same person who had decorated the wall calendar – had drawn a smiley face on the toe of the left boot. Graydon took one look and began to shake his head.

"No. I have standards," he said.

"Then wear the puke shoes," said Christopher, who had clearly had enough.

Sabretooth nodded in approval. "I like you, kid."

Graydon's lips twisted in annoyance, and he thrust out a hand.

"Fine. Give me the boots and a little privacy. I need to change," he said.

As Graydon made his wardrobe switch, Eva sidled up to Sabretooth. She thought that a little advance planning might help avoid some arguments, especially from Graydon, who seemed determined to make trouble. He disliked mutants, and therefore he seemed to consider it his job to act like a spoiled brat.

She didn't know what to think of him. From across the ocean, he'd seemed a monster in the making, powerful and suave in his tailored suits, preaching hatred with a honeyed tongue. Her mother had always changed the station when he'd appeared on the TV, to Eva's great relief. But now, he was one face in a horde that hated her, and it all seemed so stupid. His good opinion was the least of her worries. At least that's what she kept telling herself. But she had to admit that his behavior rankled.

"So the X-Copter is out on the water," she said quietly.

"Yeah?" Sabretooth replied.

"I figure we should be able to get there in a couple of minutes. Do you want to go back the way we came? I figure we should plan in advance since Graydon's acting like a two year-old."

Sabretooth smirked. "Don't write him off just yet. He's a brilliant strategist. If he's acting the fool, he's got a reason for it."

"Yeah? He must like getting slapped around then," she said archly.

He laughed, and she looked at him askance. She'd thought he was joking, but he seemed to mean the compliment. She hadn't expected the mercenary to respect anyone, let alone the mutant-hating politician. Graydon must be paying him a boatload.

"So about the chopper?" she persisted.

"Look, kid, I like your thinking, but we're not going back to the chopper yet. There's something we need to pick up back at the museum first. I'm not leaving without it."

With that, Sabretooth turned around, looking toward the corner behind the shelving unit where Graydon hid to change his clothes. He picked up an empty Styrofoam cup and threw it at the politician's head. It bounced off his hair and onto the ground.

"You done or what?" he said. "Let's get this show on the road."

Graydon emerged wearing the jumpsuit, the boots, and a long-suffering expression. He'd found a package of wet wipes on some random shelf and made some attempt at cleaning the jumpsuit, leaving damp streaks across the fabric but accomplishing little else.

"You missed a button," said Christopher, reaching toward him. Graydon sidled away, clearly not wanting to be touched, and the healer subsided, shrugging. "Never mind, then. So where are we going now?"

"Well, I thought we were leaving, but apparently Sabretooth needs to get some mystery thing from the Grace Museum first," said Eva, folding her arms to underscore her displeasure. "Because apparently we want to get caught by the cops."

"Honey, if we work together, the cops can't hold us," said Sabretooth.

"Yeah, that'll happen," said Eva. "We've got one guy who dislikes mutants, and one guy who has a secret mission that he refuses to talk about because he doesn't confide in – what did he call us again, Christopher?"

"Newbies," Christopher supplied scornfully.

"Newbies. But wait a second. Who came here to pull his butt out of the fryer?"

Christopher pretended to think. "You know, I think that was us."

She feigned surprise. "You know, I think you're right!"

"Ha ha, aren't you two funny?" said Sabretooth. "But this isn't a game, kids. You want to play in the big leagues? Remind me again who was just puking his guts out a minute ago?"

Christopher swallowed. "Yeah, well, about that..." Eva's stomach sank. Based on his nervous expression, whatever he had to tell them wasn't going to be good. He looked around. "Wait a minute. Where's Graydon?"

Eva couldn't believe it. The politician had been there just a moment ago, and in that jumpsuit he should have been quite visible. Somehow, he'd managed to sneak out of the room while they'd been arguing. He'd done it with no mutant abilities, just determination and skill. She was equal parts annoyed and impressed.

Sabretooth definitely fell on the annoyed end of the spectrum. He punched the broken computer screen, sending a shower of sparks to rain down on the desk. Then he roared in frustration.

"He can't have gone far," she soothed him. "We'll find him."

Christopher nodded. "Split up, or stick together?"

"Stick together," Sabretooth growled. "I don't want to risk losing the two of you as well. I might be able to sniff him out."

"I might be able to sense him too," said Christopher.

This statement made Eva stop in her tracks. She hadn't realized that his abilities extended so far. He'd never seemed to be able to track people before. Once, when all of the students had been out hiking, Benjamin had gotten separated from the rest of the group, and Christopher hadn't seemed to know where he was. Had his abilities grown since then, or had he been holding out? If so, why?

"You can sense where people are just by... like, sniffing out their life force or something?" she said, not quite knowing what terminology to use.

"Not with most people," he said. "But Graydon is unique. That's what made me toss my cookies all over his shoes."

"You're feeling better now, though, right? Will tracking him make you feel worse?" she asked.

"I'm doing OK, thanks. I grabbed an extra drink and put it in my pocket if I get the shakes again. So like I was saying–"

"Will you two quit your yapping so we can go?" Sabretooth snapped.

Without waiting for a response, he marched out of the office with the air of someone who has just about reached breaking point.

"I guess I'll tell you later," said Christopher quietly.

Eva nodded. She wanted to know what he had to say, but she didn't want to push Sabretooth. He seemed to be a millimeter away from losing it, and it made her nervous.

If she'd known how to contact Cyclops, she might have considered it. Sabretooth had his moments, but she didn't trust him. This rescue mission hadn't gone at all like she'd expected it to. She'd thought they would sweep in to help and then head back to school to receive their accolades, but things hadn't gone that way at all. Sabretooth clearly had his own agenda, and she didn't like being led around on a leash. Graydon clearly hated them all, and she had no idea why they were protecting him given that he'd dedicated his life to exterminating people like them. Sabretooth was muscle for hire, sure, but the guy hated mutants. They must have been awfully desperate to agree to work together in the first place. The whole situation stank as bad as Graydon's slippers, and she could have used some good advice. But the old X-Copter remote didn't offer access to the comms unit, so they couldn't radio in until they got back to the chopper.

Cyclops was probably having a fit. They'd landed and gone radio silent for at least an hour now. Frankly, she was surprised he hadn't shown up with Illyana in tow to pick up his wayward students. Either he trusted them, or he'd decided to let them lie in the bed they'd made for themselves. She wasn't sure which option would be preferable, to be honest. She wanted her independence, but if Cyclops and the rest of the instructors marched into the parking garage right now, she'd feel at least a little relieved.

Outside the office door, Sabretooth hunched over, inhaling the exhaust-filled air. He growled low in his throat, a frustrated noise that emanated from deep within him. Christopher scanned the area, and he shook his head at her wordlessly. He had nothing.

"OK," said Eva, keeping her voice as light as possible. "He's probably trying to get out of here, right? So he'll either have gone for the stairs, or he'll be going up the ramp. Which way do you want to look?"

Sabretooth sniffed again. "Ramp," he said.

He took off, not even bothering to check if they followed. Christopher rolled his eyes, and Eva smiled a little as they trailed along after him. After every few steps, Sabretooth stopped to scent the air. When Eva tried to ask him if they were on the right track, he fixed her with a glare that froze the words in her throat. Seems he didn't feel like chatting.

They rounded a corner. Just a few feet away sat a serial killer van with whited out windows, parked too close to the neighboring sedan. Eva hated when people did that. Apparently, so did Sabretooth, because he stiffened like a dog on point and then started toward the van. They followed, jumping at the distant slam of a car door.

Sabretooth darted in front of the van and came out holding one of Graydon's vomit-covered slippers. He stared at it for a moment with an almost comical level of shock before he threw it on the ground.

"Damn it!" he snarled. "He's trying to throw me off the scent. When I find him, I'll..."

His eyes glowed, a red fury building in their depths. Eva had no desire to see all that pent-up anger unleashed. She didn't think he'd care if they were his friends or not if that happened. She had to calm him somehow.

"He's trying to jerk your chain," she said. "What does he want, Sabretooth? What is he trying to get?"

"The Box..." Sabretooth hissed, slamming his fist into his open hand. "Of course. He's trying to delay us to get to the Box."

"What Box?" she asked, hoping that maybe for once he'd answer, but of course that didn't happen. He shoved her aside in his hurry to get past, and she slammed against the sedan, rocking it slightly. He didn't even slow down.

"You OK?" asked Christopher, his brows furrowed.

"Peachy." She dusted off her palms. "Let's go find that Box."

"What Box?" he asked.

"Exactly!" she said. "I love being kept in the dark, don't you?"

"Will you two shut up and come on?" asked Sabretooth.

He already stood by the door to the stairway, holding it for them. They hurried through the door before he lost it completely, and it clanged shut behind them.

CHAPTER 15

When Eva, Christopher, and Sabretooth emerged back out onto the street, they found that the police presence hadn't abated much. Instead, the cops milled about, trying to look busy while clusters of reporters clutched umbrellas as they took eyewitness accounts on nearly every corner, bright lights blazing and cameras rolling as they tried to make sense of the morning's wild occurrences. Sabretooth took one look at the crowds and hunched into the depths of his trench coat. Between his size, his teeth, and his wild hair, he stood out in a crowd. Anyone who got a good look at him would instantly know that he wasn't a garden variety human. They had to stay inconspicuous, or they'd never make it to the Grace without getting into yet another altercation with the police.

"Are you sure we can't go without your mysterious Box?" asked Eva, eyeing the chaos.

"Even if we could, I'm not leaving without Graydon," answered Sabretooth.

"He's kind of a weenie," offered Christopher.

Sabretooth paused. "Yeah, but he's my weenie." He paused a moment longer, realizing that that hadn't come out right. "I mean, he's our weenie."

"I think that line would work better if you called him a jerk," Eva suggested, her lips quirking. "Or a moron. Anything but a weenie, really."

"Definitely," said Christopher, snickering.

"You know what I meant!" exclaimed Sabretooth. "Now quit it, before I knock your heads together. We can't leave without Graydon. Period. You sense anything, kid?"

Christopher looked around. His face tightened for a moment, and his hand went to his stomach, almost reflexively. Eva wondered if he was feeling sick again, and she almost asked about it, but one glance at Sabretooth's stormy expression convinced her that this wasn't the time.

"I feel something, but I can't tell where it's coming from," he said. "I might not know until we're right on top of him. Sorry. That's probably no help."

"Keep trying," suggested Sabretooth.

"You should probably stay out of sight," Eva interjected. "If these reporters catch sight of you, they'll have a field day."

He preened. "I am photogenic. But yeah. I'll keep out of sight. I can move quieter than you yokels. You walk like a herd of stampeding rhinos."

"Hey! We've been practicing," Eva protested.

"Practice more," he countered.

Christopher forestalled yet another burgeoning argument by waving Sabretooth away and grabbing Eva's arm. He led her out onto the path toward the Grace, and Sabretooth faded into the greenery like a jungle cat on the hunt. Even though Eva knew he was there, she had a hard time spotting him as he moved soundlessly through the soggy underbrush. She hunched against the continuing drizzle and gave up trying.

They made it most of the way to the Grace without incident, and Eva began to get a little cocky. They were going to waltz right through this huge crowd without being noticed. If anyone realized she and Christopher were friends – or at least temporary traveling companions – with the infamous Sabretooth, she'd have a hundred cameras in her face in seconds. But no one realized they were missing the story of a lifetime. Or the story of her lifetime, anyway.

As they approached the side of the building, however, Christopher began to retch again. He staggered toward a trash can, holding onto the sides for dear life. All she could do was rub his back and try to look casual. A cop gave them a suspicious once-over, and she shrugged.

"Must have been the food truck hot dog," she said.

After a tense moment, the cop moved on down the path. Eva scanned the tree line, wondering where Sabretooth was exactly, but she couldn't tell. It was probably for the best. If she couldn't spot him and she knew he was there, no one else would be able to either.

"Is he OK?" asked a nearby woman with tawny skin and a pouf of brown hair tied back with a bright scarf.

"He'll be fine. He ate a bad hot dog," said Eva.

"Oh my god. I love your accent!" said the woman. "Are you Australian?"

Eva pasted on a smile. She didn't understand the American fascination with accents, but she'd run into it before. The best thing to do was not to make a big deal out of it.

"Sure am."

"I spent a few months in Brisbane working as an intern for a news station. I loved it! I didn't want to leave. What brings you to Chicago?"

Eva wondered what this friendly woman would do if she replied, "I'm on a secret mutant mission. It involves vomiting and imaginary circuses and annoying girls named Candy." She imagined that all of that friendliness would dry right up, but maybe not. Not every human she met was anti-mutant, right? Her mom had accepted her, no questions asked. Another wave of homesickness overtook her, so strong that it surprised her. She wanted to go back so badly that it hurt. But she couldn't. She'd endanger her mom, and it rankled. Why couldn't everyone just accept her mutations the way her mom did?

Some of her conflicting emotions must have shown on her face, because the woman was watching her with concern. She forced herself to smile.

"Sorry. The time difference really has messed me up. I just zoned out there. I'm here on vacation," she lied brightly.

Christopher had stopped shaking now, and she paused to check on him, leaning over the trash can to murmur in his ear.

"You OK there, bud?" she asked. "You need anything?"

"Nope. It's the same thing as before," he said, shaking.

"Do I need to call for help?" she asked, putting a little added stress on the question, hoping he'd know exactly who she meant.

"No, not yet." He straightened a little, wiping at the back of his mouth with his hand.

"OK. I'm right here if you need me." Eva turned back to the woman, who seemed reluctant to leave. "Did you need something?"

"Actually, my name's Sarai, and I work for KTL news, and I'm doing a piece on the events from this morning. Did you see anything? I think your accent would make for good TV, and you've got the personality for it."

"That's kind of you, but I don't think I should. My friend's not feeling too great," Eva demurred.

Sarai glanced at Christopher, who took a can of soda out of his pocket. "He seems fine to me, and you're not going anywhere. Please? You'd really be doing me a favor."

Eva hesitated. They didn't have time for an interview, but they also didn't have time for an argument, and arguments drew attention. The cops had nearly arrested them after their altercation with Candy. Sarai seemed like the persistent type; she wouldn't give up easily. Maybe the best thing to do would be to give a noncommittal interview to placate her.

"I didn't really see anything," said Eva. "I'd like to help, but I'm not sure I could tell you any details that would make for good TV. I got here after everything was over. I had to hear it all from a friend."

Sarai shrugged. "But you saw the chaos afterwards, right? The people on the streets? The fear and nervousness? At this point, anything is better than nothing, and I've got nothing. I'd really appreciate it if you helped me out."

"No."

Suddenly, Sabretooth stood next to her. He appeared so quickly that Eva couldn't have said where he'd come from. It was as if he'd appeared out of thin air. Sarai's eyes went wide, and all of the color drained from her face. For a moment, it looked like she might faint.

"What the hell are you thinking?" he asked Eva. "You know how dangerous it is for people like us to plaster our faces all over the news?" He jabbed a clawed finger toward Sarai. "This nice lady will sell your mug for her chance at fame. The minute she realizes that you're not a vanilla human like her, she'll turn on you. They all do."

Sarai took a stumbling step backwards. Her high heel caught on the cracked concrete, nearly toppling her over. She righted herself, not taking her eyes from Sabretooth as she continued to back away.

"I wouldn't do that..." she whimpered.

"Of course you wouldn't." He grinned. The expression made Eva think of wild animals showing their teeth in feral, threatening leers that had nothing to do with mirth. "You mess with my girl here, you deal with me, you got that? She's mine. And nobody messes with me and mine. If they do, I rip their heads off."

That was too much for Sarai. She let out a startled bleat and took off running. One of her fancy designer shoes fell off. She took a single step back for it, but decided against it after a nervous glance at Sabretooth. Instead, she leaped into a waiting van, woke the startled driver, and urged him onto the street, nearly causing an accident in the process.

Eva pushed Sabretooth back into the bushes, looking around frantically to see if anyone had noticed. Seconds later, a pair of mounted officers rounded the corner. She tried to look casual. Christopher stood up hastily, kicking the shoe off the pavement and tossing his now empty can into the trash. The officers glanced at them as they clopped past but said nothing.

"What the heck were you thinking?" Eva hissed at the bushes.

The bushes said nothing. She thought about sticking her head in, but the cops might notice, and she didn't want to draw their attention. Christopher nudged her shoulder.

"It's not worth arguing over," he said. "Time's wasting anyway. Come on." She nodded, and they continued down the path. They didn't make it more than a few steps when he added, "Besides, I think he's right."

Eva startled. "Beg pardon?"

"Sabretooth was right. Being on TV isn't smart for people like us. Every time we turn around, it seems like somebody else wants to kill us. Anti-mutant activists. Sentinels. Psychotic super villains. Advertising our presence seems foolish under those circumstances, you know?"

"But I wasn't going to advertise. I was going to play stupid," she said. "Give me some credit. I was going to talk about how everything was so loud, and so scary, and I was so glad the cops were there, and that was it. What harm could that do?"

He shrugged. "Maybe I'm paranoid, but I bet you S.H.I.E.L.D. has files on all of us. I bet a lot of people already know who we are. The minute we went out in public with Cyclops, things changed. It would be naïve to think that they didn't." He paused, his face stricken. "I sound like a jerk. I didn't mean to call you naïve. I'm sorry."

"I think I get what you're saying," she responded quietly. "No offense taken. Heck, maybe you're right. I was just trying to avoid drawing more attention. I thought turning her down would make more of a scene, so I went along with it."

"I can't blame you for that. I was trying to get information out of Candy and ended up nearly getting us arrested, so I'd say we're even."

They grinned at each other.

"We make quite the team," said Eva, holding her hand out.

Christopher slid his palm over hers. "That we do."

"So what's up with all the puking? Something's wrong, isn't it? Are you using your abilities too much? Overextending? I need to know what's happening, Triage."

The use of his X-Men name made Christopher's grin widen, as Eva had intended. But she wanted him to know that she took him seriously too. He'd done a lot that day, healing multiple significant injuries all in fairly quick succession. She didn't want him to think that she was criticizing, but she needed to know what was happening.

He seemed to get it. He nodded soberly, his face drawn in thought.

"It's about Graydon," he said. "His energy's off. Something's wrong with him, and it's making me nauseous every time I come into contact with it."

Before he could elaborate further, Sabretooth leaped onto the sidewalk in front of them. His nostrils flared and his eyes were wild as he hunched on the sidewalk, his claws held at the ready. Near the entrance to the Grace a few yards ahead of them, a few onlookers screamed, running for cover. A horse reared up onto its hind legs and bolted, despite the efforts of its mounted officer to keep it under control.

Another pair of cops started toward them, drawing their weapons. At least they kept them pointed at the ground this time, but Eva had had enough of this whole gun thing. Her pulse thumped, but, for the first time, she felt just as angry as she did scared at the sight of the weapons. She was tired of being threatened every time she turned around. If she could get away with it, she'd bubble every person with a gun on sight.

"Hey, you!" shouted one.

Sabretooth paid them no attention. His eyes raked the ornamental bushes that ran alongside the museum, behind Eva and Christopher. He inhaled deeply, suspiciously.

"What is it?" asked Eva, looking back toward the cops. So far, they'd kept their weapons pointed at the ground, but the moment they aimed, she intended to freeze them. She'd had enough.

"Something smells fishy," said Sabretooth. "I don't like it."

Christopher edged in front of Eva, and she glanced at him.

"Why do you keep doing that?" she asked.

"All that testing Cyclops did indicates I'm near impossible to kill," he said simply. "I'm assuming you're not. So I'll shield, you bubble."

She nodded. That made sense, and she was relieved to learn that the decision hadn't been based on ridiculous male chauvinist crap. She would have had to hit him over the head for that.

"Hey!" the cop repeated, closing in fast. "We're talking to you."

"Go back the way we came," Sabretooth ordered, ignoring

the cops as he continued to scan for whatever had spooked him. "Around the corner."

They didn't argue. Sabretooth had to have been in thousands of fights, and since he was still breathing, he had to have won most of them. If he had his hackles up, they'd be crazy to argue. They retreated cautiously around the corner, and the police officers followed, shouting at them to stop. Eva's heart pounded in her chest. She didn't want to be shot. Regardless of what Christopher had said, she didn't want him to be shot either. Sabretooth would probably be fine if he took a bullet, but it would piss him off, so she thought it would be best if all shootings were avoided on principle.

Sabretooth guarded them the entire way, his back arched in a savage hunch, his claws and teeth bared and at the ready. Still, when the attack came, it took him by surprise. A tawny shape, almost the exact same shade as his hair, launched at him from above and landed on his back. He snarled in pain, and the creature snarled right back. The two of them rolled off the sidewalk and into the dirt, kicking up dust and bracken as they fought ferociously for dominance.

Eva and Christopher jumped out of the way, looking around wildly for additional attackers.

The cops rounded the corner.

"What the heck?" exclaimed the one on the left, moments before a second yellowish-brown creature darted out of the bushes, slashing at him with saber-like fangs. Blood spurted. It was over in seconds.

The remaining cop bolted, running like his life depended on it, which wasn't too far from the truth.

The large striped cat watched him go, ears twitching idly

as it contemplated pursuit. Eva couldn't believe her eyes. It looked a bit like an oversized tiger that had gone through the wash too many times, with faded out stripes and a glossy coat matted down by the fitful rain. It had a muscular forebody built for both speed and force. Enormous fangs jutted from its mouth, which opened to roar in challenge as it tensed in preparation to pursue its fleeing prey.

It was an honest-to-goodness saber-toothed tiger.

Eva stared at it longer than she should have, trying to convince herself that what she was seeing was indeed real. The cat shouldn't exist, but here it was. She was torn between the agitation that came with imminent battle and awe at the magnificent creature that stood before her, its eyes glowing an eerie green as it watched the cop run away.

As magnificent as the tiger might be, Eva couldn't let it run free to maul and kill. Christopher and Sabretooth had a point: the cops weren't their friends. But the fact that they'd turn on her and her fellow mutants didn't give her the excuse to do the same. Those decisions would take her down the same road as Magneto and the Brotherhood had gone down years ago, and she couldn't let that happen. Her mother would be mortified. She would do the right thing, even when it hurt. Even if it meant helping people who wouldn't do the same for her.

Acting on pure instinct, she put up a time bubble just as the cat leaped. It moved with a speed she didn't anticipate. She missed. The cat yowled, pulling up short and turning to inspect the glistening blue bubble, its hackles raised. It sniffed and pawed at the iridescent surface. Eva didn't like it when people – or saber-toothed cats, for that matter –

touched her time bubbles. It felt vaguely invasive, like they were going through her underwear drawer.

"Stop that," she said irritably.

The tiger's head whipped around to stare at her, the police officer and the time bubble forgotten in an instant. Its glowing green stare bore into her, and she wondered what magic animated its body. It had to be magic, right? Saber-toothed cats were extinct, and no living thing had eyes like that. It regarded her with detached hunger, and its ears twitched with renewed excitement. Maybe she ought to rethink her stance on cats touching her bubbles. Maybe it could touch her bubble as much as it wanted to.

It began to stalk toward her, crouching low and placing one paw after another on the ground, belly nearly grazing the wet sidewalk. Its eyes pinned her. She'd never understood why prey froze in the sights of a predator. When she was a kid, every time she had to watch one of those boring nature shows at school, she'd wanted to shout at the screen, "Run, you idiot! He's going to eat you!" For the first time, she understood why they locked up like that. Her fight or flight system did just that as the cat drew closer. It knew it had a job to do, but it also knew that fleeing would be futile. This cat would outrun her effortlessly. She couldn't fight it off. She would end the day as kitty chow, and there wasn't a single thing she could do about it.

For the umpteenth time that day, Christopher stepped in front of her as the saber-toothed tiger closed on her. He held no weapon, and he'd clearly come to the same conclusion she had about their non-existent chances of outrunning the deadly creature. The only thing he could do was shield her with his body, allowing the cat to tear into him. The idea terrified her, and he clearly felt the same. He shook from head to toe, but he didn't hesitate.

She had to do something. She couldn't let Christopher die for her. He might be nearly impossible to kill, but that wasn't the same as immortal. She tried to bubble the cat, but she just couldn't focus. Although she'd been working towards controlling multiple bubbles at once, it sapped her strength badly, and she struggled to hold two at once. Either she would have to wait until the first one dissolved on its own, or she had to pop it. But fear gripped her with such force that she had trouble concentrating, and her mental hold slipped off no matter how hard she tried. With every second that passed, the cat stalked closer and closer.

"You leave her alone," Christopher said, like he was scolding a household pet.

The cat tensed, gathering all of its considerable strength. It leaped onto Christopher's chest, its claws piercing his flesh. He cried out, falling to the ground, putting his hands on either side of the creature's massive head. The tiger yowled and thrashed, but still Christopher held on. Their eyes were locked in some invisible struggle. Eva wanted to help, but she didn't know what to do. Sabretooth could offer no assistance; he still fought the other saber-toothed cat on the opposite side of the clearing. So she stood there, frozen with indecision. Her body broke out into a cold sweat, and she bit the inside of her cheek, urging herself to move. Do something. But if she did the wrong thing, it could mean their deaths.

Christopher retched, his body convulsing, but still he held on. Was he trying to heal the tiger? That didn't make any sense to Eva, but it looked like the same reaction he'd had when he tried to heal Graydon.

With a mighty roar, Sabretooth lifted the other saber-toothed cat up over his head and slammed it down over a park bench, breaking its back. The mighty mutant bled from what looked like a thousand scratches, and his chest heaved as he panted for breath, but he had triumphed once again. He threw back his head and bellowed in victory as the body at his feet disintegrated, leaving nothing but a pile of dry bones, empty fur, and dust.

"Sabretooth, help!" Eva cried.

His head whipped around, and it only took moments for him to assess the situation. He grabbed a rock off the ground and flung it at the cat with impeccable aim. It pinged off the animal's shoulder, drawing its attention away from Christopher.

"Here, kitty, kitty, kitty," said Sabretooth.

He beckoned to the cat, eager to fight once again. A gleeful light played in his eyes as he licked blood from his lips. The tiger approached him, but instead of the graceful, slinking approach that it had made toward Eva, it now staggered on unsteady paws. Its fur appeared patchy now too, and as she watched, bits of it fell out in uneven clumps to be carried off by the wind. Sabretooth's tense eagerness relaxed as he watched the cat, and he seemed almost disappointed at losing the opportunity to do battle with it.

Halfway across the clearing, the sabre-toothed tiger shuddered, fell on its side, and went still. After a moment, it dissolved just as its companion had, leaving only bones and fur behind. Sabretooth tilted his head, studying the pile for a moment, then nudged it with the toe of his boot.

"Well would you look at that," he said, wonder in his voice. "Did you do that, kid?"

"The other one fell apart too," said Eva, pointing toward the pile.

"Huh. Never seen that before."

Eva hadn't either, but she was more concerned with Christopher right now. He had raised himself up to sit while she'd been distracted, which would have been a relief if he hadn't been clutching his stomach in obvious pain. Blood trickled from punctures in his suit. She went to her knees beside him but didn't know what to do.

"You OK?" she said. "Are you gonna be sick?"

He shook his head. "I think I got it, but I need a minute."

As Christopher caught his breath, Sabretooth pulled Eva aside.

"He OK?" he asked.

"He says he is, but I'm not sure."

"What's your gut say? You know him better than I do."

She considered this. "He's obviously hurting, but at this point, he's determined to go on. If it was really bad, I think he'd bow out and tell us to go on without him."

Sabretooth nodded. "That's good enough for me. I'll get him up then."

He walked over to where Christopher was still slumped on the sidewalk. He leaned down and held out a hand, being careful with his claws.

"Let me give you a hand," he said.

Christopher considered the offer for a moment. It seemed to take some effort for him to gather the energy to take the offered help, but he did it. Sabretooth hauled him to his feet and stood there a moment, offering a little extra support and stability. Then, he stepped closer. Eva couldn't help it. She listened in.

Sabretooth said, "I saw what you did there, kid. That was brave of you. Good work."

Then he clapped Christopher on the shoulder, nearly knocking him back off his feet. Christopher smiled tremulously. Eva couldn't tell if it was out of weakness or emotion, and she didn't feel like it was her place to ask. Instead, she cleared her throat and rubbed at her own watery eyes.

"So can we get that Box thing and get out of here already? I am so over this day," she declared in a shaky voice. "It sucks."

"You can say that again, missy," said Sabretooth.

Eva opened her mouth to say it again, and Sabretooth bared his teeth at her.

CHAPTER 16

The fight with the saber-toothed tigers had made a lot of noise, and it was only a matter of time before the cop that had escaped managed to convince his fellow officers that he wasn't completely nuts. He'd return with backup. Even if the other cops didn't exactly believe his story about giant prehistoric tigers dropping from the sky, they were already on high alert. They'd come to check it out, and Christopher thought it would be better if the mutants had gotten far away by then.

"We should go," he said, swallowing hard.

His stomach had settled into a slow roll, like the last day of the flu when you thought you might stomach some saltines or ginger ale but you definitely weren't ready for a full-on spaghetti dinner yet. Thin tendrils of that same tainted life force that filled Graydon seemed to permeate the air here. He could feel them on his skin, a creepy crawly feeling that he disliked intensely. If this was how Sabretooth felt with his enhanced senses, Christopher didn't know how he handled it. It would drive him mad.

Perhaps that explained a few things about Sabretooth's behavior, come to think of it.

Eva nodded. "You feeling up to this?"

"I'll manage."

She followed Sabretooth toward the front entrance once again, but Christopher stopped short. He looked along the featureless side of the brick building. Bushes and ivy lined the sidewalk in what looked like an unbroken line all the way to the corner, but there had to be a door down there somewhere.

"Wait a second," he said. "When we were talking to Candy, she mentioned that her sister went out through one of the emergency exits. If we waltz up to the main entrance, we're going to have to walk through a bunch of cops. I'll bet you Graydon didn't do that. He knows they're not going to open the doors for anybody, so there's got to be another way in. Remind me why we're not going around the back again?"

Sabretooth paused further up the sidewalk, shrugging. "I figured it would be more fun this way."

"More fun?" Eva demanded. "You're kidding me."

"Hey, I get bored. Everyone's got to have hobbies."

Eva gave Christopher a long-suffering look, and he smothered a grin. Sabretooth had to be joking. Although he didn't look like it. The more Christopher thought about it, the less certain he was…

It didn't matter.

"If we find an emergency exit, you can break down the door, right?" he asked Sabretooth.

Sabretooth scoffed. Clearly, he wouldn't even dignify this question with an answer.

"It'll get us to that Box quicker. That's good, right?" said Christopher.

"And Graydon too," Eva added brightly. "We'll find him, and we'll finally get out of here."

Sabretooth nodded. "Yeah, yeah, you're right. I'll have some fun some other time, I guess. I did get to fight a real saber-toothed tiger after all. How ironic is that? I should have gotten a picture."

"Very ironic," said Eva, deadpan.

Christopher led them down the path as they chatted. He wanted to get this over with, just so his stomach would settle. He didn't care how upset Cyclops would be; he intended to stop somewhere on the way back. He would buy a real meal that didn't come between two pieces of bread, and he would eat the entire thing. Somehow, he had the strange sensation of being starving and not wanting to eat ever again, both at the same time. It didn't fall at the top of his list of his favorite experiences. Not even close.

The Grace Museum was bigger than he remembered. They walked for a long time around the curving length of the building without seeing a single door, and Christopher began to wonder if maybe he'd made a mistake. Maybe all of the emergency exits sat on the other side of the building for some unknown reason having to do with building codes. Just as he gathered up the courage to tell the others to give up and turn around, he saw the outline of a russet-colored door set into the wall ahead.

He jumped up and down, pointing in excitement.

"Look! Look!" he exclaimed.

"It's a door," said Eva, looking at him askance.

Sabretooth patted him on the shoulder. "He doesn't get out much, does he?"

Christopher thought about clutching at his stomach again and making them feel guilty about teasing him when he'd repeatedly sacrificed his welfare for their safety. It wouldn't be much of an act, after all. But he blushed instead.

"I just want to get home before I puke again, guys," he said. "At this rate, I'll hork up my spleen before this is all over."

His earnestness seemed to work better than the stomach-clutching would have. Even Sabretooth had the grace to look sheepish.

"You feeling OK?" he asked.

"Not great," Christopher admitted, "But I'm holding on. The faster we move, the better."

"Can you feel Graydon yet?" asked Eva.

Christopher shook his head. "Not with all this interference. I should be able to tell when we get closer to the Grace, though."

"Let's get you in there, then," said Sabretooth.

He squared his shoulders and charged at the door, ramming it with all his might. The reinforced metal flew off the hinges with a squeal of protest. The security system let out a fading electronic whoop, and Christopher tensed, expecting the full lights and siren treatment, but it fell completely silent instead. He peered around Sabretooth's bulk, trying to figure out what had happened. The interior of the museum was a vast black chasm, with only the dim red glow of the security lights in the distance offering any illumination whatsoever.

"The lights are out," said Christopher.

"Good job stating the obvious, kid," replied Sabretooth. "That might have something to do with the giant robots with the lasers that were here earlier. They probably took out the power."

"That's good for us. No alarm," said Eva. "So, where's this Box of yours?"

Sabretooth stepped into the Museum and looked around. They stood in one of the natural history wings, in a room full of fossils in glass cases. Under different circumstances, Christopher would have loved to read every single placard, but he didn't have the time. He ran his fingers over a trilobite fossil and marveled at it. He was touching something millions of years old. How amazing was that?

As Christopher examined the exhibits, Sabretooth looked at the signage.

"The Box is in the Evolution of Mutants exhibit. This way," Sabretooth said, gesturing for them to follow.

As they wove their way through rooms full of fossils, Christopher fell into a broody silence. Something had been nagging at him, and the trilobite brought it to the forefront. The saber-toothed cats had been extinct for thousands of years, and they'd crumbled into bone, almost as if they'd never been alive in the first place. It led him logically to places he wasn't sure he wanted to go, but he had no choice.

The soft sound of crying interrupted this disturbing chain of thought, pulling him out of his reverie. He had fallen behind Eva and Sabretooth, who had hurried ahead to consult the map at the next intersection and seemed to be arguing over it. He ducked around the corner, gesturing wildly for silence and finally catching Eva's attention. He held his finger to his lips, and she clamped her hand over Sabretooth's mouth mid-rant. From the looks of things, he nearly bit her hand off before he realized what she was doing. Then the two of them slinked back to join Christopher.

"What is it?" whispered Eva.

They wouldn't believe him if he told them, so he just pointed. He could barely believe it himself, and he'd seen it with his own eyes. A pair of what looked like honest-to-goodness Neanderthals with loincloths wrapped around their waists carried a long stick on their shoulders. Tied to the stick and ready for roasting was a museum security guard. He was old and frail, with deep lines on his liver-spotted face.

Christopher had heard him whimpering around the cloth tied over his mouth.

Eva's eyes filled with tears, and she took an involuntary step forward as if eager to help him right now. Christopher had to grab her arm and hold her back, shaking his head.

"What?" she asked.

"Not a good idea," he responded, pointing.

The slumped bodies of a few other prehistoric men and women littered the carpet nearby, testament to a quick and brutal battle. Christopher had only caught the end of it, but he'd been impressed.

"There are a few more of them hiding in the displays," he whispered. "They throw spears. They ambushed the other prehistoric people and took the guy."

"Bad luck for him," said Sabretooth. "We need to get going."

The two students stared at him like he'd suddenly grown horns.

"You can't be serious, mate," said Eva.

"We don't have the time to waste on this," Sabretooth argued. "You heard him. They have an ambush set up. One of us takes a spear to the throat, and then Chris here has to heal us. He's been puking left and right as it is. It's not worth the risk. But if you want, you can go out to the doors and fetch the cops. Chris and I will go on and get the Box."

"It's Christopher. Not Chris, remember?" Christopher said.

Sabretooth sighed. "Whatever."

"Splitting up is a bad idea," Eva argued. "If we do that, we have to find each other again. That takes time, and we've wasted a ton already. Can't we free the guy without fighting them?"

"You could bubble them," suggested Christopher. "Buy some time. Call the cops and let them handle it."

"Then the cops know there's someone else here. I don't want to advertise our presence," said Sabretooth. "Right now, it's nice and quiet in here, and I'd like to keep it that way."

Christopher nodded thoughtfully, looking around the room. An idea had begun to form in the depths of his mind. It just might work…

"So I bubble them?" asked Eva. "I just can't sit back while they eat some poor old guy. I mean, we've got to have standards."

"Yeah, yeah. I know. I wouldn't have let them cannibalize the guy. Not really," Sabretooth replied, although Christopher wasn't sure whether to believe him or not.

"Wait." Christopher held up a finger. "I might have it."

Eva perked up, listening eagerly as he explained his plan in simple terms. They didn't have much time. The Neanderthals moved with swift efficiency to prepare a bonfire using sticks from one of the exhibits. They would be finished in minutes.

Sabretooth stood guard as the two students snuck down toward the Neanderthals and their intended lunch. Christopher knew he didn't approve of yet another delay in their schedule, but Eva was right. They had to have standards. He just couldn't abandon somebody to such a horrible fate. If that meant he puked his guts out again, so be it. Sabretooth had put his foot down on the topic of the Box; he and Eva had put their foot down on the subject of the guard. Now they were even.

The guard continued to squirm against his bonds as the prehistoric hunters built the fire, communicating in grunts and gestures. A pair of them stood guard, spears at the ready. Eva moved like a shadow, darting from display to display in quick, furtive movements. Christopher did his best, but he'd never been the fastest. His overcoat kept brushing up against the displays, making the slightest of noises. At some point, one of the Neanderthals would hear him. He stopped his approach, hoping that he would be close enough.

He crouched down and mashed the buttons on the display. If the power had been up, a recording about the use of tools by the Australopithecus, likely read by a narrator in a bland monotone, would have played over the speakers. With the power down, all that came out when he pushed the button was a single garbled syllable at high volume. It startled the Neanderthals; they grabbed their spears and grunted aggressively as they searched for the source of the noise, but Christopher was already on the move. He moved to another display and pushed another button, producing another earsplitting syllable. They nearly jumped out of their skins.

He would have felt guilty about using technology to frighten a bunch of prehistoric people except for the part where they were going to eat a frail old man for lunch. A little fear wouldn't hurt them, and it was a lot better than letting Sabretooth knock their heads together. He continued on, pushing buttons on various displays, drawing them further and further away from the man on the spit so that Eva could free him. Then he pushed a button that emitted a clap of thunder. Perhaps the Neanderthals worshipped some lightning deity, or maybe they'd just had too many bad experiences standing on top of hills during thunderstorms, but they panicked. En masse, they ran from the room, hooting and clutching their spears.

Slowly, Christopher straightened from his semi-stealthy crouch to look after the Neanderthals with a puzzled look.

"I guess they must really hate lightning," he said. "Too bad we don't have Storm here. They would have peed their loincloths."

"Yeah," said Eva. "You OK there, mate?"

She loosened the gag from the guard's mouth, and he greeted her with the widest grin Christopher had ever seen. It brightened up his face despite the tear streaks.

"Thank you, young lady," he said. "I thought I was a goner."

"We got you," said Eva. "Gimme a second, and I'll find some way to cut you loose."

She turned to look at the displays, but before she could take a single step, Sabretooth stalked forward. His claws flashed. SNIKT! SKIKT! In their wake, pieces of rope pattered to the ground.

"Can we go now?" Sabretooth growled.

The guard went pale. He took his hands from the stake and sat upright, massaging his wrists. "You're mutants, aren't you? The ones they warn about on the news. You folks shot up the place earlier today."

"I didn't shoot anybody," said Sabretooth, baring his teeth. "They shot at me."

Christopher stepped between them. He wanted to avoid a confrontation. It felt like everyone they met hated them on sight, and it was beginning to get discouraging.

"We don't mean any harm," he explained. "We've got a friend who's lost in here, and he might be in danger."

"Oh." The guard considered this for a moment before getting to his feet in slow, painstaking stages. Eva offered a hand, but he waved her away, not unkindly. "I've got it, young lady. I've got it."

Once he finally made it to his feet, he looked them over. He flinched as he got a good look at Sabretooth, but otherwise he made no reaction. Then he said, "So you think your friend is in danger, but you stopped to help me instead? Why would you do that?"

Christopher blinked. "You were about to be eaten, sir."

"Nobody should have to go through that," added Eva.

The guard arched one of his bushy eyebrows at

Sabretooth, who hitched a shoulder.

"The kids are stubborn. I would have let you handle it. You're a grown man," he said.

The guard huffed. "Well, at least you're honest. I believe you. But I really ought to call this in. If I were a suspicious man, I'd think you were trying to steal something, sneaking around the museum while it's closed like this."

"What?" Eva demanded. "After we just risked our lives to save you?"

"Eva, simmer down," Christopher said, patting her on the arm.

"Wait. What did you say?" said the guard, coming to attention.

"Huh?" asked Christopher.

"What's your name, young lady?" the guard persisted.

"I'm Eva," she responded in some confusion.

He swallowed hard. "You know, I'm not a religious man, but I recognize a sign when I see one. You can go."

"Just like that?" Christopher asked cautiously. It seemed too easy.

The guard nodded. "I won't tell a soul you were here. Lock me in the maintenance closet if you think I'm lying. There's one right over here. I'll show you."

"Why the change of heart?" asked Christopher.

"My wife's name was Eva. She died a year ago today. She'd say this was a sign, and I sure could use one." The guard shook his head in wonderment. "You know, I always said mutants couldn't be trusted. I even voted for that anti-mutant candidate a few years back. What was his name?"

"Graydon Creed?" asked Eva.

"That's it. But Eva said I was an old fool." He shook his head, his eyes welling again. "Looks like she was right. If I show you where that closet is, can I trust you to come let me out again once you find your friend?"

"Of course you can," said Christopher.

He held out a hand, and when they shook, it felt really good. Like they'd both learned something about trust.

"That was real touching," said Sabretooth from the hallway. "Are you coming, or am I leaving without you?"

CHAPTER 17

As they wandered the darkened halls of the Grace Museum, Christopher could feel a familiar presence a short distance away, in the direction of the Evolution of Mutants exhibit. The exhibit teemed with the twisted life force that had been making him feel so awful, and for the first time he realized why: because this life force had been perverted by some strange magic he didn't understand.

He nodded, swallowing against the sensation of bile in his throat.

"Graydon is in there." He pointed. "But like I was trying to tell you before… Wait!"

Sabretooth didn't stick around to hear anything else that he had to say. The moment that the word Graydon hit the air, the elder mutant took off, hurrying toward the Evolution of Mutants exhibit like someone had lit him on fire. Christopher wanted to finish the conversation, but they had to follow him. Someone had to keep him in line.

"We'll talk about this later," he promised Eva, and she nodded.

They hurried after him.

Christopher took one step into the exhibit and immediately began to wish that he could have seen it when it was intact. The first display charted the evolution of mutant DNA up to M-Day, when most of the mutant population had been wiped from the earth in one catastrophic magical swoop. The bottom half of the display had been obliterated by a laser blast, making it completely illegible, but Christopher didn't have the time to stop and read anyway. He would have liked to come back and take a look around, though. Maybe talk Cyclops into a field trip for the school, since the material here really did relate to their field of study. But it would take the Grace some time to rebuild after the extensive destruction that had occurred here.

One side of the room had completely caved in, leaving a pile of rubble, twisted metal, and exposed wiring that made him grateful that the electricity no longer functioned. Life-sized models of various mutants stood against one wall. Juggernaut's head had been blown off his shoulders, but he still loomed over Christopher. He even dwarfed Sabretooth.

In the center of the room, a large cluster of glass cases contained artifacts that scientists had found to contain particles of mutant DNA. Placards explained how materials from space may have caused mutations in normal humans, and how collecting and studying these artifacts could potentially help scientists understand how mutations worked and eventually how to control them. Christopher wasn't sure if that was a good thing or not, but it definitely interested him.

Then he realized that one of the cases on the far end had been cracked open. Graydon Creed was trying to sneak away from it with a metallic box tucked under one arm. It was approximately the size of a tissue box, with a raised glyph decorating each surface. The glyphs shimmered in the dim red glow of the emergency lights. Christopher's eyes had adjusted to the low illumination, so it stood out. It seemed as if the glyphs sucked up what little light was available, storing its energy.

Before Graydon could make his getaway, Sabretooth stepped into his path, crossing his arms and making his muscles bulge impressively. He grinned, showing his incisors.

"Going somewhere?" he asked.

Graydon had the gall to look casual, tucking the Box more securely under his arm and striking a thoughtful pose as if for some invisible camera.

"I thought I might take a walk," he said. "That parking garage was a bit stuffy, and to be honest, your personal hygiene leaves something to be desired."

"What?" demanded Sabretooth.

"I realize you're not used to spending time in more civilized circles, but have you considered a clinical strength deodorant? Your body odor could take out a wild bull. Although perhaps that was the intent."

As he spoke, Graydon edged toward the exit, clearly hoping to distract Sabretooth enough to make his escape. But if anything, his barbed words only made the mutant more desperate to keep him in check. Sabretooth dogged his every move, looming over him as they exchanged insults.

Eva and Christopher watched as they bickered, neither one of them insane enough to interfere.

"This is ridiculous," Sabretooth finally said. "Give me the Box."

"Why should I? It doesn't belong to you. I rightfully stole it!"

"Well then, I'm stealing it back from you."

"Go find your own Box!" Graydon demanded.

Eva put up her hands and looked at Christopher as their voices grew louder and louder.

"I really don't want to get in the middle of this, but if they keep screeching at each other, somebody's going to come looking," she said.

He nodded.

"I can't figure them out," she continued. "They talk like they hate each other, but Sabretooth risked everything to save Graydon. You don't do that for somebody you hate."

"You just described half of my family members," Christopher joked.

Eva snickered. "Yeah, no kidding. So you've been trying to tell us something about the Box. What's going on?"

"You know how I keep puking? That's never happened to me before. Graydon's life energy is like swimming in a polluted lake. To make matters worse, once I got in, I couldn't get out. It was like a sinkhole pulling me in. I think I would have been stuck if he hadn't shoved me away."

"That sounds bad," she said, raising an eyebrow.

"Very."

"Damn."

"The saber-toothed tiger felt like Graydon does, and

when it died, it fell into dust, because it wasn't really alive in the first place."

He stared at her significantly, hoping she would understand what he was trying to tell her. He didn't want to have to say the words aloud, not outright. But she blinked at him, shaking her head.

"Please tell me you're kidding," she begged.

"I wish. Those tigers disintegrated into bones and pelts. The same things that the Grace puts up. They have saber-toothed tigers on display. I've seen them. They also have Neanderthal hunters, like the ones we saw trying to cook that guard for lunch."

"So somebody magicked those tigers and the hunters back to life?" she said thoughtfully. Her eyes settled on Graydon, and she frowned. "I don't like where this is going."

He hung his head. "Yeah."

He just couldn't bring himself to say it. Not yet. Because maybe he was wrong about Graydon. The politician might not be likeable, but that didn't mean Christopher wanted him to be a zombie either.

Sabretooth and Graydon argued on. In fact, they seemed to rather be enjoying themselves. Venting off some steam. However, they were shouting so loud that the floor had started to tremble, although that didn't entirely seem possible, even for Sabretooth. But the glass case standing a few feet away visibly shook in a rhythmic tempo that increased at a steady rate.

"Uh, guys?" he said, raising his voice. Sabretooth and Graydon paid him no attention. They were having too much fun arguing. "Guys?" he shouted. "I think we have a problem!"

They fell into a sudden, shocked silence.

As soon as they stopped shouting, the thunderous footsteps in the distance became immediately audible.

"What the heck is that?" demanded Sabretooth.

Christopher closed his eyes and shook his head as the pounding grew closer. He had the sinking feeling he knew what was making the noise, because he knew the Grace's collection well. He'd bought a book about it during his visit.

Last year, the museum had added an extraordinary find – the largest and most complete Tyrannosaurus rex skeleton ever discovered. They'd named it Bob. They'd put Bob on permanent display as the shining star of the Grace Museum's collection, and he loomed fifteen feet tall at the center of the dinosaur atrium. Although Christopher had left his dinosaur days behind him, he'd read all about it.

Somehow, he knew before the enormous creature turned the corner. Perhaps he was getting better at sensing the shape of the energy emitted by the Box, and something so incredibly massive had to register on his radar. Maybe he was just being fatalistic and expecting the worst possible thing to happen.

Regardless of the reason, when the enormous undead Tyrannosaurus turned the corner and fixed its beady eyes on them, he wasn't surprised at all. Muscles bulged under the scaly hide, and the entire form seethed with that familiar magic.

"It's Bob, the undead T-Rex," he said, as if you ran across those every day. "We should run now."

CHAPTER 18

The walls of the Grace Museum shuddered and cracked as the Tyrannosaurus thundered toward them. Its eyes glowed with an eerie green light that reminded Christopher of the strange shimmer on the glyphs that decorated the Box and the unnatural glow of the saber-toothed cat's eyes. He didn't have to concentrate to sense the twisted life magic that animated its limbs. It made him queasy. His heart raced in his throat, and he felt nearly faint with fright. If that thing got too close, he would toss his cookies all over the place, even though he was fairly sure there were no cookies left to toss.

Christopher expected Sabretooth to argue with the suggestion that they should run from the attacking dinosaur. But the giant mutant took one look at the rampaging beast and nodded.

"Running sounds smart to me," he said. "We'll table the argument."

Graydon clutched the Box like he expected someone to rip it from his hands at any moment.

"I'm keeping a hold of this," he declared.

"Who cares?" asked Eva. "Come on."

They sprinted from the room. It was a futile exercise. The dinosaur would catch up with them soon enough. As they ran, Christopher racked his brain for options. Electronic whines and lighting sound effects wouldn't scare this creature off, but they had to do something, or they'd end up as dino chow. His breath already came in ragged gasps. He wasn't in bad shape, but his body had been through the grinder already today, and it had reached its limit. It needed rest and fuel before he could push it much further.

"Can you bubble him?" he asked Eva, clutching at the growing stitch in his side.

She glanced over her shoulder, her eyes wide.

"He's awfully big," she said nervously. But then her lips firmed, and she nodded. "But if that's what I need to do to get us out of here, I'll make it happen."

"You're not alone," he said. "We have to work together. It'll take all of us to take Bob down."

"The giant dinosaur's name is Bob?" asked Sabretooth. His shoulders shook with silent laughter as he loped along, devouring the ground with long, easy strides that Christopher envied. The mercenary seemed completely unfazed by the enormous predator giving chase behind them, which he envied even more. Did Sabretooth even feel fear?

"Yeah."

Bob picked that moment to burst through the wall right above Graydon's head, taking them all by surprise. He tried to snatch the Box from Graydon with his sizable teeth, but the politician fell over backwards and the dinosaur missed by a hair. Graydon let out an inarticulate yell of panic and scrambled to his feet, and Bob gave immediate chase.

"Bob's chasing the Box!" yelled Eva in a burst of inspiration.

"What do I do?" exclaimed Graydon, running for his life with the Tyrannosaurus hot on his heels.

"Throw a long pass!" Sabretooth directed, holding out his hands.

Graydon tossed the Box in a perfect spiral across the long gallery. As soon as the artifact left his possession, the dinosaur lost all interest in Graydon. Bob's head turned to follow the Box as it flew through the air and thunked into Sabretooth's arms. The mutant took off running in the opposite direction.

"That's the plan!" yelled Christopher. "We need to weaken it. Set up traps and bubbles, and pass the Box from person to person. Once it's taken some hits, I should be able to finish the job. I hope. We can't just bubble it and leave it to come after us later."

"Good idea, kid," said Sabretooth, tucking the Box securely into his leather jacket. "On it."

"Bring him through that archway at the end of the gallery," instructed Eva, pointing toward the entrance to the Natural Evolution Hall. "It's too small for him. He'll get stuck, and I can bubble him there."

"Got it, missy," said Sabretooth.

He led the dinosaur the long way around, giving the rest of them time to get through the archway first. At one point, he leaped over a pile of debris without slowing down in a display of agility that could only have been accomplished by a mutant with enhanced physiology. Bob stomped on the debris, smashing it to smithereens as he pursued his quarry. Sabretooth looked back, rolling his eyes.

"Show-off," he muttered, and then leaped through the archway.

The dinosaur followed, crouching to fit through the narrow opening. Its wide body wouldn't fit. It tried to ram through, knocking chunks out of the wall. The building rumbled, and bits of plaster pattered down on the floor as the animal mindlessly began to batter his way through.

"Eva, you'd better freeze him before he brings the ceiling down on us," Christopher suggested.

She nodded, clenching her jaw in concentration. Her face went pale, and he thought he saw the vague outlines of a bubble wavering in and out of existence around the dinosaur, but he wasn't sure. Bob continued to batter at the entryway. Stone crumbled. The dinosaur was almost through, and the bubble still failed to materialize. Christopher began to worry that maybe Bob was too big to fit. If that was the case, what would they do?

"Eva?" asked Sabretooth. "You got him?"

She wavered on her feet but continued to hold her hands out toward the Tyrannosaurus.

"I'm so close," she said as a thin trickle of blood began to run from her nose. "Almost got him."

Christopher reached toward her hesitantly, worried. "You need help?" he asked, but she shook her head.

"Almost got it," she repeated.

"Aw, heck," muttered Sabretooth. "It's too late. Graydon, catch!"

He tossed the Box back to Graydon and launched himself at Bob just as the Tyrannosaurus wrenched itself through the entryway in a spray of rubble. Sabretooth landed on the creature's torso, holding himself aloft with his claws buried deep in its flesh. Bob reared back, roaring in pain. Christopher clapped his hands over his ears, but that didn't help at all. Bob had some lungs on him.

"I'm sorry," said Eva, stricken. She wiped her face with the back of her hand and seemed dazed as she looked down at the red smear of blood. "I really tried. I've never bubbled something this big before."

"It's OK, Eva. It was a lot to ask," said Christopher, rolling up his sleeves. It was up to him now.

Sabretooth climbed up Bob's body as the T-Rex tried desperately to dislodge him. Graydon stood nearby, clutching the Box. He intercepted Christopher as he crossed the room toward the ongoing struggle. His face was drawn with worry as he watched Sabretooth scale the giant prehistoric beast.

"How can I help?" he asked. He looked torn for a moment but then thrust the artifact toward Christopher with a convulsive movement. "Do you need the Box? Take it."

Christopher gently pushed Graydon's hands away.

"I can't believe I'm saying this, but I need you to take the Box and hide. Not too far. If Bob gets loose, you don't want to be on your own. But you can't stay here. We don't know what will happen if Bob gets his claws on the artifact, but we can't risk it. You understand?" he said.

Graydon nodded, beginning to back away, but Christopher put a hand on his arm before he got too far.

"If you run, I'll find you," Christopher said. "Please don't make me do that."

Graydon glanced back at Sabretooth. Something had changed. For the first time, he'd lost the air of revulsion he'd worn every time he addressed any of the mutants. Christopher had no idea what had happened to cause such a difference, and he had no time to ask, even if Graydon would have confided in him.

"I won't," Graydon said simply.

Then he hurried away with the Box in hand.

As they'd talked, Sabretooth had scaled up Bob's long torso. Now he clawed at the mighty creature's eye socket, ripping long rents in the scaly hide. Bob whipped his head back and forth, thrashing in pain. Sabretooth went flying, impacting hard against the ceiling and then crashing to the floor. He lay there for a moment, motionless as his accelerated healing worked overtime to try to fix him. As Christopher hurried toward them, his heart in his throat, Sabretooth began to stir. The T-Rex stomped on him, crushing his body with its massive weight. Sabretooth's face went immediately slack, and he collapsed back down to the ground once more, limp and still.

"No!" Eva shouted. She began pelting the dinosaur with rubble from the pile, throwing with the impeccable aim of a girl who has spent many a summer at softball camp. A chunk of stone hit Bob right in the eye, making him shriek. He thundered toward her, completely forgetting about Sabretooth in his anger and pain.

Christopher darted forward as the dinosaur lumbered past. He leaped onto the massive foot and put his hand onto the scaly hide. The dinosaur was cold to the touch. It felt like a leather jacket on a rock wall, not a living being of flesh and blood. The ever-present flow of tainted magic filled him, twisting his insides, but this time, he knew what to expect.

He'd done this before and he'd survived it. He would do it this time too, until there was nothing left of the T-Rex but a pile of bones.

During his struggle with the saber-toothed cat, he'd realized something. A normal living creature was connected to their life force, but these creatures were connected to something else. He'd found a way to sever that connection, but it took time and severe, draining effort. To do so with the dinosaur would strain him, but he had to try. He dug in, ignoring his heaving belly and the queasy feeling deep in his bones, and began to work. The energy overtook him in a rush, nearly knocking him out, but he held on.

It was working. The dinosaur felt its strength ebbing, and it did everything in its power to dislodge him. It stomped its feet, making his ears ring. It spun around in dizzying circles so he had to hold on for dear life. It pitched its body back and forth, trying desperately to reach him, but its struggles became increasingly weaker as he sapped its strength.

Then, just as with Graydon, the flow of power changed. He felt the moment when it began to clutch at him, trying to pull him into its depths. Now, instead of trying to dislodge him, it tried to suck him in. He heard words in the distance, spoken by a deep and booming voice. He'd heard that voice somewhere before, but he couldn't place it. He strained to make out the words. If only he could get a little closer...

Then someone grabbed him, and his senses snapped back to his body, taking him by surprise. He found himself lying on his back on the ground, looking up at Eva. Littering the floor around him were hundreds of enormous bones. He had unmade the dinosaur.

"Christopher? Can you hear me? Are you OK?" Eva asked, worried.

He took a moment to gather himself and consider her question. His head spun, and it felt strange to be aware of his body again, but it seemed like everything was intact. His stomach wasn't too sure about things, but that he could deal with. He nodded and tried to look reassuring.

"My insides want to become my outsides, but otherwise I'm OK. What happened?"

"I pulled you away. You said you couldn't get free when you tried to heal Graydon, and I figured the same thing might happen again, so I took a chance on it." She looked around at the pile of bones. "I think it paid off."

"Yeah."

"Can I help you up?" She offered a hand.

He shook his head, and she retreated with an expression of hurt on her face.

"Eva, I like you a lot, so I'm going to ask you to go away now. There are only so many times that you should have to see me vomit in one day."

She snickered. "You keep this up, and I'm going to suggest that they change your X-Men name from Triage to Puke Bucket."

He had a witty retort for that, but it would have to wait until later. He got to his feet and staggered toward the trash can, holding his hand over his mouth. He probably had nothing left to heave at this point, but better safe than sorry. Eva stood out of the way and kept the rest of her witty comments to herself.

CHAPTER 19

Eva didn't know who to help first. Christopher hugged the garbage can like he'd fallen in love with it and was contemplating a proposal. Sabretooth, who appeared to have survived the undead Tyrannosaurus foot stomp through sheer stubbornness, had climbed to all fours on the debris-strewn carpet but couldn't manage to make it any further. He wavered there, shaking his head as if to clear it. She had no clue where Graydon had gone. The jerkface had probably run off with the Box again, knowing him.

She sighed and dusted off her hands before marching over to Sabretooth. He'd been hurt the worst, so it seemed like the most logical place to start.

"Do you need anything?" she asked. "Want me to help you up?"

"Just give me a minute," he muttered. Then, to her surprise, he added, "Thanks. You did a good job there. What's your name again?"

"Eva. Eva Bell," she replied, feeling rather flattered.

"You got a mutant name yet? Don't let Cyclops pick it. If

you look up the word 'lame' in the dictionary, you'd find a picture of Scott Summers. If you need one, let me hook you up instead."

Sabretooth sat back on his haunches and wiped his face. He looked at his hand, stained with blood and dust, with a confused look that clearly said he didn't quite remember what had happened. Eva's heart went out to him.

"They call me Tempus, on account of the time bubbles. I don't think that's too silly, do you?" she asked.

He considered, rubbing his chin. With every passing moment, he looked less dazed. Animation returned to his face, and he looked around, reorienting himself. But all the while, he kept up the casual conversation, pretending that everything was fine. Stalling for time. She didn't have the heart to call him on it.

"That's not bad, actually." He stood. Stretched. Eva could hear the POP-POP-POP of his spine as it adjusted back into place. He sighed with obvious relief. "Now that's more like it."

Christopher finally extricated himself from the garbage can and trudged toward them. Eva's mother always loved to say that she looked like death warmed over. If she didn't have her hair perfectly done or her makeup on just right, she pulled out her favorite phrase even if Eva thought she looked just fine. For once, the saying fit. Christopher looked exactly like death warmed over. Dark circles ringed his eyes, and his face had gained an ashen tint. But he grinned with delight as he saw Sabretooth on his feet.

"I'm glad you're OK," he said.

"You sure you're OK, kid?" asked the older mutant, his face drawn in concern. "You don't look too good."

"I feel like death warmed over," said Christopher.

Eva laughed aloud, making the other two look at her strangely.

"My mom always says that," she explained. "I was just thinking about it, and now you said it. Don't mind me. I'm probably hysterical."

"You and me both."

Graydon's dry voice took them all by surprise. He climbed down the pile of rubble on the far side of the room where he'd been hiding. The Box slipped from his grip and rolled down before him, coming to a sliding stop on the floor. He picked his way down with surprising nimbleness. He'd never seemed particularly athletic to Eva, but then again, she'd only ever seen him as a mutant-hating politician. There had to be more to the man than that, didn't there?

He picked up the Box and ambled over, taking in their various expressions of shock and surprise. He offered them a thin-lipped smile in return.

"You all thought I'd run, didn't you?" he asked.

"I wonder why," said Sabretooth dryly. "Oh, I know. You hate our guts."

"Only in general terms," admitted Graydon.

Sabretooth's eyes lit up, but he tried to play it cool. "Yeah, I get that. I'm glad you're safe, and not just because you brought that Box back."

Graydon's eyes roved over the room. If it had been damaged before, now it was obliterated. The dinosaur's bulk had crushed nearly every remaining artifact and display, leaving only the occasional piece intact. Eva felt a little sick as she looked over the destruction.

"That's astounding," said Graydon. "How did you defeat something so powerful?"

"He did it," said Eva, pointing at Christopher.

"Well," Christopher demurred, "Sabretooth weakened it. Eva slowed it down. You helped get the Box out of the way. Then I sealed the deal, that's all."

Eva giggled. "Sealed the deal? You sound like a car salesman."

"Can you get me a good APR?" asked Graydon, joining in on the joke to the shock of everyone involved.

Christopher stuck his tongue out at them. Sabretooth made a big show of rolling his eyes and throwing his hands up into the air.

"You see what I have to put up with, Bob?" he asked the nearest pile of bones. "A bunch of children." As if in response, the floor rumbled, and Sabretooth's eyes went wide. "Hey now," he said warningly, kicking at the bone. "Stay where you are, Bob. We don't need to go for round two."

The floor rumbled again.

Graydon brushed plaster dust from his hair, looking up at the ceiling. Hairline cracks began to crawl across the surface, and a distant rumbling suggested that something was happening. It didn't sound good.

"I don't think it's the dinosaur," he said. "I think it's the Grace. It took a lot of structural damage during that fight, and Bob took out a few galleries on its way to us, too. I think we need to get out of this building before it falls on us."

"We can't forget that guard," Christopher reminded them.

"Right. Back the way we came?" asked Eva, starting in that direction.

"You won't make it out that way." Graydon started down a different hallway, urging them to follow. "There's an emergency exit just down here."

It felt like a huge risk. He had hated them from the start, and perhaps his new attitude was just an act, calculated to make them follow him into certain death. The thought of putting her life into his hands did not feel like a bet that Eva wanted to make. It somehow made her feel less safe than leaving it all to chance. But the other two started to follow, and there wasn't time to argue. The building shuddered with increasing intensity, and a steady rain of plaster and paint began to patter down around them.

"OK," said Eva, hurrying after them.

They rushed through rooms full of smashed galleries and past an empty display that had once housed a pair of saber-toothed tigers. Eva would have stopped to marvel at it if she'd had the time. Instead, she let out a delighted squeal that was cut short as a large chunk of ceiling collapsed onto the empty display. She scrambled backwards, a stray piece of stone flying at her face, slicing her cheek.

"You OK?" Sabretooth shouted, catching her.

She nodded wordlessly, clapping a hand to her bleeding face. He shoved her back onto her feet and they ran on, unable to risk slowing for even a moment.

The tremoring of the building intensified, and ahead of them, the doorway leading to the next gallery began to collapse in on itself. Sabretooth put on an inhuman burst of speed, sprinting ahead. The wall began to disintegrate into giant pieces, slabs of marble toppling in slow motion toward the ground. Sabretooth reached the doorway just in time to save it from being buried under a pile of rubble. He put his shoulder against the largest stone and shoved with all of his considerable might, holding it aloft. His enormous leg muscles bulged. Veins popped. He let out a mighty roar of effort, trembling with strain.

"Go!" he yelled.

They needed no further urging. First Graydon clambered through the gap between Sabretooth's legs, then Eva, and finally Christopher escaped into the chamber beyond. Once they were all clear, Christopher called to him.

"We're good. Come on!"

Sabretooth released the stone and dashed free as fast as he could, but it wasn't quite fast enough. One of the jagged pieces of marble sheared a strip of flesh off the side of his bicep, digging in deep. He grunted in pain, flinging himself free. The rest of the ceiling came down on him faster than even he could roll with his mutant reflexes. He would be pinned beneath tons of marble, and Eva worried he wouldn't be able to regenerate if his head was crushed. As Cyclops had reminded them frequently, Christopher could heal a lot of things, but a crushed head wasn't one of them.

The giant piece of marble froze inches from Sabretooth's face, suspended in a glistening bubble. Eva strained with all of her might, pulse pounding, her fingers stretched to their limits. Her teeth were bared in a rictus of concentration as she held a few tons of stone off the ground in her time bubble. She could feel her hands tremble as she reached out toward the bubble, trying desperately to keep hold of it. It was the biggest one she'd ever made, its contents heavier than she'd ever held, and she'd done it just in the nick of time.

Sabretooth sucked in his stomach and squirmed out from underneath the time bubble. He eyed it as he did so, as if he expected it to fall at any moment, but it remained in place, suspending the heavy stone in time. Eva lowered her trembling arms as he stood up next to her and the rest of the group joined them to marvel at the sight.

"How long will it stay like that?" asked Sabretooth.

"A few minutes, maybe," said Eva. "With a bigger bubble, it may degrade more quickly. We should move on to be safe."

He nodded. "Thanks for the save, Tempus." He put a teasing amount of stress on the name.

"We're even, Sabretooth," she responded with a grin.

"Enough witty banter already." Graydon turned his back on them. "You're making me regret not leaving with the Box."

"You have a thing against witty banter?" Eva asked as she followed him from the currently quiet building.

"It clashes with his rep," said Christopher.

Graydon opened his mouth to argue, considered, and then closed it again. "He may have a point," he admitted. "I concede."

"You should write this down. Commemorate the day," suggested Sabretooth.

"Get it bronzed," added Eva.

"OK, now you're starting to tick me off," grumbled Graydon. "Stuff it."

"Sorry," said Eva. "You still got the Box?"

He patted his dingy jumpsuit. It had acquired a new set of stains atop the old ones, dust and blood and sweat layered on top of the motor oil and unidentifiable crud that had already stained the once-bright fabric.

"I got it," he said. "Where we going next?"

"Let's get that guard out of the supply closet first. I'll bubble him so we can get a head start, just in case he decides to sic the cops on us after all. Then we'll find a place to plan where the sky isn't going to fall on us," she suggested.

"If you jinxed us, and the sky falls, I'm going to be very put out," he said.

"That sounded like witty banter to me," she teased. She would have said more, but he glared at her, and she decided to quit while she was ahead.

CHAPTER 20

The mutants emerged from the back of the half-collapsed museum and into the nearly empty employee parking lot. A pair of cars still sat in their stalls, but both had the derelict look of abandoned and forgotten vehicles. One sported a bright yellow boot on the front tire.

For once, their luck held. No one witnessed their exit from the building. No police officers watched them duck the caution tape that had been hastily strung around the building. No news reporters ran over to demand an interview with the survivors of the astounding collapse of the famous Grace Museum. They hurried across the lot toward the comparative safety of the park on the opposite side, only relaxing once they hit the tree line. Sabretooth leaned against a tree, taking a much-needed breather. Christopher toppled onto the soggy grass, not caring at all if it got his coat all damp. Eva flopped onto a handy bench. Graydon just stuffed his hands into the pockets of his jumpsuit and waited.

After a couple minutes, Sabretooth raised his head,

sniffing. "Do I smell meat?" he asked eagerly.

Eva took a big whiff. "Hot dogs, I think," she said. "It looks like the snack shop next to the baseball diamonds is open." Then she patted her pockets. "But I've got zero cash."

"I didn't bring my wallet," said Christopher sadly. "I don't think I had much cash left anyway. I didn't have much time to pack when I left college."

Sabretooth shook his head in exasperation. "You're all freeloaders, and you owe me." He dug in his pocket and came up with a battered wallet, which he offered to Eva. "I think out of the lot of us, you're the most presentable. People tend to be scared of my pretty face; Graydon looks like he rolled in a garbage heap, and Christopher looks like he's been sick for the last month. You mind taking orders and grabbing us some grub?"

"Deal."

She snatched the wallet out of his hand before he could reconsider and took everyone's orders. Then she hurried toward the snack shop, which was doing brisk business. The early evening games were just getting started now that the rain had finally let up for good, and parents and kids milled around the baseball complex, getting snacks and drinks before their games started.

Eva hadn't been around a crowd of people like this since she'd left for the school, and the noise took her aback for a moment. She nearly got leveled by a boy on a scooter who zoomed past her, almost running over her foot. Under normal circumstances, it would have annoyed her, but today, it felt nicely normal.

The line for the snack shop stood six people deep, but it

moved at a brisk pace, and she didn't have to wait long to place her order. The boy behind the counter was incredibly cute. He looked a bit like a young Cyclops, with a strong jaw and short brown hair, and he smiled at her charmingly when she approached the counter, leaning toward her on his elbows.

"What can I get you?" he asked. As she ordered, his eyes grew wider and wider. "Man. That's a lot of food," he said, frowning. "The boss usually asks teams to place their orders in advance so we don't run out of dogs. I'll make an exception for you just this once, but make sure you remember for next time, OK?"

"Oh, it's not for a team," she said. "It's for my... family. We're here from Australia."

"You must have a big family, then," he said. "That'll be forty-two seventeen."

His fingers brushed against hers as he took the money, and he looked straight into her eyes. Had he done it on purpose? Was he flirting? She'd always been good at flirting, but now it worried her. She could just imagine Sabretooth putting this guy's head in his mouth because he decided the guy had gotten too fresh. Or worse. She could imagine much worse if she put in a little effort. She had to make him stop flirting before something awful happened.

"Oh yes. I have a giant family," Eva babbled. "They're polygamists. Most people don't realize that we have polygamists in Australia. But we do. Polygamy is... just great. I really recommend it."

The guy's eyes went wide as he began piling hot dogs onto the counter.

"You don't say. Are you going to want a bag for all this?" he asked, avoiding her eyes with all of his might.

"Yes, please. That would be kind of you," said Eva, blushing bright red.

He handed her the bags of hot dogs and drinks and immediately looked toward the next person in line. "Next, please!" he called, ignoring her with firm deliberation.

Her cheeks still flaming, Eva noticed an empty picnic table right at the edge of the baseball diamonds. She waved her hands over her head until she caught Christopher's attention and ushered the group over.

"How about this?" she asked. "Sabretooth can sit with his back to the diamonds. We don't have to eat on the ground this way, and we're a little less conspicuous. If we have a picnic in the grass without a blanket, that looks weird, don't you think? Plus, it's still pretty wet."

"Makes sense to me," said Graydon, sitting down.

"I don't care, so long as I can eat," said Christopher, joining him.

Sabretooth didn't even speak. He sat down and devoured the first of six hot dogs in a single bite. Eva didn't know how he managed to fit the whole thing in there. For a while, there was nothing but silence as they chowed down. Everyone except for Graydon, who didn't eat a thing. Eva noticed it, but if he didn't want to draw attention to his status, she wasn't going to bring it up.

Finally, the food was gone. Christopher sat back and let out a long and contented belch. Sabretooth slouched in his seat, resting his head on his palm. Graydon watched the first inning of the game opposite their table with an inscrutable expression.

"OK," said Eva. "What now?"

"We need to do something about the Box," said Christopher. He looked better now. The rings under his eyes now looked less like he was critically ill and more like he'd had a few poor nights' worth of sleep. "It's dangerous."

"How did you find out about it in the first place, Sabretooth?" asked Eva curiously.

He hitched a shoulder. "From S.H.I.E.L.D. I got a little birdie in their offices. Maria Hill was complaining about how the Box was too dangerous to be included in the exhibit, and she was trying to get it pulled. That got me curious, so I decided to check it out."

That story had a lot of holes in it, if you asked Eva. If Sabretooth had simply been curious about the Box, why had he risked his life to go back for it after the Sentinels had shown up? People don't take chances over curiosity, no matter how stubborn they are, and Sabretooth didn't seem like the kind of guy to needlessly risk his own skin. The story also conveniently skipped over all mention of how Graydon had become involved. Apparently, they were supposed to believe that he'd conveniently shown up and gotten blasted by Sentinels, who had also conveniently shown up, and Sabretooth had felt so guilty about it that he'd risked life and limb to set things right. It didn't add up, no matter how she sliced it, but now wasn't the time to point that out, so she simply nodded.

"Did she say anything about how it works?" she asked instead.

"I wish. I would have swiped the file if I could have, but

they've got that place locked up tighter than Fort Knox," he said.

Now, this sounded like the truth. Sabretooth glared at the Box, which sat atop the picnic table in one of the paper bags from the snack shack. It looked too strange to leave out in the open, and they stood out enough among the milling baseball families as it was. Sabretooth had done his best to hide his face and claws, but they'd still amassed a collection of strange glances from harried parents with wagons and kids in tow. Graydon's stained jumpsuit, Christopher's goggles, and Eva's multicolored hair stood out in this crowd.

"Damn," Christopher muttered.

"So, is that what we're left with?" asked Eva. "We call S.H.I.E.L.D. for help?"

Graydon recoiled.

"Over my dead body," Sabretooth snarled, slamming a hand on the table.

A toddler walking past on the nearby sidewalk burst into tears.

"I'm so sorry," Eva apologized to his glaring mother. "We're practicing lines for a play."

The mother took one look at Sabretooth's furious expression, grabbed the kid's hand, and hurried away. She looked about ready to burst into tears herself. Eva balled up one of her hot dog wrappers and threw it at the mercenary. It hit him between the eyes and fell onto the table, and he bared his teeth at her a little.

"What was that for?" he demanded.

"You scared the heck out of that woman!" she said.

"Well, that's not my fault. This is my face," he protested.

"Enough, guys," interjected Christopher. "That's enough. We've got to figure out what to do, and I don't think that calling S.H.I.E.L.D. should be on the list of options. You've seen what they're like, Eva. They don't bargain."

Eva thought back to her first run-in with S.H.I.E.L.D. She'd been brand new to the school, so eager to prove herself. When they'd shown up to intercept the students on a mission, she'd been delighted. She'd assumed they would work together. But the agents of S.H.I.E.L.D. tried to arrest them instead, right there on the spot. Maria Hill said they'd have the opportunity to defend themselves later, but that didn't do any good when the clock was ticking and someone needed saving. What happened to innocent until proven otherwise, or did that only apply to non-mutants these days? Eva wasn't automatically guilty just because she went to some school, or because she had a mutation in her DNA!

No, Maria's prejudice had blinded her, and S.H.I.E.L.D.'s resulting hardline tactics had put Eva at odds with some of her childhood heroes who worked for them. The Avengers probably hated her now.

"I get what you mean," she admitted. "Agent Hill is awful. But is there somebody higher up on the food chain that we could go to?"

But Christopher shook his head without even considering it. "I don't think that matters," he said. "If we call them, we lose control of the Box, and that's dangerous. I mean, I think it's dangerous for Graydon. I think the Box is keeping him alive."

Eva didn't know where to look. She couldn't meet Graydon's eyes. He infuriated her, and he'd been wrong about mutants, but she'd started to hope that maybe he was beginning to realize that. To make matters worse, Sabretooth wore an expression of intense sorrow. The kind of look you only wore at someone's funeral. He brushed a clawed hand over his eyes, shoved up from the table with sudden fury, and stalked off into the trees. Graydon watched him go without a word.

Eva's stomach sank. To her surprise, she felt a deep swell of sympathy for the both of them. If anyone had suggested that she would feel this way just ten minutes earlier, she would have laughed at them, but now she could have hugged them both.

"What is he to you?" asked Christopher.

Graydon still didn't speak.

"Are we sure?" Eva asked. "I mean, really sure?"

The politician met her eyes, and for the first time, she could see how all of his swagger and bluster had been hiding a deep reservoir of fear. He gripped the edge of the table as if he worried some inexplicable magical phenomenon might come along and carry him away at any moment, and he'd be powerless to stop it.

"I know something's not right," he said. "I feel…" He shook his head as if to drive away some thought he couldn't bear. "I don't feel right. And I can hardly remember anything from the past few years other than my nightmares."

"When you snuck away from us to take the Box, why did you do that?" asked Christopher.

Graydon swallowed hard. "It almost felt like it was calling

me. I had to have it. I can't really explain why."

"That's because the magic from the Box is feeding you," Christopher explained. "I didn't realize that's what I was sensing at first, but it's the only explanation that makes sense."

"So that's good, right?" asked Eva, hoping against hope.

Christopher held a hand up and wiggled it back and forth. "So-so. Because we don't have any way to control it. It's just pouring out magic. That's what animated the dinosaur."

Sabretooth finally returned, his hands in the pockets of his jacket. His face was drawn and resigned. He'd gotten control of himself again, although he clearly wasn't happy about it. Eva considered reaching out to him, even if it was only to pat him on the shoulder, but he wasn't the sort who would welcome comfort, regardless of how badly she wanted to offer it. At this point, she had to admit that she needed some too. Every time that it seemed like the story couldn't get more tragic, it did.

"It brought back the tigers too," Sabretooth added, clearly having heard every word they'd said. "So it'll keep raising the dead. Is that what you're saying? Is there a way to contain it, kid? Limit its effects to Graydon only?"

Christopher considered. "Maybe? But this is above my pay grade. Somebody like Illyana might have an idea of how to do it."

Sabretooth's eyes lit up. "She's a powerful sorceress. You think she could jimmy up some spell that could limit the effects of this thing?"

"Maybe. Or maybe she and I could do it together. It feels like the artifact emits a weird blend of life essence and magical power, so it might take the both of us. There's only so much I can do with it alone."

Eva contemplated the Box, which sat in its paper bag on the table. No one walking by could have realized that the plain bag contained such a powerful item. It could raise the dead. If its power continued to spread, dinosaurs could once again walk the earth, terrorizing the populace. Creatures long extinct could rise once more. It sounded like a great idea at first, but Eva had seen plenty of movies, and she read the newspapers. She knew what happened when people messed around with nature. It rarely ended well. Besides, if it ended up in the wrong hands, the bad guys could do all kinds of awful things with it. They couldn't afford to let that happen.

"So it sounds like we need to contact Magik?" she asked. "That's our next step?"

Christopher nodded. "Sounds smart to me. We can't throw Graydon under the bus, but we can't leave this thing unchecked either. It's too dangerous."

Sabretooth gave a clawed thumbs-up. After a moment, Graydon relaxed his desperate grip on the table and reluctantly agreed too. Eva pushed away from the table and began to gather up all of their garbage, eager to get moving.

"Excellent!" she said. "So we'll head back to the chopper. The comms unit won't work until we get inside, but once we're there, Illyana should be able to get right to us in a jiffy. To be honest, I'm not entirely sure why they haven't shown up already. I bet Cyclops is throwing a hissy fit and a half right about now."

She finished stuffing all of the trash into one of the empty bags and then paused. Everyone else stood motionless, staring at the ground.

"What?" she asked.

Then she looked. The grass in a wide ring around their picnic bench had wilted and died. At the edge of the blighted area stood a tree. The half that stood inside the blight was gray and dead, while the half that stood outside bloomed riotously. It was as if two different trees – one alive and one dead – had been spliced together by some mad scientist with an inexplicable agenda.

The Box affected plant life too.

"Damn," murmured Eva.

A chill ran through her as she stared at the half-dead tree. Moments earlier, she would have said she thought the situation couldn't have been more urgent. They'd already had plenty of pressure on them between their need to get back to the school, the threatening presence of the cops, Christopher's deteriorating condition, and the repeated appearance of things that wanted to eat them. But the fact that the Box also killed things made it a hundred times worse in Eva's opinion. If it made the grass sick, would it also do the same thing to the baseball players and their parents? She pictured the city, devoid of all life from the smallest sprout to the teeming throngs on the streets to the tallest animal in the zoo, and she swallowed against a throat suddenly gone dry.

"We need to keep this Box away from people," she said. "That park is full of kids."

Christopher met her eyes and nodded in instant agreement. She didn't have to explain the logic. He got her line of thinking without the need for further elaboration.

"I think you're right. We can't take the Box through those crowds. It seems to be getting stronger, and it's not worth the risk. But we can't leave it unattended either, so I say we split up," he said.

"I'm not leaving the Box," Graydon said promptly. "No way."

"So you stay with him, and Eva and I go to the chopper." Sabretooth cracked his knuckles as if preparing for a fight. "Let's go."

"Wait." Eva held up a finger. "I think Christopher should go with you, and I should stay with Graydon and the Box."

Christopher arched an eyebrow. "Not sure I'm following that logic," he said.

"You can explain all of this Box stuff much better than I can. Cyclops is going to be ticked off, and he'll need to be convinced. I can freeze the Box to keep it from killing anything. If that hurts Graydon, I can bubble him too. I've got it covered."

Christopher hesitated. "Could I... could I talk to you a minute?"

"Sure thing."

He pulled her off to the side as Sabretooth watched. Eva was fairly sure that his enhanced senses could pick up every single word no matter how far away Christopher walked, but maybe that was just paranoia. Christopher stopped near a bush that still bloomed with bright pink flowers, although if they didn't do something about the Box soon, it too would die.

"I'm worried about leaving you with Graydon," Christopher said bluntly. "It's not that I don't trust you. I've seen what you can do in the Danger Room, not to mention in Limbo. But he's never liked mutants, and I'd be worried about leaving either one of us alone with him. I'd be more comfortable if you let me take the risk. My mutation makes me harder to kill, if it comes down to it."

She kissed him on the cheek, surprising them both.

"You're sweet. I'm not particularly close with my brother, but I've got his back no matter what, because he's family. You remind me of him. Half the time, I want to kick you in the head, and the other half the time, I'd shank someone if they looked at you funny," she said.

"Thanks, I think?"

"You're welcome. But I'm still staying. This makes the most sense, and you know it."

He scowled. "I don't like it. I know he's gotten nice all of a sudden, but that doesn't just happen. People don't change like that."

"I know. Either something changed him, or he's acting." She caught his eye. "I'm not a complete idiot, you know. Maybe I bounce around like a manic pixie dream girl half the time, but I have a head on my shoulders, and occasionally I even use it. I got high marks in my first and only semester at uni, you know."

"Heaven forbid."

"Right?" She grinned, but it faded quickly. "I'm going to try and talk to him, and then I'll bubble him and the Box together. You should try talking to Sabretooth too. There's a lot going on here that they're not telling us. We're not going to get anything from them unless we divide and conquer."

"I don't like it. It's risky."

"I'm sorry, but you did sign up for the X-Men. I think you're gonna have to get used to risk."

"I'm the healer. I stay behind on the X-Jet with the rest of the support personnel, and after the big guns go in and do the real work, I come in and I mop up. You know how this goes," he scoffed.

"After the events of this morning, if you try to tell me that you haven't earned your X, I will laugh right in your face, Christopher Muse. And then I'll get Sabretooth to do it. And I bet he has bad breath."

"Hey!" Sabretooth yelled, confirming her suspicions. "I heard that!"

"But I'm right," she insisted.

"Yeah, yeah. If you're done having your moment, can we go now?" he asked, approaching them. "That tree is going to fall over if we don't do something about the Box."

They eyed the tree. They'd only been talking for a few minutes, and it had already died. The circle of death had spread beyond the tree, creeping another ten feet or so up the grass. Eva marched back to the table and gestured to Graydon. He stood, clutching the bag containing the artifact.

"OK," she said, "let's do this."

CHAPTER 21

Sabretooth scouted out Eva and Graydon's hiding spot. Although the park was huge, it didn't offer many options when it came to heavily wooded areas, but he still insisted on scoping out the territory for potential danger. At first, Eva thought the whole thing a waste of time, but then Sabretooth dismissed the first stand of trees as unsuitable after a single deep inhalation.

"What's wrong with it?" she demanded, eager to get moving.

"Decomp," said Sabretooth.

"What?"

"There's a dead dog over there. Big one. I can smell it from here. You want to deal with it when it gets up and wants a treat?" Sabretooth snapped.

He seemed extra grumpy all of a sudden, and it worried her. She knew he was hiding things from them. She might be a newbie, but she hadn't been born yesterday. Sabretooth had acquired the Box for a reason. He and Graydon were working together for a reason. She had her suspicions, but she hadn't quite put all the pieces together in a way that made sense yet.

"No. Sorry," she said, placating him.

"Good. Now let me scout out the next one and quit nagging me about it, will ya?"

None of them nagged as he evaluated and discarded the next two options as not providing sufficient cover and being too close to the park entrance. Finally, they found an option that satisfied even Sabretooth's exacting standards. The deep copse of trees provided heavy cover, with few walking trails. Sabretooth smelled no traces of major predators, and after he'd spent a little time in the area, he scared off any smaller animals. He didn't smell any recent bodies, although any wilderness would have plenty of bones buried deep in the dirt. Eva would need to keep the Box contained to avoid raising them.

Before Christopher and Sabretooth left, she bubbled the Box. Christopher kept an eye on Graydon as she did so, just in case the bubble harmed him in some way. Graydon swayed as the translucent bubble popped into existence, but otherwise he didn't react.

Christopher grabbed him by the elbow.

"You OK?" he asked.

"I can tell the difference," Graydon admitted. "I feel tired now. Like I've just run a long race. But I can deal with that. You two can go now."

"You sure?" Sabretooth asked gruffly.

"Yeah."

Graydon sank down to the leafy ground, leaning against the trunk of a convenient tree. After a moment, Eva sank down next to him. The other two mutants hesitated, exchanging glances.

"I guess we should go," he said.

"You be safe," Sabretooth ordered.

"Don't worry about us," Eva said staunchly.

They left.

It took some time before the crunching sound of their footfalls faded in the distance. Eva and Graydon sat in silence. She didn't know what to say. If she'd been stuck here with Christopher, she would have chatted easily, but Graydon didn't encourage easy speech. Something about him made her want to clam up, but she needed to get him talking. Too bad she didn't know how. He certainly seemed different from the man who'd preached mutant genocide, but as she'd told Christopher, she knew not to take that at face value.

"I thought they were never going to leave," he said wearily.

She snorted. "Yeah. I haven't known him very long, but I've noticed that Christopher likes to talk everything through three times before he does it. He's a planner."

"That's not a bad person to have on your side. Planning saves lives."

She nodded, and once again they fell silent. She watched him out of the corner of her eye, alert for signs of weakness or duplicity.

"I'm not going to fall apart," he said with obvious annoyance. "Or explode. You can relax."

"Sorry. I'm annoying when I babysit too. I hover. Which may explain why I was rarely brought back a second time."

"Caring too much may be a character flaw, but it's better

than caring too little. I've been accused of that many a time."

"You don't seem like the demonstrative type," she admitted.

"No, I never have been. I'm more the go-getter. And you're the idealist, yes?"

She hitched a shoulder. "I sure was when I got to the school, but I'm not sure how long that'll last. You can only see your childhood heroes get taken down a peg so many times before you have to reevaluate those tendencies, you know?"

He chuffed in amusement. "Things never go the way we dreamed they would when we were young, do they?"

"Nope. I'd demand my money back, but I don't know who to ask."

She said it lightly, but it wasn't a joke. Out of all of the people in the world to confide these thoughts to – thoughts she'd never spoken aloud to anyone – Graydon Creed wouldn't have been at the top of the list. But he seemed different now. He no longer overflowed with anger and showmanship. She reminded herself that she still needed to exercise caution, but she had to admit that she wanted this to be real. She didn't want to bubble him when there was still a chance that they could truly work things out. She wanted to believe that he could see the error of his ways.

When she'd urged Christopher to use this opportunity to probe for information, she hadn't exactly expected success. But now that Sabretooth had gone, Graydon truly seemed like a different person. One she might even grow to like. She really hoped he didn't leap up and try to kill her, because it would really ruin the moment. She snorted at the thought.

"What?" He lifted his head slightly to look at her.

"I hope you don't try to kill me while the others are gone, because I'm actually starting to like you a little," she said honestly.

He chuckled, settling back down into place.

"I won't say I haven't thought about it, but I'm too tired," he responded, yawning. "Maybe after I have a nap."

"Don't you dare go to sleep!" she demanded, bolting upright once again to check on him.

His eyes were still open. They looked up at her with bemusement.

"Why not?" he asked.

"Because it might be dangerous?" she asked.

"That's for concussions, I think."

"No, you idiot. I can't look in every direction at once. If someone decides to attack us, and you're catching up on your beauty sleep, they'll walk right up to us."

"That's not a bad point, I suppose. Although I resent the implication that I need beauty sleep."

He sat up and settled himself against the tree again. She returned to her spot, facing the other way. But now that she'd moved, she couldn't get comfortable. No matter how she arranged herself, bark poked her in the back. If she shifted to avoid it, stones poked her painfully in the hips. She huffed in annoyance, settling herself for what felt like the millionth time.

"Hey, Eva?" asked Graydon.

"What?" she snapped.

"Speaking of getting attacked…?"

She sighed, prying a stone out of the ground and throwing

it out of the way. It nearly pinged off the time bubble. "Yeah?"

"I think there's something moving out there."

She froze. Her eyes roamed the trees but found nothing.

"Where?" she whispered.

He pointed.

For a moment, she didn't see anything no matter how hard she strained. Then, the light through the trees glinted off something moving through the underbrush. Something metal. She swore under her breath. This could mean nothing good. Sabretooth had reported no trails through that area, and a normal hiker wouldn't make such an effort to go unnoticed.

She swallowed against the lump growing in her throat. Retreat or stand their ground? If they ran, she would either have to lead their pursuers to Christopher and Sabretooth or risk not being able to find them later. She didn't like either of those options, but she didn't like fighting unseen opponents on her own, either. It scared the crap out of her.

Graydon waited calmly, looking to her for leadership despite the fact that he must have had quite a few years on her. But he trusted her call. Maybe she should too. She thought about how scared she'd been in Limbo, and how once the Stepford Triplets had helped her overcome her fear, she'd been able to stand strong against Dormammu's faceless hordes. She thought about the look of terror on Christopher's face when Emma Frost had plunged that knife into her chest. But they'd done the job despite their feelings, and she would do this one too.

"Can you climb a tree?" she asked Graydon quietly. "I'd like to hide you away safe."

He frowned. "I can climb one, but I won't." So much for following her lead. "You can't expect me to just sit here. I think there's more than one of them out there, and if we take them on one at a time, we're weaker. I intend to survive today. It's a bad call."

She swallowed hot words of protest, Christopher's warning about him ringing in her ears. Graydon seemed to read her mind. He sighed, a bit of his old haughty attitude creeping back into his expression.

"If I wanted to do you harm, I would have excused myself to take a leak and let them sneak up on you," he said. "Don't think I didn't consider it. But again, it's a numbers game. We're safer together for the moment."

After a moment's consideration, she nodded. But she couldn't help asking one corollary question.

"Why do you hate us so much?" she blurted.

He blinked. "I…"

She shook her head. There wasn't time for it, no matter how badly she wanted to know. Over his shoulder, she saw them moving through the trees: two figures in shades of metallic purple, their robotic bodies moving with a surprising fluidity given their automated origins.

Sentinels.

She wasn't surprised. After all, they'd already been at the Grace once that day, so they either had some beef with Sabretooth or interest in the Box. Maybe both. More than anything, she wondered what had taken them so long to return. Then she marveled at the fact that, while she was afraid at the prospect of facing them, she felt a bit calmer at the onset of each battle. The fear still lingered, but she was able to control it better, setting it to the side while she took care of business.

Based on what she could see through the underbrush, these were different from the Sentinels that she'd seen when they were picking up the other students. Cyclops had explained that there were many different generations of the mutant-killing robot line, each with its own features and capabilities. These Sentinels looked a little boxier than the ones she'd seen before, their lines a bit more angular. She hoped that meant that these were older models with fewer features, like their X-Copter, and that they'd be a bit easier to dispatch. It would be nice to have some luck on their side for once.

She and Graydon ducked behind the tree, and she eyed the Box, still encased in the time bubble. She was actually rather proud of that bubble. It had held for a while and was still going strong, but it would pop sometime soon. She had to assume that the Sentinels would immediately lock in on the Box when that happened. It could serve as a good distraction if they timed it right, and she murmured this suggestion to Graydon.

"Not a bad idea," he responded. "Allow me to elaborate..."

When the time bubble popped and the Box fell to the ground, the Sentinels began to stomp through the trees, making a beeline for the artifact without any concern for the wildlife they trampled en route. Eva bubbled one of them, allowing the second to close in as they'd planned. As it drew closer, she picked up the Box and tossed it to Graydon. It wasn't the perfect spiral that he'd thrown earlier;

she didn't know how to do that. But she'd played plenty of softball, and she had good aim. He caught it easily, and the Sentinel's head swiveled to follow the Box. As they'd hoped, the robot didn't take aim at him, not wanting to risk damage to the precious artifact. Instead, it tromped in his direction, intending to capture and kill.

<<Surrender the artifact, Graydon Creed.>>

The Sentinel spoke in an emotionless monotone all the more threatening for its lack of humanity. It would kill them both and not suffer a single moment of regret over the action. It was what it had been built for, after all.

With its massive stride, it closed the ground quickly. Graydon did his best to evade it, darting in and out of the trees. Now that the Box was out of the bubble, his strength had started to return, but Eva worried that it wouldn't be enough. Her heart beat in her throat. The killer robot closed in on him as she watched, wondering if she should abandon the plan and freeze it before it was too late. It was one thing to suggest maneuvering the Sentinels into position to shoot each other, but another one to sit idly by while Graydon risked his life to make it happen. If he died, she'd never forgive herself. Regardless of his flaws, he deserved a chance at redemption.

<<Surrender the artifact or face immediate extermination.>>

The Sentinel reached toward him, and Graydon leaped out of the way. Metal fingers snagged on the dingy fabric of the jumpsuit.

"No!" Eva exclaimed, taking an involuntary step forward. But there was nothing she could do now. The Sentinel stood so close to Graydon that she wouldn't be able to freeze it without catching him too. That would only delay the inevitable. She clenched her hands, digging her nails into her palms, as Graydon threw himself forward. The jumpsuit ripped free. She felt her limbs go limp with relief. He clutched the Box, scrambled to his feet, and ran for the tree line.

The angles were perfect. She had to act. She'd been practicing her time bubbles, but never with the precision she needed at this moment. But she would make it work. She grabbed onto the bubble that held the second Sentinel and twisted with her mind. It popped, releasing the metal monster. It completed its step and halted in confusion as it registered the new locations of the Box and the mutants.

<<TIME ANOMALY DETECTED. BOX OF PLANES LOCATED.>>

This Sentinel sounded exactly the same as the first one. Eva wondered if they ever got confused in conversation, or if they had some kind of hive mind that allowed them to all think together. She thought that would get awfully boring.

Graydon threw the Box up into the air, as high as it would go. The Sentinels tracked it, completely dismissing Graydon and Eva in their eagerness to obtain the Box. They wouldn't be ignored for long.

Eva bubbled the Sentinel standing next to Graydon. She felt the first stirrings of fatigue, but she pushed them down and firmed her hold on the bubble, locking the robot in space and time. It would not move until she allowed it to. Their survival depended on it.

Graydon yelled, "Now, I'll destroy the Box!"

It was such an ineffective super villain thing to do. Eva knew that megalomaniacs couldn't help but gloat over their intelligent plans and prove themselves the smartest people in the room, but it still struck her as incredibly stupid. Luckily, the Sentinel didn't stop to psychoanalyze Graydon's actions. A hatch opened in one of its arms, and a laser cannon popped out with a whir and a click. It would only take a moment for it to sight on Graydon. She had to time this perfectly.

The translucent bubble popped into existence around the second Sentinel. It wobbled as Eva fought for control, trying desperately to maintain both bubbles simultaneously.

Graydon caught the Box and began to run.

With a sigh of relief, Eva released the first bubble. It took a fraction of a second for the Sentinel to realize that Graydon was only yards away. It lurched into action, trying to intercept his escape attempt.

Eva waited for just the right moment. Then she released the second bubble.

The moment the Sentinel was released, it fired at the space where Graydon had been standing. But now, the other robot stood in his place. The laser blasted its head into pieces, and the Sentinel let out a startled electronic bleat before Eva bubbled it a second time. Then she laughed.

"You OK?" she called.

"Just fine."

Graydon twirled the Box on one finger like it was a basketball. "Nice work with the bubbles. Highly finessed."

She shrugged modestly. "Yeah, well, it was a good plan. We work well together."

He nodded, seeming just as surprised about it as she felt. Then he looked over her shoulder once again. "I hate to interrupt this lovely moment that we're having, but I think we've got more company. Think you can do that again?"

"Nah." She grinned, flush with pride at their success. They'd defeated the Sentinels all on their own, without Sabretooth or Cyclops or any help at all. She felt exhausted and sore, and she'd pulled a muscle in her shoulder, but she couldn't have been happier. "I think we can do better this time."

CHAPTER 22

After they left Eva and Graydon, Christopher followed Sabretooth, trying to mimic his silent method of moving through the trees, but he quickly realized that his body couldn't do those things. It would be like trying to mimic the motions of a high-performance car, so he went back to trying not to sound like a herd of animals.

Sabretooth led him through the park, past baseball diamonds full of screaming parents and bored children, past the delicious smelling hot dog stand, and through the skate park. He kept his head down and his shoulders hunched, his long blond hair hanging down to hide his face. No one bothered them. Christopher had to walk quickly to keep up. Sabretooth took huge strides.

"Do you think they're OK?" Christopher asked.

"Huh?"

"Eva and Graydon. Do you think they're OK?"

"Wouldn't have left them if I didn't."

"You don't really worry, do you?" Christopher shook his head. "I wish I knew your secret. I worry about everything."

"No real mystery to it, kid. Once you make a decision, there's no looking back. When you've lived as long as I have, you realize the only thing you get from looking back is regret. The only way through is forward," Sabretooth said gruffly.

"That's… that's some good advice," Christopher said. He was honestly more than a little shocked.

"Pay me a quarter, and I'll call it even." Sabretooth grinned.

"You're not as crazy as they say you are, you know that?" Christopher said, emboldened.

"Oh, yes I am." Sabretooth stopped, grabbed Christopher by the shoulders, and turned the younger mutant to face him. "I meant what I said. I do what I need to do to survive, and I don't second guess myself. Sometimes that means thinking about one thing: me. Fact is, I could never hack it as one of you do-gooder X-Men types."

"I think you're a better guy than you let on," said Christopher, staunchly.

"You think? Summers has called me a lot of things over the years. Like a 'criminal,' and a 'wildcard,' and my personal favorite, a 'menace to society.' But I think he's a blowhard with a bad haircut, so I guess we're even." Sabretooth began walking again. "I'm a bad guy, kid. But even bad guys can do the right thing every once in a while, if you give them the right reasons."

"And Graydon is the right reason, huh?" said Christopher. Sabretooth didn't reply.

"I'm going to assume that you heard me, with your super-sensitive hearing and all. So I must be right." Christopher sighed. "I don't know what's going on, and I know I'm just a newbie, but I'm going to help anyway. I think Graydon's going to need it. I'll do everything I can to make sure he's OK. It's like you said before. Nobody messes with my people. Even when they're jerks."

"Yeah," Sabretooth said gruffly. "I appreciate it."

They continued on in companionable silence to the harbor. The water was choppy, and as they approached, it began to drizzle again. Sabretooth looked up at the early evening sky and growled as if this might make it stop. It didn't. The water was all but deserted except for the gulls; they swooped and cawed, searching out a few last tidbits. Christopher saw a few larger freighters far out to sea, but otherwise the docks and the bay remained largely deserted. He took Sabretooth down toward the end and pointed out the direction of the chopper, pulling the remote from his pocket. All he had to do was push the button, and it would land right on the sand next to them. Easy peasy.

He pushed the button. Nothing happened.

"You have got to be kidding me," he muttered, pushing it again.

"Does it need new batteries?" asked Sabretooth. "Want me to hit it and swear a little? That works with my TV."

"The button lights up when I push it, so I know that it's working. Something's wrong."

"Did someone steal your invisible chopper?"

Christopher looked up and down the beach as if he might spot some handy explanatory sign with bullet points that would tell him what had happened to the X-Copter and what to do about it. Sadly, no sign popped up. No tour guide with informational pamphlets sprang up from the sand. He would have even made do with a nice portal opening up and spitting out all of the instructors from the New Xavier School, who would then order him around and make all of the big decisions, leaving him to follow in their wake with the burden of decision-making removed from his shoulders. That last option would likely come with a lecture and a variety of disapproving looks, but he would gladly endure them all if only it meant that he could relax a bit. All of this responsibility really wore on a person. He could have used a nap.

He sighed. "I guess we should make sure it's still out there. I could see if there's a boat that we could borrow."

"You mean steal."

"Borrow. We'd return it."

"Kid, do you know how to hotwire a boat?" Sabretooth asked, arching a brow.

Christopher blinked, looking toward the marina. A variety of boats floated there, tied to the docks in peaceful quiet. He knew nothing about boats. He just figured he'd grab one of the smaller ones.

"What do you mean, hotwire? I figured I'd grab a rowboat. Or a kayak. Something with paddles. Who said anything about hotwiring? I mean, have you met me? I'd have no idea where to even start," he said.

Sabretooth snickered. He tried to hide it, turning his head away and covering it with a very transparent cough, but he was one of the worst actors Christopher had ever seen.

"Go ahead," Christopher said sourly. "Laugh at me. I can take it."

Sabretooth laughed outright. "Come on," he said. "That's comedy gold right there." He punched Christopher on the shoulder, nearly sending him into the water. "Lighten up, kid. You gotta quit taking yourself so seriously."

Christopher wilted. He didn't mind getting made fun of; that wasn't what bothered him. He just wanted to go back to school. He'd had enough of feeling sick and lost and scared, and he was ready to be done now. Besides, he'd proven himself, right? He'd saved Emma in the Danger Room, and if that wasn't enough, he'd taken down a freaking dinosaur. If anybody had earned a little R & R, he had, if only the stupid remote would cooperate.

Sabretooth studied him, his head tilted to one side. "Hey," he said. "Don't worry about it. I'll just swim it. No boat hijacking necessary. But you got to hold my coat, OK? This is my favorite one, and I'll be ticked if something happens to it."

"The water's probably freezing," Christopher protested.

Sabretooth grinned. It seemed like he was actually looking forward to this, which provided yet more evidence that he was borderline insane.

"Nothing like a nice, brisk swim to wake a man up," he said.

Hope rose in Christopher's belly, but logic quickly quashed it. "How are you going to find the chopper if you can't see it?" he asked.

"Water on the hull of a heavy object has a specific sound to it," Sabretooth explained. "All the stealth technology in the world can't cloak that if you know what to listen for. Lucky for you, I am a man of extensive experience and skill." He preened.

"You're pretty modest, too," Christopher said.

Sabretooth shook a finger at him. "Watch it, kid. You keep that up, and I'll toss you in the drink instead and let you go fishing for the chopper."

He stripped off the jacket and tossed it to Christopher, smacking him in the face with the sleeve. Christopher didn't dare to complain about it, though. He felt like he'd pushed his luck hard enough with Sabretooth. The animalistic mutant wasn't exactly what he'd expected. He'd had this image of a wild and aggressive creature that acted only on instinct and delighted in violence, one that had no understanding of culture or relationships or even real emotions. He didn't know why he'd thought that. Maybe because he'd read all of those stories about Sabretooth's years as a killer for hire and the trail of blood he'd left behind him.

Now he realized that the truth was much deeper. Just as Cyclops wasn't the perfect hero that Christopher had wanted him to be, Sabretooth wasn't all bad either. He could still care about people despite himself, joke around, eat eight hot dogs in one sitting, and other things that normal people did. Christopher had made the lazy assumption that someone like Sabretooth would do nothing but kill things simply because he had fangs and claws. Because he was the infamous Sabretooth, and a legendary mutant like that would never do anything mundane.

It was the same mistake Graydon had made, making assumptions about Sabretooth because of what he was.

The revelation left him flushing with shame as he clutched Sabretooth's coat. The muscular mutant failed to notice his embarrassment. Sabretooth tied his hair back and stripped off his boots. The wind whipped his face as he stood there for a moment, silhouetted against the sky, and he turned and winked before diving into the waves. Christopher held the trench coat tighter, trying to protect it from the spotty rain. It smelled like wood smoke and leather soap and gunpowder. Something crunched when he tucked it under his arm. Unable to resist the pull of curiosity, he reached into the pocket to find a packet of dried apple slices. He would have expected bullet casings and knives, if he'd guessed on the contents of Sabretooth's pockets that morning, and he felt ashamed of himself for it.

He couldn't even see Sabretooth. His eyes scanned the choppy waves with no luck, and he tented a hand above them to protect them from the mist, hoping that would help, but no joy. He'd really begun to worry when a tawny head popped up a few yards from shore. Sabretooth took a few steps onto the sand and shook like a dog, spraying water everywhere. The chains around his neck jingled.

"Well?" Christopher asked hopefully.

Sabretooth hadn't been gone long, so that had to bode well. He must have found the chopper quickly. He could take Christopher out there, and they'd call Cyclops, and this whole thing would be over soon. Christopher could feel the tension draining from his shoulders already.

"I found it easy enough," said Sabretooth, rubbing his hands together. "Damn, it's cold. Let's head up toward the bathrooms. They might have one of those hand dryers I can stand under for a minute."

"Sure thing."

Christopher gathered up the clothes and his staff,

following Sabretooth up toward the nearby building. As impatient as he was, he couldn't begrudge a minute or two to warm up. They were minutes away from success, after all. A brief detour wouldn't matter that much.

They reached the bathrooms only to find the men's room door secured with a heavy padlock. Sabretooth took a moment to glance around and make sure there were no inconvenient onlookers and aimed a well-placed kick at the heavy door. It released with a boom and a clang. He gestured to Christopher with a flourish.

"After you," he said.

Christopher went inside, happy to get in out of the wet. He hung Sabretooth's jacket over one of the stalls and availed himself of the facilities while Sabretooth dried himself off. By the time Christopher had finished washing his hands, he couldn't resist his eagerness any longer.

"So can you take me out to the chopper after we're done here?" he said eagerly. "How do you think we should work this?"

But when he turned to face Christopher, Sabretooth wore a drawn and serious expression.

"You're not gonna like this, kid," he said. "To be honest, I don't either."

Christopher sagged against the nearest stall door. "What's wrong this time?" he asked.

"I couldn't get to the X-Copter. I can tell it's there, but I can't get to it. There's a force field around the chopper. Probably explains why your remote won't work too. It shocked me something fierce when I tried to break through it. I had to turn back. Figured I wouldn't do anybody much good if I shocked myself unconscious and drowned out there."

"A force field? Come on! Can't we catch a freaking break?" Christopher threw his hands up. He couldn't believe what he was hearing. He had just about had it with this mission, and the constant setbacks and… everything. If he could have quit, he would have given it serious consideration at that moment. But he didn't even have that option, and it made him so frustrated that he wanted to scream. He clenched his fists and paced for a long time.

Sabretooth let him stew. He didn't try to soothe his temper or offer empty platitudes. He just waited until Christopher's fury slowly faded and logic took over once again.

"Why would somebody put a force field around the X-Copter?" Christopher finally asked in a quiet voice.

"That's a good question, isn't it?" Sabretooth nodded. "Almost seems like somebody doesn't want us leaving with the Box, huh?"

Christopher opened his mouth to answer, but he had no good response for that. He fell back into a deep and pensive silence as Sabretooth turned the dryer on again.

CHAPTER 23

By the third – or was it fourth – wave of Sentinels, Eva and Graydon had their approach down to a science.

Graydon had a knack for getting the robots to do just what he wanted at precisely the right time, and he manipulated them deftly into the right position for Eva to freeze them in place. Eva felt as if her control with her time bubbles grew by the minute, even if she tired along with it. She might need a nice long rest at the end of this, but she began to think that her dreams of helping Jean Grey and the rest of the time-displaced mutants weren't so far-fetched after all.

It was as if she could sense the strands of time just beyond the confines of her bubbles. All she needed to do was expand her abilities and find a way to pluck them. In just one short day, she'd managed feats she'd considered impossible, so why not this one too?

Together, they dispatched the final pair of Sentinels in a masterful stroke, timing the bubbles with such perfection that the robots took each other out in a simultaneous blast of laser fire. Sparks arced into the air as the metal monstrosities toppled over in slow motion. Graydon applauded, and Eva curtsied, then she turned around to scan for more.

"Is that finally it, then?" she asked. "I hope so, because I'm pooped."

"For the moment, at least," he said. "I don't mind a breather myself. I'll admit that I'm not used to all of that running."

"And on an empty stomach too," she said, shaking her head.

It seemed like he ought to topple over at any moment from low blood sugar. He'd been running circles around the Sentinels for the past ten minutes or so, and he hadn't eaten anything since she and Christopher had arrived. She'd been healed a few times in the past, and she'd been ravenous afterwards. Christopher had said her body was replenishing the energy it had used to repair the damaged tissues or something to that effect.

But Graydon wasn't injured after taking on so many Sentinels despite his lack of mutant abilities, super-powers, or any weapons at all. She had a pulled muscle and a singed bit on her arm where one of the Sentinels had gotten off a shot that landed a bit too close for comfort. But Graydon was fine. Not hungry. Not tired. Not hurt.

Actually, not really fine either, come to think of it. She couldn't bring herself to face it, because after everything that had happened, she found herself pitying him.

"I'll take a quick look around to make sure there aren't any more of them," she offered, changing the subject. He settled himself back down at the base of the tree, ready to spring up again at a moment's notice if needed. "But before I go, I probably ought to bubble the Box again."

He grimaced. "Is that truly necessary?"

She looked up at the tree. Since the Box had been in rather continuous motion over the past few minutes, its effects seemed to have been more widespread than when it had sat motionless on the park bench. However, the leaves still drooped noticeably, and black rot hugged their edges. He followed her gaze and sighed.

"I suppose I don't need to ask. Go ahead. Do what you must," he said.

She searched for something kind to say but came up largely empty. So she encased the Box safely in its bubble, double checked on both of her charges to ensure their safety, and then made a quick circuit around the area to verify that there weren't any stray killer robots lurking out there that they'd missed. It didn't take long, and she didn't dawdle. The skies had opened up again, releasing a spotty rain that chilled her to the bone and made her glad for the warmth of her overcoat. She clutched it tightly against her body and returned back to the tree, hoping that Christopher and Sabretooth would be back soon with good news and perhaps even reinforcements.

That didn't happen, but Graydon perked up as she approached, which made her feel strangely flattered. He sat upright and called out, "All clear?"

"For now, at least. You doing OK?"

He actually seemed to consider the question. "Well enough. I'm proud of us. How many of those Sentinels do you think we destroyed?"

"Eight? Nine? I lost count. Whoever sent them is going to be ticked. Who do you think it was?"

He shrugged. "Someone else itching to get their hands on the Box. Could be S.H.I.E.L.D. Sabretooth said they wanted it, remember?"

"Yeah." She sat down next to him, hugging her knees to her chest. "You warm enough?"

He eyed her, a brow arched. "You will not offer to share your coat with me, young lady. I forbid it. A man has to have some standards."

She snorted. "So you're determined to freeze just to prove that you're macho?"

"So what if I am?" he demanded.

She couldn't tell if he was kidding. She laughed anyway, and after a moment, the corner of his mouth quirked up despite his evident efforts to keep it under control.

"You know, you're not so awful for a mutant-hating politician," she said. "But you never did answer my question."

"Why I hate you, you mean?" He sighed. "Mutants are unknowable. Full of limitless potential, which means that you could be staring a nuclear bomb in the face and not know it. We have rules to control access to weapons of mass destruction among the populace, and I believe that those laws are necessary to create a safe and civil society. But with mutants, we have weapons of mass destruction walking among us, wearing our skins. We cannot see them or identify them. We cannot know who they are until they identify themselves, and therefore, we must take action to protect ourselves."

"Against criminals, sure. But I'm no criminal, Graydon. Christopher isn't one either," she said sadly. It felt futile to say it, but she had to try.

He offered her that faint smile again. "I notice you said nothing about Sabretooth."

"I don't know about him," she admitted. "But he risked his life to help you, and I don't get the idea that he sticks his neck out much. Why did he do that?"

Graydon fell silent, looking down at the ground. She wondered if maybe she'd pushed him too far. She'd finally gotten him talking, and instead of smoothing things over, she'd antagonized him. So much for her stellar interpersonal skills.

But then he spoke up, taking her by surprise. "I used to think that I was entirely justified in my hatred," he said quietly. "I lost things – people – to mutants, and nothing anyone can do will ever get them back. So I used my connections and had them build me an armored suit, and I hunted your kind for a while. They called me Tribune. I was good at it. Then I became a politician, and I rallied the world around a platform of hatred. It worked all too well."

He fell silent again. Eva didn't want to ask, but she had to know. "What changed?" she asked.

"Everything is different now." He lifted his tortured eyes to meet hers. She saw a world of pain and loss, one in which hope had fled and nothing remained but the determination to endure. "Eva, I think I died."

She'd known it herself for a while, but hearing him say it in such a broken voice made her want it to be a lie. "Maybe not," she urged. "There could be another explanation."

"No. The Box sustains me. It brought back the dinosaur. Dead. The tigers. Dead. The hunters. All dead. It kills the living and brings back the dead. I have no need to eat or drink because I'm not alive. That assassination attempt was successful. I remember it. I remember every moment."

He closed his eyes in remembered pain, hanging his head. Eva didn't know what to do. She wished Christopher were here. He was good with this kind of thing. He empathized. But she would have to do. She shifted closer, putting her shoulder against his.

"I'm sorry," she said simply. "I believe you."

"That's kind of you."

"So is it just a blank up until you showed up at the Exhibit?"

He raised his head. Now the heavy secret was off his shoulders, he looked better. Still exhausted. Still sick – or like the walking dead, to be more accurate. But he met her eyes without smirking or scowling.

"No. I've come back a few times since then. I don't really understand it. There are big blank spots where I'm fairly sure that I'm just dead, and then random points where I'm up and moving with no idea of what's going on. The last time, a sorceress raised me and made me into her slave." He shuddered. "This one hasn't been a walk in the park, but I'll take it over that any day."

Eva pressed a hand to her open mouth, horror curdling her insides. "I have nightmares about this sorcerer," she admitted. "Dormammu. He pulled us into Limbo and trapped us there, and it was the most awful experience of my life. I've never felt despair like that before."

"So you do get it," he said. "I can't go through that again, Eva."

She nodded. "I wish I could help."

"It's funny you should say that," he said. "I was going to ask you for a favor."

"Name it."

She meant it, too. How could she turn down a request from a dead man? His story had tugged at her heart. Something told her that every word was true. He wasn't alive. Graydon had been right; Christopher had all but said it aloud. But he was too tenderhearted to hit Graydon with the truth before he was ready to admit it.

Graydon's stormy blue eyes met hers. "Let me leave with the Box. Please. Before it's too late."

Eva stared at him, shock freezing her in place. She didn't know what to say. Sabretooth would kill her. Christopher would kill her. Cyclops would kill her. She couldn't think of a single person who would think this was a good idea. Could Graydon be joking? When she finally did find words, they tumbled out in a confused heap.

"Wait, what?" she said. "Take the... what?"

"I've changed my mind. Let me take the Box and leave."

He stared her down intently while she wondered what she'd gotten herself into, and what on earth she should do about it.

CHAPTER 24

Christopher paced the length of the dock, twisting the strap of his goggles between his hands. He didn't know what to do. They'd expected this excursion to be so easy: land the X-Copter, pick up Sabretooth, and take off again. He hadn't anticipated all of these complications.

He didn't know how to deactivate a force field. Eva wouldn't know either, and what was Sabretooth going to do, growl at it until it decided to turn itself off? Or maybe Graydon could insult it until it decided to go away. That would work out just great. All they could do was sit here and wait until Cyclops decided to pick them up. If he ever did. He might decide that they didn't deserve to be students any more since they couldn't follow basic directions.

Wait. Would he really do that? Christopher didn't think he'd just abandon the X-Copter like that, but would he boot them over this? Cyclops seemed like a fairly nice guy, but he'd made it clear that he was fighting a war. When Fabio had wanted to go home, Cyclops had taken him there to prove a point, and it hadn't gone well, putting Fabio's family at risk and bringing S.H.I.E.L.D. agents into their house. He might just decide to make an example of them too. Maybe the instructors hadn't come to the rescue yet because they were watching right now. Letting him squirm a little before they came to the rescue. His head whipped around as he searched the shore for them, but he saw only Sabretooth.

"You're gonna break those goggles," he said.

"Huh?"

"The goggles. That strap will give if you keep twisting it like that."

"Oh." Christopher forced his hands to relax. "Yeah. Thanks."

He returned to the dock, where Sabretooth sat on a bench under a convenient overhang, and sat down. The goggles thumped to the ground. He let his head fall into his hands.

"This is hopeless," he moaned.

Sabretooth snorted.

"You give up too easy, kid," he said.

Just like that, Christopher had had enough. He felt like he'd done more than his fair share. He'd been a team player, even when the other players on the team had treated it like a summer camp. He'd taken care of his part of the work and done a damned fine job of it too. He'd been supportive and positive, and what had it gotten him? Zero respect. Sabretooth called him "kid" all the time despite the fact that he could go to a bar and order a drink. He might be new to the X-Men, but that didn't make him a baby, and it didn't give Sabretooth the right to treat him like one. He had just about had it.

"Yeah?" he demanded. "Well, please enlighten me, O great and powerful Sabretooth. If you have some secret force field busting abilities that you've kept up your sleeve for some reason, by all means, let's see them. I'm prepared to be impressed."

"I don't like your tone. You better watch it," Sabretooth warned, his eyes beginning to glow.

"Or what? You'll claw me up? Ooooh, I'm scared." Christopher waggled his fingers in Sabretooth's face. "But I'll heal, and you'll still be a grown man with all this skill and power who can't control himself to save his own life." He shook his head sadly. "You know who you remind me of? My pops. He couldn't control himself either, and sometimes I hated him for it."

As soon as the words left his mouth, he regretted them, and not just because he expected Sabretooth to explode into a violent rage. Things would be broken. He would be lucky not to be hit. But what made him feel worse was that he liked Sabretooth despite the man's many faults. He didn't know what had made him say such an awful thing, and he instantly wanted to take it back, but once it was said, he couldn't undo it. Too bad Eva couldn't rewind time as well as freeze it. That would have been a handy skill to have right about now.

But Sabretooth didn't fly off the handle, and somehow that made it worse. Instead, he hunched into himself, his muscles balling into tense knots. His fists became tight balls of tension. His head disappeared into humped shoulders as his body curled.

"You're not the only one," he growled, his voice shaking and distorted with anger.

"What?" Christopher asked, reaching toward him. "Look, I'm sorry, but–"

"Don't touch me!"

Christopher snatched his hand back.

Sabretooth stood up and stalked to the end of the dock without another word, and as much as Christopher wanted to follow him, he felt like that would be a bad idea. So he waited as the wind whipped at his face and rain pattered down in fitful spurts for the umpteenth time that day. Worry nagged at him, gnawing at his stomach. He would have given anything to start this day over again. There were so many things he would have done differently if given the chance, but he would just have to muddle through and hope it would be enough. He put the goggles back on his forehead and hoped for the best.

After a few minutes, Sabretooth returned. He sat back down on the bench and said, "I could swipe someone's phone, and you could call Summers for help."

"Beg pardon?" Christopher asked, confused by the abrupt change of subject.

"I could steal a phone," Sabretooth repeated with infinite patience. He was acting as if nothing had happened, as casual as you please.

"No good. The Institute is in the middle of a frozen wasteland. There's no reception."

Sabretooth's jaw tightened, but he didn't complain. "OK, what about a car? We'll drive you back."

"Would we make it over the border?"

Christopher didn't love the idea, but at this point, he was a beggar. He couldn't afford to be a chooser too. But the school sat in the wilds of Canada, and his mind immediately began to run through the difficulties. There would be checkpoints. Customs. He didn't have his ID, and they'd be driving a stolen car and transporting an illegal artifact. It didn't sound like the best idea he'd ever heard.

"There are ways," Sabretooth answered evasively. "If you have connections. I could get you there, but we'd have to go the long way around. The crossings around here are too heavily monitored. There's no way we'd get across."

"I'm just not sure if they'll let us back in if we come back without the X-Copter." Christopher frowned. "I think they would, but…"

"I hadn't thought of that," Sabretooth admitted. "OK, scrap that idea. You'd probably spend most of the trip puking your guts out, anyway, and I'd rather not have to deal with the smell. We could try to radio the school, but finding a system that will transmit that far will take time, and then we've got to luck onto a channel they're listening to. I think that puts us back to Plan A."

"I'm afraid to ask, but what's Plan A?"

"We steal a boat, go out there, and I try to break through that force field. If I fall apart, do me a favor and put me back together?" Sabretooth stood up and began walking as if the whole thing was a done deal. His voice carried back to Christopher on the wind. "Maybe you hate me sometimes, and I don't blame you for that, but I don't think you want me dead."

"I don't hate you," Christopher called, hurrying to catch up with him, but Sabretooth didn't answer.

It turned out that Sabretooth knew how to hotwire a lot of things. He led Christopher onto a motorboat with a fishing

charter logo on the side and showed him how to pry the
cover off the electrical compartment and find the correct
wires to start the motor. He explained everything in simple
and easy-to-understand language, covering safety concerns
first, then the basics, and then extra details and nuances
about different types of motors that Christopher might
encounter later. By this time, the motor hummed quietly,
and Sabretooth popped the cover back into place and patted
it gently.

"So there you go," he said, teasing. "Next time you come
across some gangsters, you'll fit right in."

"You're a good teacher," said Christopher.

"Thanks, Chris."

Christopher considered protesting the nickname but
decided not to bother. Sabretooth hadn't called him "kid,"
so his point had been made. He'd better stop while he was
ahead.

"So what's the plan here?" he asked.

Sabretooth put the boat into gear and deftly steered them
out of the mazelike harbor. Christopher remained tense,
waiting for some random sailor to emerge from a nearby
boat and immediately recognize them as thieves. Then
there would be a boat chase, if the movies were right about
these things. But no one appeared, and the only noise was
the insistent cawing of the gulls as they huddled together
against the wind. To be honest, he was a bit disappointed.
He would have enjoyed a little boat chase, at least in theory.

"I'll get us right up near the chopper," said Sabretooth.
"We'll anchor ourselves nearby, and I'll try to batter through
the force field. It'll get rocky, but I picked us a nice, steady

boat. Not one of those narrow buggers that'll tip over at the slightest nudge. We'll be fine."

Somehow, that reassurance failed to have its desired effect. Christopher eyed the water and decided that discretion was the better part of valor. He took one of the life vests off the rank beside him and began to adjust the straps.

"Didn't you hear me? I said we'd be fine."

"Oh, I heard you loud and clear." Christopher tried on his vest. "I'd offer you one, but I know you're too manly to wear safety equipment, and I don't think they have one that would fit you anyway."

"You calling me fat?!" Sabretooth demanded, grinning.

"Nah. Just big boned."

Christopher grinned back, and just like that, everything was OK between them again. Sabretooth steered the boat out toward the X-Copter. The choppy water quickly set them to rocking. Christopher had been raised as a city boy, and as a result, he hadn't been on many boats, but to his surprise he found that his stomach tolerated the tilt and roll of the craft without much trouble. It was quite a relief. He'd had enough of puking for one day. Heck, he felt like he'd reached his quota for the next year.

It only took them a couple of minutes to cross the open expanse of water. Christopher was sorry the trip was over so quickly. He found that he enjoyed the white noise hiss of the water against the hull and the rhythmic splash of the waves as they crested and fell. His cheeks began to go numb with the cold, and the wind blasted tears from his eyes, but he could have stayed there forever. When they bumped up against the invisible bulk of the force field, he felt a pang of disappointment, although he tried to hide it.

Sabretooth didn't seem to notice. He pointed toward a device in the stern of the craft.

"Push that red button there to release the anchor," he said.

"You seem to know your way around boats," Christopher observed.

"When you do mercenary work, you learn a lot of things. I can teach you to survive in the wilderness with nothing but a canteen and a book of matches, if it comes down to it."

"That sounds like fun."

"Trust me; it isn't."

Christopher chortled, warming to the conversation. It reminded him of the rare evenings when his dad had been stable and talkative. He'd invite Christopher out to the garage to work on one of their old, broken-down cars. He'd promised to fix one of them up for Christopher when he turned sixteen, but none of them ever saw the road. Most of the time, his dad didn't even touch them. He was too busy battling monsters that Christopher couldn't see, couldn't touch, couldn't fight for him. Pain and PTSD sent him deep inside himself where his son couldn't follow. But on rare occasions the monsters would recede, and his pops would invite him to the garage, and they'd both crack open a drink in a glass bottle glistening with sweat, and his pops would show him the parts of an engine or teach him how to replace spark plugs. Nothing huge or melodramatic ever happened on those nights. They just talked. Pops taught him about cars, and they chatted while they worked. It was nice. The way things should have been.

This conversation reminded him of those glorious

moments somehow. He didn't want it to end. But before he could ask another question, Sabretooth had turned away and begun contemplating the empty space where the chopper presumably sat. The water seemed calmer, the waves less choppy.

"I think if we balance out the boat, that'll be better than getting into the water," he said.

"What's that?" asked Christopher.

"Either I try to crack through the force field from out here, or I climb back down into the water and do it there. If I stay up here, you have to try and counterbalance me, and there's a risk that I could send you flying, but I've got a better angle at it. If I go into the water, you're safer, but if I get knocked unconscious, you've got to haul my butt back onto the boat, and I'm not light. I've got to be honest: I don't like either option."

"Stay up here." Christopher said after a moment's thought. "I've got a flotation device on if I do go overboard, and I can swim. So I think it's worth having the better angle."

Sabretooth nodded. "You're the boss." He considered the boat again. "If you stand down at that end, and I go over here, we should be good. When I touched the force field before, it shocked me wicked hard. I don't want you anywhere near it when I hit it. There's gonna be some blowback."

Christopher went to the spot that Sabretooth indicated, watching with concern as the mercenary mutant lifted a clawed hand, trying to judge the distance to his imaginary target. Then, inspiration struck.

"Wait!" said Christopher. "I just had an idea. There's some fishing equipment in the locker next to the anchor. They got harpoons. Why not use one of them instead of sticking your hand into the force field?"

Sabretooth considered. "That's not a half bad idea."

Christopher pulled one of the harpoons out of the locker. The small, spear-like object was heavier than he'd anticipated, and he fumbled it a bit before tightening his grip. Then he gave it an experimental spin. Unlike his staff back at school, the harpoon was terribly unbalanced, but he thought he'd be able to work with it in a fight if he had to. Good to know.

"Any time now," Sabretooth prompted.

Flushing in embarrassment, Christopher tossed the weapon to Sabretooth, who caught it one-handed and made it look easy. He tested the long length of wood and took a moment to judge the angles before preparing himself to strike.

WHOM!

The thick harpoon impacted against the invisible barrier of the force field. Christopher felt the blow deep in his bones, a vibration down in his marrow. It seemed like even his teeth shook in their sockets. The boat slid backwards, and an electric shimmer in the air outlined the shape of the force field for just a moment before it disappeared again. Sabretooth gritted his teeth, shifting the harpoon in his grip. The metal tip smoked where it had impacted the magical barrier.

"Good idea, kid," he said, indicating the harpoon. "You OK back there?"

"Yeah."

Sabretooth struck again. The first time, he'd been testing

the weapon and the balance of the boat, but this time, he put the full force of his might behind the blow.

WHOOOOMMMM!

This time, Christopher felt a pulse of familiar magic grip his heart and squeeze it painfully. For a second, he couldn't breathe. White spots danced around the edge of his vision, and he struggled to keep his grip on consciousness. He gasped for air, sagging against the side of the boat. It rocked as a wave hit them, sending him overboard. The cold water smacked him, and his brain froze in shock and panic. The vest brought him immediately back up to the surface, where he weakly spluttered out water. He bobbed there, flailing in helpless desperation.

"Sabretooth," he croaked, but his voice was too feeble to carry over the wind and waves.

WHOOOOOMMMM!

The harpoon struck again, and Christopher's vision went dimmer. He couldn't feel the tips of his fingers. He tried to speak but couldn't make his mouth form the words. His lips had gone numb too. He heard the slap of water against the hull of the boat but didn't know where the edge was. He lacked the strength to haul himself aboard anyway. Sabretooth wouldn't know what had happened to him. Hopefully the vest would hold him afloat long enough for him to be saved, but he wasn't even sure about that. Right now, he could barely hold his head out of the water. He even struggled to breathe...

"Kid? Chris? You OK?!"

Sabretooth's desperate face filled his field of vision as the color slowly began to leach back into the world. Christopher became aware of heat in his hands as Sabretooth massaged warmth back into his fingertips. He struggled to move his mouth and finally managed to force out a single word.

"Thanks," he said.

Sabretooth's face relaxed slightly.

"Don't mention it," he said, sitting back on his haunches. "What the hell happened?"

"That force field is tied to the Box. When you hit it, it hurt me."

Sabretooth went pale. His eyes blazed yellow in a suddenly white face. Without another word, he leaped to his feet, leaving Christopher lying on the deck, and ran to the wheel, turning the boat on. The engine roared to life, and he flicked it into gear and started back to shore while Christopher still struggled to sit up.

"What is it?" Christopher asked.

"Graydon," said Sabretooth, his expression grim. "If it hurt you when I hit the force field, what did it do to him?"

CHAPTER 25

In the wake of Graydon's shocking request, Eva didn't know what to do. She couldn't let him just waltz out of here with an artifact that raised the dead. It would be only a matter of time before some random undead beastie would take his head off. Other people would die too, and she'd be at least partially at fault. Plus, Sabretooth would probably kill her. But Graydon didn't seem to be joking. In fact, he looked like he wanted to fall on his knees and beg, and that tugged at her heartstrings.

"Graydon," she said gently, "you must not have thought this through."

"Of course I have. I'll have to go somewhere remote. I need to be near the Box, and the Box needs to be as far away from living things as possible. I'm thinking the desert makes the most sense. It won't be the most comfortable existence, but it'll be mine. Please help me make it a reality. It will cost me a lot to beg, but I'll do it if I have to."

"You know I want to help, but I can't do that if I don't understand what the heck is going on, Graydon. I have to admit that right now, you sound insane."

He chuckled, looking down at himself, clad in a ripped and stained jumpsuit, his normally immaculate hair tousled and dirty. Blood smudged one cheek. He couldn't have looked any more different from the perfectly poised, impeccably coiffed politician he'd once been.

"I look the part too, don't I?" he said. "But I don't feel insane. For the first time in my existence, I feel like I'm starting to see clearly. I just need a little more time to figure things out, but that's the problem. Time is exactly what I don't have."

"What do you mean?" she asked cautiously, eyeing the bubble where the Box still sat, safely frozen in time.

"I don't understand what's been happening to me," he explained. "I keep getting brought back due to circumstances outside of my control. I don't understand how or why this is happening, which means it could end at any moment. I have no idea how much time I've got left. I've got to seize the opportunity to figure things out while I've got it, but I can't do that with Sabretooth hanging over my shoulder. He's… It's…" He paused to search for the right words. "If I stay here, he'll do whatever he thinks is right. I won't even have a say in it."

"He cares about you. Even I can see that."

"Sure he does. And he'll protect me no matter what. I won't have any choice in the matter." Graydon sighed. "It's not that I don't appreciate it, but I've had enough of being used. That's what this would be, even if it was kindly meant."

"Look, I get that, but I can't let you gallop off into the sunset with the Box by yourself." He opened his mouth to protest, but she held up a finger to forestall him. "Let me finish. It's not about a lack of trust. It's not my judgment call to make. I don't own the Box, so who am I to say whether you should be trusted with it or not? But I'm also not a complete and total jackwagon, or at least I try not to be. And only a complete and total jackwagon would let someone wander off into the desert alone with no food, water, or money. Not only is that an awful thing to do to somebody, but it also means that once you're gone, there's a dangerous artifact just sitting out there in the desert, waiting for somebody to come along and pick it up. I like nothing about this plan. This plan sucks rocks."

As she spoke, Graydon's eyes grew progressively larger, and finally he nodded, holding his hands up. "Fine, fine. I get it. It was a bad idea. But I have to do something. You do see that, don't you?"

"Sure, but why go to all that effort just to be a hermit? I'll give you some private time here. I could maybe keep Sabretooth off your back, too. Would that be enough?"

He began shaking his head even before she'd finished the sentence. "Afraid not. He's just so huge. I don't mean in the physical sense. Even if you did manage to keep him from interacting with me directly, I'd feel him when he's near. He has an aura about him." He sighed. "I sound ridiculous."

"No, you don't."

Eva knew exactly what he meant. Sabretooth had defied many of her expectations. He was capable of kindness when she'd expected nothing of the sort from him. He had a wicked sense of humor that had shocked her. But still, throughout this entire day, she'd never lost the sense that she stood in the presence of a predator. Maybe it was in the way that he scanned every space they entered as if he claimed it for his own, or the way he stared down at everyone he met in a silent struggle for domination. He didn't even seem to realize that he did these things. As a result, her hackles went up every time he came anywhere close, so she knew exactly what Graydon referred to. Sabretooth was truly equal parts man and animal. Neither side of him would ever fully dominate the other, but to discount either of his facets would be a fatal mistake.

Graydon watched her expression intently. "So you do understand," he said, breathing out in what looked like relief. "Thank goodness. Will you help me?"

She licked her lips, which had suddenly gone dry. "We'll figure something out," she promised, not knowing what.

The lack of commitment seemed to discourage him more than anything. He slumped back against the tree, staring at the frozen Box with obvious longing. Eva racked her brain for a solution that would check all of the boxes – one that wouldn't leave Graydon alone and vulnerable, anger Sabretooth and send him on a rampage, get her and Christopher into even more trouble, or expose more people to the Box's magic. It seemed like a solution should be simple, but she couldn't come up with it. She was just so drained after everything that had happened. Maybe she needed a little time and a clear head, and then the answer would become obvious. She hoped so, because despair weighed on her, and it looked like Graydon felt the same.

He cocked his head then, listening intently. The sudden movement drew her attention and she followed suit.

Perhaps he'd heard Christopher and Sabretooth returning? It would be a relief to be able to finally leave. But she didn't hear footsteps. Instead, she heard a faint hum, and she leaped to her feet and scanned the sky for the X-Copter.

But she saw nothing, and as she looked over the unbroken gray expanse of clouds, she realized that it didn't sound like the chopper anyway. It was too high pitched and much too close by. It grated on her eardrums, growing in intensity with every passing moment.

She clapped her hands over her ears, but that failed to provide any relief. Beside her, Graydon had climbed to his feet too, and he gritted his teeth against the pain. She could feel her bones vibrating.

"What is that?" she shouted, trying to be heard over the deafening whine.

Graydon shrugged helplessly, looking around for the source but coming up empty.

From its spot on the ground inside the time bubble, the Box flashed with a bright white light. Eva experienced a dim echo of impact, like when the bottom half of her face had been nicely numbed at the dentist but still she felt a vague rummaging about as the necessary work was accomplished. The bubble vibrated visibly now, letting off curls of steam. She had the strong idea that touching it would be a very bad idea indeed. It glowed as if it would be burning hot to the touch.

The Box flashed again, brighter this time. Graydon winced, putting a hand to his forehead. Eva's attention went instantly from the scorching hot surface of the time bubble to him.

"You OK?" she demanded.

"Just a blinding headache all of a sudden. That's all," he said through gritted teeth. "Keep an eye on the bubble. Please, whatever you do, don't let it pop. I have the distinct feeling that would be a very bad idea right now."

She couldn't have agreed more, but the bubble had reached a critical point of instability. It vibrated uncontrollably, hissing and burning a visible scorch mark into the grass underneath it. She reached out tentatively, trying to take a mental hold of it, and immediately drew away as even the slightest contact sent white-hot bolts of pain through her. Apparently the heat wasn't just physical. She couldn't reinforce the bubble. It was just a matter of time before it blew. But perhaps if she was on the ball, she could replace it with another bubble quickly enough that whatever was going to come blasting out at them would still be contained.

She readied herself and tried to look confident. Based on Graydon's worried expression, her efforts were less than successful.

"Maybe we should take cover," he suggested.

"That isn't a bad idea," she admitted.

But the phenomenon failed to repeat itself. The Box emitted no more waves of power. Unfortunately, the time bubble continued to quake, and although Eva couldn't reach out to test it, she knew that it had been strained to its limits. Tentatively, she began to form a second bubble, layering it atop the first one. Perhaps she could sandwich them one on top of another like layers of an onion and keep the Box contained that way. As the new bubble solidified into shape, Graydon nodded his approval.

"Smart thinking," he said.

Moments after she'd formed the second bubble, the first one winked out of existence, sending a wave of magic impacting against the new one.

WHOOM!

The bubble rocked visibly, its surface darkening from a translucent blue to a deep and vibrant violet within seconds. She would need another one, much more quickly than she would have wanted. She wouldn't be able to keep this up for long, but giving up wasn't an option. Desperately, she began to form the shape of another time bubble in her mind.

"They're coming!" Graydon shouted, pointing through the trees.

At first, Eva's stomach fell, anticipating yet another problem to add to the already full stack of troubles on her shoulders. But then she saw them. Sabretooth sprinted at full speed toward them, with Christopher huffing and puffing along behind him as fast as he could go. But his fastest gallop couldn't match Sabretooth, who had gone to all fours and ate up the ground in long, bunching strides that reminded Eva of a cheetah running across the African prairie. He was just that fast.

Relief coursed through her. This wasn't another problem; this was the cavalry coming to the rescue. She didn't know what they could do to help, but at least if more Sentinels poured out of the trees, she could focus on her bubbles and know that they'd watch her back.

"Are you OK?" Sabretooth shouted, his eyes wild.

"The Box went haywire," Graydon explained, indicating

the steaming time bubble containing the artifact. "Eva is trying to contain it, but it's a losing battle. It's been burning through her bubbles almost as fast as she can make them."

Eva thought this summary sounded just about right. Good thing, too, because she had her hands full. She let another bubble loose, barely containing the shockwave as the previous one burst. She shook her head, spots dancing in front of her eyes. That had been close.

Christopher staggered up to her, holding his side. "Are you… OK?" he panted, doubled over. "We… came… as… fast… as…" With every word, he grew increasingly more unsteady, and his pauses for breath took longer and longer.

Finally, Sabretooth clapped him on the shoulder and said, "Take a breath, bud. You galloped all the way here. You earned it."

Christopher nodded and sat down right on the spot. It looked like his legs had given out underneath him.

"This might be my fault," Sabretooth explained. He briefly described how they'd discovered the force field and tried to batter through it, and the effect that striking it had had on Christopher. "So we ran all the way back here. Chris stuck with me the whole way. He couldn't keep pace, but he never lost me entirely. I've outrun trained military men before. He's got some guts." He turned an admiring look towards Christopher, which faded slightly when he saw that the younger mutant had collapsed onto the grass. "I thought he'd puked them all out."

"Ha ha. Very funny," said Christopher weakly.

Eva released another bubble. This time, she managed to hold both bubbles together for a good second before the first one popped. She felt a wave of triumph, but she'd begun to develop one heck of a headache.

"This is all great, but can we come up with a plan here?" she said.

"A plan?" asked Sabretooth, sounding honestly confused. "What do you mean, a plan?"

She couldn't believe her ears. Did she have to do all the thinking around here? Christopher would be helping if he wasn't so exhausted. She couldn't hold that against him. But Sabretooth wasn't a stupid man. He should have understood what she meant.

"What we're going to do about the bubbles!" she exclaimed.

"There's nothing to be done," he said. "Let it pop. We should take cover. Be ready for what happens. But you're not going to contain it indefinitely. Better that we choose the time for it to pop then have it overtake you and risk your incapacitation."

"I hate this plan."

He shrugged. "You fight enough battles, you realize there's no such thing as the perfect one. Just the one you got." He indicated the glowing time bubble. "Is that thing gonna blow?"

She hastily put up another bubble just in time. "I see your point. Once Christopher's recovered, let's do it. The more of these I make, the more tired I'll be."

"I'm good," said Christopher. He looked much better now. Much less green around the gills, as Eva's mother would have said.

"OK." Sabretooth looked around. "We're going to want

some heavy-duty shelter. That bubble looks hot. It could go through trees like butter."

"Maybe behind that boulder?" Christopher suggested, pointing toward one of the stone clusters that dotted the area. "Rock won't burn."

"My thoughts exactly. Let's make sure there's enough room for all of us."

The two of them hurried around the boulder. Moments later, Sabretooth jogged out, his expression alarmed.

"There are dead Sentinels over here," he reported.

"Oh, yeah," said Graydon. "Eva and I took down eight or nine of them. We lured them out with the Box, and then when they tried to shoot me, she froze them in place. Then we maneuvered them so that when the bubbles popped, they shot each other instead. We got pretty good at it by the end there."

Sabretooth wore a fairly stunned expression. Christopher couldn't help but laugh at it, and Graydon smirked.

"Nice work," Sabretooth finally said.

"I thought so too," Graydon replied with false modesty.

CHAPTER 26

The magic from the Box came in nonstop waves, and little spots had begun to dance at the corners of Eva's vision as she struggled to contain it. By the time the other mutants led her to their hiding spot behind the boulder, she could barely remain upright. She'd never made so many time bubbles in such a short period, and the constant surges of magic inside them drained her in ways that she didn't entirely understand. She just knew that she wanted to take a break now.

They ducked down behind the broken husks of the Sentinels, trusting that their armored bodies would provide some additional protection from whatever came out of the bubble, and they waited. This time, when Eva felt the bubble go, she did nothing. A wave of heat passed over her, and she could hear the crackle of burning things, but she kept her head down for the moment, reveling in the sensation of release. Her temples still throbbed, but she could relax for just a moment, and so she stretched out on the ground, closing her aching eyes.

When she finally lifted her head, she saw Graydon and

Christopher stamping madly at some smoldering bushes, trying to avoid a full-grown fire. Sabretooth stood nearby, sniffing the air, all senses alert for danger. The Box sat at his feet, seemingly inert. However, Eva didn't trust that for a moment. Who knew what kind of magic spilled from it even now? But Christopher didn't seem alarmed, and she hoped that if something was happening with the Box, he'd warn them.

He noticed her stirring and finished kicking dirt over the bush before coming over to check on her. He hunkered down in the dirt, his shoulder grazing hers.

"How's the head?" he asked.

"Still attached. How's the stomach?"

"Not thrilled to be this close to the Box, but I'll manage."

Sabretooth gave one last sniff, shrugged, and joined them. "Well, that was anticlimactic," he said. "The Box lit a few things on fire, but otherwise it seems to be business as usual."

"I'll take it," Eva said, rubbing the bridge of her nose.

"Nice work, Bubble Girl," said Sabretooth with obvious admiration.

"No. Nuh uh. You did not just call me Bubble Girl."

"That's your X-Men name, isn't it?" he replied with exaggerated innocence.

"It's Tempus. Say it with me. Temp. Us."

"I dunno. Bubble Girl has a much better ring to it. It's perkier."

Eva began to laugh. "I don't care who you are, buster," she said, "but I will rip out your throat if you call me that one more time."

"Whoa, whoa," said Christopher, who still sat between them. "I do not support any throat ripping. Veto on the throat ripping."

But Sabretooth just grinned, warming to the banter. "I'd like to see you try. Bubble Girl."

"Enough," she said. "Give me a minute to make my legs work, and we can go."

They decided to check out the force field around the X-Copter together. Splitting up had done them no good, and if Cyclops was going to come search for them, he'd start at the chopper. Eva would just have to freeze the Box if anyone got too close. It wasn't an ideal plan, but it was all they had.

"Cyclops will want to take the Box, you know," Sabretooth said to Graydon. He sounded all casual, but the stiff set of his shoulders looked anything but.

"I wouldn't be surprised," Graydon responded.

"I'm not going to be one of Scott's little yes-men. I'd last about ten minutes before I wanted to knock his head off his shoulders."

The corner of Graydon's mouth turned up. "Ten? I wouldn't give you five."

Sabretooth snorted. "You're OK with giving it to him? I won't be able to watch out for you."

"I think it's for the best," Graydon said cautiously.

Sabretooth nodded, and after a tense moment, Graydon walked off.

Christopher watched all of this, unnoticed, from a spot on the ground only a few yards away. He debated whether or not he should say something. After all, he'd obviously caught what was meant to be a private conversation, and the polite thing to do would be to pretend he hadn't heard a thing. But how much had he missed with his pops because he'd been afraid to say what was on his mind, and now it was too late? He didn't want to make that mistake ever again.

Cautiously, he joined Sabretooth. At first, he just stood there, hoping to comfort the larger mutant with his presence. But Sabretooth didn't pay him any notice. Instead, he just hunched miserably, staring out at nothing. He had to say something.

"You OK?" he asked, which was stupid. Of course he wasn't OK. That couldn't have been more obvious.

"Could you do me a favor, Chris?" Sabretooth asked unexpectedly.

"Sure," Christopher said. Then he immediately felt the need to qualify the offer. "I mean, if I can."

"If Graydon does go back to that school with you, could I give you a number to call and let me know how he's doing? Nothing sensitive. I don't want to get you in trouble with Summers. Just... how he's doing."

Christopher's heart went out to him. "Sure. No problem. I could even put him on the line for you if you wanted."

"No. Don't tell him I'm checking up on him at all." Sabretooth's voice was gruff. "It would only upset him." He ran a hand over his face, which looked unusually haggard. "We should get out of here before we're attacked by a bunch of killer undead daisies or some ridiculous nonsense like that."

He smirked at Christopher, but it felt forced. Christopher

wanted to say something, but what? He had no idea how to fix this problem. Heck, he had no idea what the problem was, only that it felt all too familiar. Maybe he was just taking his own past, his own trauma, and pasting it onto Sabretooth. In that case, he really did need his head examined. Or maybe it was just stress. Stress was a handy excuse for just about anything.

Sabretooth arched a brow, waiting for a response.

"Sure. I'm happy to help," said Christopher. It was the easiest thing to say. Maybe that made him a coward, but if he found something more substantial to do later, he would do it. That would have to suffice.

Sabretooth's beefy hand clapped him on the shoulder. "Thanks, Chris. Let's get going."

"You took the words right out of my mouth."

"Lead the way."

Christopher was happy to do just that. He led Sabretooth over to join the others, and they walked past the boulders with him in the lead right up until the moment when he smacked face first into something. He backed up a step, his nose smarting and his eyes watering uncontrollably, and tried to figure out what had happened.

"Ow," he said.

"Your nose is bleeding." Sabretooth stiffened, instantly on high alert. "Another of those magic wave things?"

Graydon checked on the Box, which was safely tucked back down in his jumpsuit. "You'd think I would have felt something."

"No," Christopher confirmed. "I ran into something with my face."

He pinched his nostrils, and his fingertips came away streaked with red. This made no sense. He looked around. The space before him appeared completely empty, with nothing that could have hit him. He saw nothing on the ground that could have been thrown at him while he wasn't paying attention, and he thought he would have seen it even if he wouldn't have been able to duck out of the way in time. But he'd seen nothing in the moment before impact.

"Another one of those invisible force fields?" Sabretooth suggested.

Christopher tilted his head to see if he might glimpse something when the light hit it just right, but still no luck. He began to put his hand out, moving with slow caution, but Sabretooth grabbed it before he could move more than a few inches.

"No, this thing packs a punch. Let me," he said.

"You were trying to break through it, but we're not doing that any more. If it's linked to the Box, it might be susceptible to my abilities. I should at least try it," Christopher responded.

"If you're going to do that, one of us should be ready to pull you away if it goes bad," Eva suggested. Sabretooth looked confused, so she elaborated. "Sometimes when he's touched things affected by the Box, he's nearly been sucked in. He's had trouble disengaging on his own."

"And you were going to tell me this when, kid?" Sabretooth demanded.

"It didn't come up," said Christopher. "Probably because I knew you'd overreact."

"I'd do no such thing."

"Actually, he has a point," Graydon muttered.

Sabretooth held up a finger in warning. "You stay out of this. And you need to share with the rest of the group." He turned to Christopher.

"Sure. As soon as you start doing that, I'll follow your lead," said Christopher. "Now if you're done throwing your temper tantrum, I'd like to see if there's a force field here or not."

He didn't bother to wait for an answer, because he knew what the answer would be. Sabretooth would grumble and complain, but eventually he'd have to admit that Christopher was right. He didn't need a babysitter all the time.

More to the point, he didn't deserve being called "kid" again.

With caution, he reached out toward the spot where he thought he'd impacted against the invisible barrier. His fingers touched something cold and smooth and unseen. It didn't shock him, but it felt hard like diamonds. No wonder it had hurt to run his face into it. He put his palm flat against it, marveling at the firm but completely invisible surface. How far did it extend? He began to search, adding a second searching hand alongside the first.

"No shock, huh?" asked Eva.

"Nope. It feels like glass, almost." Christopher smiled a little. "It's kind of neat when you're not hitting it with your face. I'm trying to find the edge."

She nodded and reached out, moving with the same slow caution he'd used. After a moment, she stopped. "It's over here too. It's curved."

Graydon followed suit, picking an open area and moving with elaborate caution until he came to a stop some fifty yards away. "It's over here as well," he called. "I'll see if I can't find the edge."

Sabretooth watched them with his arms folded, sulking. The three of them ignored him, working their way around the circumference of the force field, searching for the exit. There had to be some way out. After all, they'd gotten into it.

Finally, after a few minutes of painstaking searching went by, he joined them, filling in the gaps and reaching up to the high points the rest of them couldn't touch. At its apex, he could just reach the top, so it had to be a good seven foot in height. The curved surface was about twenty feet across, with only grass and uneven ground inside. Just outside the border sat the boulders and the husks of the dead Sentinels they'd killed.

"It's a dome," Sabretooth said, sitting down in the dirt with finality.

Christopher had begun to suspect it sometime before, but he hadn't wanted to say it aloud. Sabretooth just threw the ugly truth right out there. No hesitation.

"Could you bubble it?" Graydon asked Eva.

She shrugged. "If I could, then what? It would freeze us too, which does us no good. There's no way to bubble the force field without affecting us as well. Sorry, mate, but thanks for the vote of confidence."

"I'll try to drain it."

Christopher knew he sounded resigned. He certainly felt that way. He'd gone into this flight thinking that his abilities were uncool and, in some ways, useless compared to what a lot of other mutants could do. But now he just wanted a break.

Luckily, Sabretooth didn't try to patronize him this time, because Christopher might have punched him in the face. He was fairly sure that this wouldn't have ended well for him, no matter how many nice moments he'd had with the elder mutant that day.

"I'll pull you back if you need it," Sabretooth said instead. He looked at Eva. "How do I know if he needs it?"

"He'll start going all clammy," she said. "Like he's about to hurl again."

"We've had lots of examples of that," said Sabretooth. "I should be able to recognize it."

"Oh, stop it," said Christopher.

"How can I help?" asked Graydon, obviously trying to forestall another argument.

"Keep an eye on the Box," Christopher responded. "If it starts doing anything odd, anything at all, get me out of there. It reacted really strongly when Sabretooth messed with that other force field, so I don't know what's going to happen here. But I don't want to stay here and wait for whatever trapped us in here to come and fetch us, do you?"

"Heck no," said Eva. "If you're willing to risk this, I say it's worth doing."

"Absolutely," said Graydon. He pulled the Box from his waistband and watched it intently. "If anything happens, I'll let you know."

Sabretooth sighed, smoothing his bloody, matted hair out of his face. His claws stuck in the tangled strands, but he didn't even seem to notice.

"Fine, fine. Whatever. Risk your life if you want. It's all the same to me," he said.

Marvel: Xavier's Institute

Christopher nodded, reaching out toward the invisible barrier once again. But before he could make contact with it, Sabretooth interrupted him.

"Hey, Chris? Be careful, would ya?" he said diffidently.

"Yeah. Sure."

Christopher touched the barrier, feeling its cold smoothness beneath his hands. This one was clearly different from the barrier that blocked the X-Copter from their reach, but they must have been generated from the same source. He wasn't willing to believe that two magic users coincidentally roamed around Chicago on the same day, having an invisible force field competition. They had to be the work of the same person. Or perhaps they were stuck in the middle, with multiple people trying to get the Box, sending Sentinels and cops, raising the dead and putting up force fields, fighting each other for dominance.

Either option could be true, so he had to be prepared for anything. He opened up, letting his power flow through him, allowing the life force to flow from his palm into the unseen barrier beneath it.

For a moment, nothing happened. Then he could feel the magic that powered the force field and the immense will that sat behind it. Once again, he could hear a faint, incessant chanting in the distance, rhythmic and guttural. The deep voice rose in volume this time, filling his ears. It seemed familiar somehow, but he couldn't place it. He couldn't move away from it, couldn't return to his body or disengage from the force field. He was trapped as the chant filled his mind and took him over, driving away all conscious thought and action.

CHAPTER 27

When Christopher opened his eyes, it took Eva a moment to realize that something was dreadfully wrong. At first she sagged with relief, because he hadn't been trapped by the force field. The emotion quickly gave way to disappointment because he must have come to the conclusion that he couldn't do anything to get them out. The pang of dismay she felt made her speak more bluntly than maybe she should have.

"Giving up so soon?" she asked. "Come on, Christopher. Please try again. I know it makes you feel ill, and that sucks, but I don't want to sit out here forever. I'm getting awfully sick of this park."

But Christopher gave no indication that he'd heard a word. He walked over to where Graydon stood staring at the Box. Christopher wordlessly snatched the artifact out of the politician's hands and began pressing the glowing sigils on the outside in swift sequence.

"What the hell?" Graydon barked.

Christopher didn't even seem to hear him. Now Eva

realized that he wasn't his usual self. The healer stared off into the distance, his eyes unfocused as his hands moved with automatic precision. His face was slack, his normally animated expression empty of thought or emotion. She snapped her fingers in front of his eyes. Nothing. Not even a blink.

"What's wrong with him?" Graydon asked.

"Whatever it is, I don't like it," Sabretooth growled.

He elbowed Eva out of the way without much grace, reaching for the Box. Before he could take it, it rose out of Christopher's hands of its own accord, glowing with an eerie green light. It began to spin, slowly at first, but quickly picking up enough speed that they all backed away, fearful of coming into contact with it. It would make a dangerous projectile at such high speeds. Christopher seemed to shake out of whatever trance he'd been in, and he looked at the Box with the same shock they all felt.

"What's happening?" he asked.

"You should know," said Sabretooth. "You're the one who did it."

"Huh?" Christopher looked honestly puzzled.

"I don't think he realized what he was doing, did you, Christopher?" asked Eva.

"Last thing I remember, I was trying to take down the force field." Christopher backed up until he bumped up against the invisible barrier, still watching the wildly spinning artifact. "Guess I don't have to ask whether it's still there."

"Yeah, well..." Sabretooth didn't sound convinced. He stepped in front of Graydon as if to protect him from whatever might happen next. "You doing OK?"

"No negative effects here," Graydon reported. Then, after a moment, he added with diffident awkwardness, "Thank you for asking."

"Sure." Sabretooth cleared his throat. "No problem."

The top of the Box opened. In all their examinations of it, no one had noticed hinges or seams. It had seemed for all intents and purposes to be one solid cube. But it opened nonetheless, spilling out more of that cold, eldritch light. The spinning slowed, leaving the Box hanging in midair as if held by some unseen hand. Then a familiar holographic figure rose from its depths, tall and resplendent in black and red armor, segmented like some giant bug. Flames rose from his head and outlined his eyes and mouth, which curled in a satisfied smile.

Dormammu.

Eva would have been happy never to see the Lord of Darkness again. After all of the students had been imprisoned in his awful realm, she'd had nightmares about him, even though they hadn't been his prisoner long. They'd stood against him and won, but only because of Illyana. Without her, Dormammu would have enslaved them for eternity in that land of flames and horror, and none of their pitiful mutant abilities would have done them any good. Seeing him again made her want to curl up into a ball and cry as the memories flooded her. She began to tremble, but she couldn't run and hide no matter how much she wanted to. The force field left her nowhere to go.

Christopher seemed to share her fear. He bit his lower lip hard as he tried to maintain control, and for one tense moment, he swayed as if he might keel over entirely. But then he steadied, gripping her hand tightly in his. The grasp hurt her fingers, but somehow the pain helped. She focused on it instead of the fear. This time would be different. If Dormammu wanted to pick a fight, he'd be on their ground this time, and even though they didn't have Illyana on their side, they had Sabretooth. Besides, she and Christopher had grown since then. They might still be new, but they'd learned so much in only a short time. Their newfound confidence would make a difference. It had to.

She stood up a little straighter and released Christopher's hand, nodding to reassure him that she was OK. They would get out of this one way or another. She had to believe that.

Dormammu surveyed them like a king looking over his subjects from atop the floating Box. He may have been only a few inches tall and slightly see-through, but he managed to look imposing nonetheless. When he spoke, his voice boomed, its timbre and volume at odds with his small stature.

"I am Dormammu," he announced. "The Dread One, Lord of Chaos, Master of the Box of Planes. Identify yourselves."

"Sorry," said Sabretooth. "I don't take orders from action figures. Are you the reason we can't leave? Because if so, I've got a bone to pick with you."

"Identify yourselves," Dormammu repeated.

"I don't think it's smart to argue with him, Sabretooth," Eva said nervously. "He's dangerous."

But Sabretooth didn't even pretend to listen to her. He wanted a fight more than anything else. His fists clenched and his lips curled away from his teeth as he glared at the hologram. She'd known it would come to this. To her surprise, she liked Sabretooth. He was like a grumpy uncle who said swear words in front of the kids and took them for rides on his motorcycle but was never allowed to watch them alone because of that one time no one ever spoke about. He just wasn't trustworthy, and now a sinking feeling in her stomach told her that things were about to go very badly indeed.

"I don't like your tone," he said. "If you're not going to let us out of here, I'm just gonna have to make you."

Before Eva could stop him, he leaped toward the Box, swiping at the hologram that hung in the air over it. A loud cracking sound filled the air, and lightning lanced from the Box, striking Sabretooth. He howled in pain. The smell of ozone and burnt flesh assaulted Eva's senses. Sabretooth grabbed at the Box again, and another flash of light threw him onto the ground. He scrambled to his feet, his hands blackened, his face twisted with fury, and prepared to throw himself at the Box for a third time, mad with rage and pain.

"Hold him!" Eva shouted, leaping toward him.

She tried. Really she did, but she weighed about as much as one of his arms, and even then, she wasn't sure which was heavier. She grabbed on, and he flung her off effortlessly. Her shoulder slammed into the force field, exploding with pain. Christopher tried too, but he was shaken off with similar ease. Sabretooth started toward the Box and Dormammu's hologram once again. His eyes glowed with murderous rage, all signs of rational thought gone. He'd held on as long as he could, but finally, he'd snapped. They had all heard what he was capable of, and although Eva now realized that this didn't mean he couldn't be funny or kind, it only took one look at him now to realize that at least some of those stories were most likely true. He was a violent killer, and no amount of witty banter would change it.

Graydon stepped in front of him. He was just a human. He had no superhuman powers or abilities to protect him from the raging mutant that loomed over him, eager for violence. Somehow, he didn't even look afraid. His eyes were clear and his expression calm as he stared up at the wild-eyed figure before him.

"You'll have to go through me," he said. "Is that a sacrifice you're willing to make, Victor? Mother was willing to throw me aside. In fact, I think she was eager to strike the blow that killed me. I didn't know she was my murderer at the time, but…" His expression creased for a moment with some vaguely remembered pain. "Someone told me. I don't remember who, but one of the times they brought me back, someone made sure I knew that my own mother killed me. So if you do it now, it won't be that bad. I'm used to being offed by my parents."

"Get out of the way!" Sabretooth roared in his face, making as if to strike him aside.

But something held him back. For some inexplicable reason, he didn't move. The mercenary had done a million horrible things in his life, and if he was given the chance, Eva knew he'd do a million more. To her intense astonishment, she realized that maybe Sabretooth had finally found his limit. He couldn't hurt Graydon. He'd reached the one line he wouldn't cross. Emotions buffeted her – pride at Sabretooth's growth, horror at Graydon's past, and a sinking dread of what would come next.

"Do it," Graydon urged, his face suddenly alight with a horrible eagerness. "You never wanted me. Send me back to Hell where I belong. Do it!"

Sabretooth's eyes cleared, and he looked suddenly disgusted. He shoved Graydon away from him, without too much violence, a master of his emotions once again.

"No," he said roughly. Then he whirled away, retreating as far as the force field would allow.

As soon as Sabretooth retreated, the fervent expression faded from Graydon's face. Eva couldn't believe how quickly it changed. Had he been acting all along? Now he watched Sabretooth with an unreadable expression. If they'd been alone, she would have offered sympathy. Now she understood his desperation to get away: Graydon was Sabretooth's son. It was obvious now. Under less chaotic circumstances, she probably would have figured it out already.

"Interesting," Dormammu said, unmoved by this raw display of emotion. "But let us resume the negotiation. I recognize two of you. You are both associates of Illyana Rasputin."

His glowing orange eyes roved over Eva and Christopher, seeming to miss nothing. Eva swallowed hard but refused to shrink under that awful gaze. Dormammu's flaming eyes brought back uncomfortable memories of despair from those moments when she thought she'd be stuck in the barren nothingness of Limbo forever, at the mercy of a sorcerer who seemed to delight in misery. It would be easy to give up now, knowing what they faced. Dormammu had the strength of Illyana Rasputin, and he was cunning and cruel. But instead of bowing before him, she lifted her chin in a gesture of blatant defiance against both him and the fear he made her feel.

"Yeah," she said. "I'm Tempus."

Somehow, using the name strengthened her anew. It reminded her that she was more than just Eva Bell now. Yes, she was still the young woman who played a wicked game of softball and liked punk music, but she could also deploy time bubbles with such precision that she could make a pair of Sentinels shoot each other by accident. She had changed so much since she'd joined the New Xavier School. Heck, she'd changed noticeably in the past few hours alone.

"I'm Triage," said Christopher, following her lead.

"I have been watching you, and you have impressed me," said Dormammu. "What of the other two? The master manipulator and the trained killer. I have yet to meet them."

They weren't bad descriptions, sadly enough. Graydon shook his head silently as if refusing the introduction, but Eva didn't think this was a hill worth dying on. What harm could a name do? They would come to conflict soon enough, but in the meantime, they needed to know more about him and what he intended.

"This is Graydon, and that's Sabretooth," she said, indicating each one in turn.

Graydon frowned a little but said nothing.

"I have a proposition. I have determined that you would make potent allies, and I am in need of support for my plans. You will serve as the keepers of the Box of Planes and do my bidding," said Dormammu.

Sabretooth opened his mouth to answer, but Eva leaped in before he could say a word. With his hotheaded nature, she couldn't guarantee that he wouldn't mouth off, and Dormammu didn't seem like the type of guy to let that slide. She had to keep him talking.

"What plans?" she asked hastily.

"You will do as I say and ask no questions," he ordered. "You have seen my power. Do not anger me."

"I can't help if I don't know what you're trying to accomplish," she replied, ad-libbing it. "I want to be useful. The X-Men don't let me do anything fun."

The fiery eyes surveyed her for a moment with what seemed like amusement. Then Dormammu nodded. "You speak sense, Tempus. My plans are simple, and there is no harm in your knowing them. The Box gives me access to multiple planes of existence. I need you to open the doors for me. Then you will be rewarded."

"That sounds like a crap deal to me," said Sabretooth. "You got no reason to keep your end of the bargain."

He didn't move to rejoin them, but he glared at Dormammu's hologram from his spot at the back of the force field, as far from the rest of them as he could possibly get.

"Do not dismiss my offer out of hand," said Dormammu. "Not before you understand its advantages. The Box sustains Graydon's life. This is why you sought out the artifact, is it not?"

"Yeah, well, I don't need you for that, do I?" snapped Sabretooth.

"Oh, but you do," Dormammu responded smoothly. "I could send a surge of power through the Box so great that his weak physical form could not contain it. He would disintegrate into so much dust. Or I could break his mind, flooding it with horrors until he was nothing but a drooling husk trapped in this body. Would you care for him then? Do you have the patience to change his diapers and spoon food into his lips, or would you leave your son to die?"

Sabretooth's expression went completely white.

"Oh yes. I heard. Graydon is your son. I am told that men will go to extraordinary lengths to protect their family. You will deal with me, or I will unleash Hell upon him," said Dormammu.

Sabretooth turned bleak eyes on his son. His lip quivered, baring one of his fangs as he struggled against his surging emotions. But with effort, he mastered himself. His expression firmed. Then his back bent as he knelt before Dormammu. Graydon's eyes welled with tears as he watched his unbendable father prostrate himself for his safety.

Eva couldn't stand it. The sight of Sabretooth on his knees offended her on a level she couldn't exactly explain. Maybe he could use a little humility, but prostrating himself in front of Dormammu? After the fiasco in Limbo, she knew what Dormammu was capable of. All he cared about was freeing himself from the restraints Magik had placed on him and grabbing power over as many planes as he could. He wouldn't keep his end of the bargain. He'd kill Graydon just for the fun of it, no matter what they agreed on. Their only hope of saving Graydon was to defeat Dormammu and claim the Box for themselves. If she froze him, maybe they could figure something out.

She did it before she could think twice. Dormammu and the Box froze in space, held tight by a small, glistening bubble. For a moment, no one moved. Then Christopher grinned.

"Nice call, Eva," he said.

"Nice call?" Sabretooth demanded, launching toward her. He grabbed her by the shoulders and shook, none too gently. Her teeth rattled together. "You've killed him!"

"Hey! Stop it!" said Christopher, trying to pull him off.

Sabretooth whirled on him. "She just doomed Graydon. Dormammu isn't just going to let this go. I've seen guys like him before. You don't know–"

"Yeah, actually we do, because we've fought him before," Eva snapped. "You can't trust him, Sabretooth. He's willing to do anything for power; we saw that ourselves. He was lying to you. He'll get what he wants and then kill Graydon just because he can, and then he'll go on a killing spree here on Earth. We can't let that happen. The only way to protect him is to take the Box for ourselves."

"Yeah," Christopher agreed. "We can keep the Box in a bubble. Eva, you'll have to watch it like a hawk, because if Dormammu gets out, he'll be ticked. We'll work on breaking through this force field."

Sabretooth seemed to consider it for a moment. His eyes flicked to Graydon, who had watched the entire argument that would decide his fate without a word. The politician seemed resigned, and Sabretooth took one look at him and instantly made up his mind.

"No."

Sabretooth struck Eva upside the head once, hard. She didn't even see it coming before pain exploded through her skull. Everything went dark.

CHAPTER 28

Christopher couldn't believe what happened next. They'd been talking about the plan when Eva captured Dormammu in one of her bubbles, taking him by surprise in what he'd thought was a brilliant move. They could have escaped and protected Graydon. Worked together. Been a team.

But then Sabretooth knocked her out cold. She dropped like a box of bricks, and for one horrible moment, Christopher thought she was dead. Blood trickled from one of her ears, and she didn't appear to be moving. But then her chest trembled ever so slightly as she breathed. She was alive. The realization made him go limp with relief. He could heal whatever damage Sabretooth had caused, and she would be OK. No thanks to Sabretooth.

He whirled around and shoved the giant mutant as hard as he could. It was like trying to push a rock.

"How could you, man?" he demanded. "She didn't do anything to you!"

"She could have gotten Graydon killed," Sabretooth snarled. "He's mine. My flesh and blood. I don't expect you to understand that."

"But..." Despair filled Christopher. "You're the one who doesn't understand! I feel like that about you, and about her, and about Graydon. I thought we were a team."

At least he had the grace to look ashamed. "I'm sorry, kid. But I didn't kill her. I knew you could patch her up, and I won't hurt either of you again so long as you don't interfere. Got it?"

Christopher couldn't even meet his eyes, but he nodded.

"I'll take her over there, so we're out of your way," he said, bitterness soaking into every word.

"Good."

Sabretooth seemed like he might say more, but Christopher had no desire to hear any of it. He had no reason to be upset. After all, he'd only met the man a few hours earlier, even though it felt like forever. But that time had meant something to him. It had changed him in profound ways that he probably didn't even understand. Learning that it had meant nothing to Sabretooth... hurt.

He dragged Eva as far as the force field would allow and got to work healing her. Sabretooth may have pulled his blow, but he'd still managed to do a ton of damage. Any more, and he would have killed her. It took some time for Christopher to bring her back. By the time he was done, the time bubble had popped. He opened his eyes to find Dormammu and Sabretooth talking again. When Eva stirred, he clapped a hand over her mouth, cautioning her to silence. She would be confused, but he couldn't risk her asking questions and attracting their attention. Not if he wanted to get them out alive.

After a moment of panic, she relaxed underneath his

hand, and he released his grip. They held onto each other and listened, trying to figure out what to do next.

"Very good," Dormammu said to Sabretooth. "I will allow this infraction this once, but next time, I shall not be so lenient. If you continue to serve me well, I can reward as well as punish. You fight with your son. I can offer you an offspring who does your bidding. A perfect, pliant child."

Graydon, who stood a few steps behind his father, blanched visibly.

"No thanks," said Sabretooth. "No cages. Not for me, and not for him."

"But that's what this is," Graydon said suddenly. "Eva and Christopher were right. Don't you see? We'll be wearing collars instead of trapped in cages, but it's the exact same thing."

"Stuff it, Graydon!" Sabretooth commanded, but Graydon kept on going.

"I want nothing to do with this poseur. He looks like a Halloween pumpkin on steroids. He's offering us a leash and collar, if not a cage. I'd rather go back to being dead than be someone's slave again. And as much as I've hated you in the past, I refuse to see you leashed. You can't do this," he said. He took an involuntary step toward his father, his expression pleading. "Please don't do this."

Sabretooth hesitated.

"Quiet," Dormammu snapped at Graydon. "Or I'll quiet you."

Graydon inexplicably smirked. "You'll only prove me right. Go ahead, and see what that gets you. He'll rip you to shreds, and I'll find my way back again somehow. You'll see.

I won't regret waiting to be resurrected again if it means you get your just deserts."

"You were warned," said Dormammu. "Now you will pay the price."

His hologram made a complicated gesture, his hands flaring into bright, fiery light. The Box of Planes brightened too, and Graydon jerked as if struck. Christopher didn't want to look, but he couldn't resist. It was like driving past a car wreck and knowing that no one could have survived but being unable to resist the urge to check anyway. He felt the life energy stream out of the Box, twisting around Graydon in a complicated pattern. It moved too quickly for his mind to unravel. When it withdrew, Graydon no longer had a mouth with which to speak. In its place sat smooth, unbroken skin. He groped at it, his eyes widening in increasing panic, and muffled sounds came from his throat but found no means of escape. He scrabbled desperately at his face.

Eva whimpered, clutching at Christopher. He had to help Graydon, even though he had no idea if his abilities extended to putting a mouth back where it ought to be. He had to try, even if the thought of approaching Dormammu's hologram made him tremble uncontrollably. But he only made it a single step before Eva latched onto him tighter, refusing to allow him to move another inch. Fear had given her a panicky strength.

Sabretooth snarled. "Put it back, or so help me, I'll…"

"What?" Dormammu remained unfazed. "What could you possibly do to my projection that would bother me?"

Graydon collapsed on the ground, tears streaming down his face as he continued to feel for the spot where his mouth had been. He didn't even seem to register their presence any more. He'd withdrawn into some place deep inside himself where he wallowed in despair. Sabretooth watched him for a moment, and once again he crumbled in slow stages. Christopher wanted to punch him in the nose – hard – but it still hurt to watch him accept his defeat. He and Eva might be able to fix this. Sabretooth probably didn't deserve it after he'd stabbed them in the back, but that didn't matter.

Christopher intended to do what was right after all, because his instructors had taught him well. Maybe he still had a lot to learn, but he was an X-Man, and for the first time, he realized that it didn't matter if he had the flashiest mutant ability or not. He still had what it took. Emma Frost had tried her best to show him that, but he'd had to learn it on his own. He would try. He'd be scared, and maybe he'd fail, but he would give it everything he had. Nothing less would do.

He gently uncurled Eva's fingers from his suit. Their eyes met. Hers brimmed with tears, and he knew his did too. They touched foreheads, drawing strength from each other. He would not let Eva fall to Dormammu. He would not let Graydon suffer. His lips firmed, and he watched as Eva's expression mirrored the growing resolve he felt. They had to do something. They had to make this right. Together.

For all of their little squabbles and disagreements, they were truly becoming teammates. Whatever happened, he knew that she would always have his back, and he would be there for her in turn. Heck, Sabretooth should be learning from them, not the other way around. Maybe then he'd get his head out of his behind for a change.

Christopher straightened, stretching out his neck in preparation for the confrontation to come. Beside him, Eva cracked her knuckles. He grinned at her. It was a grin of fear and determination and, strangest of all, of hope.

"I'll do what you want," said Sabretooth, bowing his head. "Just put him back the way he was."

"Don't!" Christopher interrupted. "Remember what Graydon said. He doesn't want this."

Graydon had stopped rocking and crying. He just sat there quietly now, listening. He neither contradicted nor confirmed what Christopher had said. Maybe he couldn't.

"Dormammu is a punk," Eva added. "He's only telling you what you want to hear. Illyana told me he'll do just about anything to get out of Limbo. He's buttering you up to get you to do what he wants, and then he'll throw you away like a piece of garbage. Go ahead. Ask him if I'm wrong."

Sabretooth's eyes narrowed, and he lifted his head to stare at the hologram with a hint of his old spark. "Well?" he asked.

"I assure you, I intend to have a lengthy and mutually supportive partnership," said Dormammu smoothly.

Sabretooth exhaled. "I believe you." Then he stood up and turned to Graydon. "But I'm not the one you need to convince. You can't con a conman. Do you believe him, Graydon?"

For one tense moment, it seemed like Graydon might not answer at all, like the loss of his mouth might have broken his mind. But then his eyes narrowed. He shook his head in a short and definitive no, and then, just in case his message wasn't clear, he made a rude gesture.

Sabretooth tensed. Father and son held each other's eyes for a long moment. Then Sabretooth's expression softened, and it was clear that he loved his son. Enough to kill for him, which was easy for a man like Sabretooth. But sacrificing his revenge was a different story.

Graydon's chin lifted. Maybe he couldn't speak, but the meaning was all too clear. They would stand together, no matter what happened. He scrambled to his feet and stood next to his father, providing a unified front. They turned to face Dormammu as one.

"I guess the deal's off after all," said Sabretooth. He turned to Christopher, immediately dismissing the holographic sorcerer. "Can you fix him?"

"Get us out of this force field, and I'll try. Illyana should be able to help us with the Box," Christopher replied.

"She can give me a ride to Limbo." Sabretooth smacked a fist into his open palm. "I'd like to have a few words in person with Dormammu. You hear that, punk? I'm coming for you."

"I hear you," said Dormammu. He sounded delighted. "I'll even make it easier for you to get here. Allow me to take down the force field."

Christopher's ears popped. He felt a sudden static shift in the air, and his heart leaped. Had it really been that easy? Eva reached out, delight evident on her face, and waved her hand around. No force field. She took a few steps and turned to offer him a cautious smile. Nothing. But it couldn't be that easy. Dormammu had tricked Illyana, and she wasn't stupid. If he was that eager to take down the force field, he had to have something up his sleeve. Some trick. Something he wanted. He just didn't know what it was.

"You will be able to get in your helicopter as well. I'll be waiting for you," said Dormammu. "I'm looking forward to it."

"You must have a death wish," Sabretooth said.

He'd returned to his old self now. He grinned at Dormammu with fierce eagerness, hunching forward as if he couldn't wait to get on with the battle. His arms twitched with adrenaline already. Christopher hoped with every fiber of his being that Sabretooth was just leading Dormammu on, but he worried this wasn't the case.

"Oh, I almost forgot," said Dormammu. "This one has outlived his usefulness."

He snapped his fingers, and Graydon Creed began to dissolve. His horrified eyes bore into Sabretooth's, and he clutched at his father as he fell into bones and dust that rained onto the ground in slow motion.

"Graydon! My son!" Sabretooth howled, trying desperately to hold him together. He scooped the jumpsuit into his arms, ashes pouring from the sleeves. "No!"

Graydon was gone.

The empty jumpsuit sagged, but its layers of stains and grime held it upright, as if someone invisible still stood inside. One of the ripped boots toppled over onto its side, spilling dust and bone fragments onto the ground.

Sabretooth fell to his knees and howled in grief and loss. He ripped the jumpsuit to shreds, venting his emotions on the fabric and sending dingy pieces to flutter on the ground.

Christopher reached blindly for Eva, tears blurring his vision. Although it would have been tactless to say so, he hadn't really liked Graydon much at first. The man had made it his life's mission to hate mutants, and he'd spent most of the day being rude to Christopher and Eva after they'd gone out of their way to help him. But toward the end there, he'd shown hints of a decent person that Christopher would have liked to know.

Maybe he'd struggled with some of the same things that Christopher had. His father hadn't been there for him either, and he'd been angry too. Maybe Christopher needed to learn from what Graydon had become. If he let his anger at his pops consume him, he could become just like the politician. But if he learned from his example, maybe he could make Graydon's life – and death – mean something. It wouldn't bring the man back, but it would give him his voice after he'd died without one. Christopher thought Graydon would have liked that. He hugged Eva a little tighter as he thought about it, feeling her tears wet his shirt.

Dormammu watched their grief, flames welling from his wide and delighted smile. Sabretooth finished destroying the jumpsuit and turned his wild eyes toward the Box. But when he leaped toward it with murder in his eyes, Dormammu simply laughed. Sabretooth's claws swiped through thin air as the hologram dissolved into motes of light. The Box's lid closed, and it fell to the ground with a thump, rolling to a stop at Christopher's feet.

Sabretooth followed it and seemed about to vent the remainder of his anger on the artifact, but Christopher picked it up first.

"Give it to me," Sabretooth snarled. His spittle sprayed Christopher's cheeks and his eyes glowed gold with barely checked fury.

"No. You break this thing, and all that magic goes haywire. There's no telling what it'll do," said Christopher.

"Exactly." Sabretooth's eyes lit up with a terrible hope. "It might bring him back again."

"You can't be serious," said Eva. "Listen to what you're saying."

"Think about what Graydon would want," counseled Christopher.

But Sabretooth was beyond rational thought. Driven mad by grief and his own twisted desires, he grabbed the Box and sprinted away at full speed. They gave chase. Christopher had kept pace with him before and felt proud of himself for it, but this time he couldn't even keep the runaway mutant in sight. Eva, who had a much shorter stride than the both of them, fared even worse. Either Sabretooth had been holding back last time or desperation had kicked him into a higher gear. Within moments, he'd disappeared into the trees.

Christopher slowed, kicking at the dirt in frustration. Eva jogged up next to him, looking towards the trail where Sabretooth had disappeared. She came to a stop, bent over and gasping for breath.

"He's gone... isn't he?" she asked.

"Yeah," he said, bleakness filling his voice. He could barely believe it. After everything they had done, everything they'd sacrificed, he couldn't believe that Sabretooth had thrown it away like that once again. Had Christopher's overtures of friendship meant anything to him? It had felt like it at the time, but maybe Sabretooth had been playing him all along.

Maybe he'd just been naïve.

"We should go back to school," he said, turning his back on the whole sordid mess and looking down at Eva's worried face. "I'm sure Cyclops and the rest of the instructors are worried sick. Let's go home."

CHAPTER 29

Christopher stalked down the park trail with a mulish expression on his face that didn't seem like him at all. Eva knew that Sabretooth's betrayal had hurt him deeply. She didn't blame Christopher for getting attached, although she felt like they should have seen it coming. After all, Sabretooth had a reputation for a reason. If even half of the stories were true, he and Wolverine were like brothers, and they'd stabbed each other – literally – more times than Eva could count. One more betrayal wouldn't even register on his radar, although it would wound someone like Christopher to the core.

She hoped it didn't change him. She'd come to the school full of hope and eagerness, and she had to admit that it had been hard to see her childhood heroes alternately jaded and faded. Maybe if she could just do the right thing, say the right thing, she could inspire them to be the people they used to be. Because she was beginning to realize that mutant powers had very little to do with what being a member of the X-Men was all about. Sabretooth remained one of the most powerful mutants she'd ever seen. Even M-Day seemed not to have diminished his potent abilities. But he wouldn't last in their school for a day. He wouldn't stab himself to prove a point to his students. He'd never think in such a self-sacrificing – if completely insane – kind of way.

Christopher was right about one thing. She'd be glad to go back to the school. Her homesickness had reached new levels. At this point, she even longed for Emma Frost's class, stabbing and all. Not that she wanted to put the training wheels back on; she felt like she'd proven that she could hold her own without a doubt. But she longed for the security that came with having a team to back her up, and she was eager to show off what she'd learned. Focusing on that took some of the sting out of what had ultimately turned out to be a mission failure. She still wanted to punch Sabretooth and cry simultaneously, but at least she could hold her head high on the way home.

But if that was true, she didn't understand why she kept looking off in the direction that Sabretooth had fled with the Box of Planes, even as she followed Christopher toward the X-Copter and their way home. She had no reason to worry about Sabretooth. He could take care of himself, and based on what Christopher had told her, Sabretooth had nearly killed her. Worrying about him was ridiculous.

Maybe she was just worried about the Box. It would be reckless to leave such a powerful artifact in his hands. He could do a lot of damage with it, and although she knew that Cyclops would do something about it, she felt a certain responsibility. She and Christopher had the ability to tackle this problem, so why were they running?

She stopped. Maybe she wanted to turn tail and go home, but she and Christopher had helped Sabretooth escape with the Box in the first place. Without them, a lot of things might have been different. They had an obligation to see this through, whether they liked it or not.

Christopher continued on a few more steps before he realized that she'd come to a stop. He turned, looking at her quizzically.

"Got something in your shoe?" he asked.

She shook her head. "We've got to go back for him," she said.

"Nuh uh. No way."

"Why?" she asked, not unkindly. "Because he stabbed us in the back? Hurt our feelings? Tried to knock my block off? I got news for you, Christopher: we're X-Men now. You might as well get used to it, because from what I understand, this kind of drama comes with the job."

"Maybe that explains why Emma's slightly unhinged," he said, with a sudden and surprising hint of humor.

She considered it. "Well, that and a lifetime of looking into people's heads." She shuddered. "I'm so glad I'm not a psychic. It's a wonder they're not all a little mad, don't you think?"

He snorted, but his expression quickly sobered. "Look, I see what you're trying to do, and I appreciate it. But I'm not sure it's a good idea. The more I think about it, the more I think he was playing us the whole time. All those jokes and camaraderie… what if it was just an act?"

"So what if it was? Does that change our responsibility? We know he has a dangerous artifact in his possession. If we leave now, he may disappear with it for good before they can get back here again to track him down. We need to get that Box back, and our messy feelings about Sabretooth – whatever they may be – aren't relevant."

Christopher shook his head slowly. "Man, I'm usually the hyper-rational one, and everyone hates me for it. For the first time ever, I understand how they feel."

"Trust me, I don't like it any more than you do."

"I'm glad you're with me, though." He grinned. "Can you imagine how awful it would be if it was just one of us here with Fabio and David complaining about tacos the whole time?"

She groaned loudly, rolling her eyes.

Christopher straightened his goggles on his forehead, scanning the trees.

"I can sense the Box," he said excitedly. "We should be able to follow its signature to Sabretooth."

"I'll bubble him, and we'll take it," she said. "There's no need to fight him. We just need to get the Box and go. If he gets his hands on the remote, he could take the X-Copter and leave us stranded here. A direct confrontation would be a bad idea."

He nodded in intense agreement. "You can say that again." She opened her mouth. "But don't. Seriously, Eva, that joke is so tired now, and we don't have the time. Come on. The Box is this way."

With Christopher leading the way, they descended down into the depths of the park once again. A long row of lampposts drove away the early evening gloom. This path wound down, taking a roundabout and scenic route through some pretty ornamental gardens and finally emerging near a group of basketball courts. Sabretooth had clearly come and gone. The bleachers alongside two of the courts had been ripped from the ground and twisted into impossible shapes. Two basketballs and a single high-top shoe sat abandoned on the court, left by panicked players too afraid to retrieve them.

On the far side of the complex, one of the fences had been torn down and shredded to pieces. Eva pointed it out, and Christopher nodded.

"Well, at least he's making it easy for us to follow him," he said. "That's nicer for me. I won't end up puking so much this way."

"Yeah, he's a stand-up guy, that Sabretooth. Next thing you know, he'll be nominated for the Nobel Prize or something."

Eva's attempt at comedy fell flat. Maybe it was the rampant destruction or the eerie abandonment of the park in the wake of Sabretooth's rampage. It seemed like there should be screaming or police or something. The unbroken quiet made it seem like everyone might be dead, even though that was ridiculous. But they continued, Christopher walking closer to her, his shoulder brushing hers. Something didn't feel right. They both sensed it.

They passed through the basketball courts and came to a large courtyard featuring an ornamental fountain at its center. The heavy stone fountain had been knocked clear off its pedestal, and water sprayed from the broken base, spattering the surrounding ground in a wide circle. There was no way around it without getting wet. They held their arms up over their heads and dashed through. Under different circumstances it would have been fun. It made Eva think of warm summer days spent sprinting through the sprinklers and sneaking frozen ices to share with her friends down the street when her mom wasn't watching. But now all she could think of was the immense strength it took to blast through all of that rock, and the unchecked aggression Sabretooth had displayed when he'd come out of nowhere to attack it.

Christopher had wandered toward the tree line, his attention caught by something on the ground there. His shoulders slumped as he looked at it, and her stomach sank as she joined him. Whatever he'd found, it didn't look good.

Dead birds littered the ground. One or two could have been a coincidence, but there had to be at least twenty of them. She saw no signs of violence, although she was no bird expert. It looked like they had made a habit of congregating here. Feathers and droppings littered the patchy grass, and empty shells suggested birdseed. Someone had been feeding them, and so they'd made the area their home. Sadness and horror gripped her by turns as she looked around the park with new eyes. Could this be why the park had fallen so silent? Could they be the only things left alive in the entire place? She thought of all the rowdy children and the boy at the hot dog stand and didn't want to believe it.

"It was the Box," said Christopher, joining her. He clenched his jaw tight as he fought to retain control of himself. "It killed them. I'm sure of it."

"I figured as much," Eva replied. "We have to stop him

before that..." She jerked her thumb toward the dead birds. "...spreads any further."

She almost asked if he sensed any other dead things. Christopher's healing abilities and work with the Box put him in a unique position. If anyone would know, he would. But she wanted to stay in the dark just a little bit longer. If Sabretooth had killed everyone in the park, they would find some way to bring him to justice, and she would face that reality when the time came. But there was no need to borrow trouble, as her mother would say. She'd spent her entire childhood pining to get away, but right now, all she wanted was to go back to the things she knew and loved. Although she'd outgrown her hometown, it felt good to think of returning there to rest and regroup before she went back out again to do her job. After she graduated from the New Xavier School, of course. Assuming that she got out of this mess without getting expelled.

"We should keep moving," she suggested. "The longer we wait, the more damage he can do."

Christopher nodded, but he didn't move. He seemed rooted to the spot, and when she looked at him, he swallowed hard.

"He's going to fight us, Eva. This is Sabretooth we're talking about. You know the things he's done. The people – powerful mutants, even – that he's killed."

"Yeah."

"I'm so freaking scared."

She looked down at her boots. Somewhere during all of this mess, she'd managed to put a hole in one of the toes. It reminded her of Graydon's awful boots and his indignation at having to wear them. But he'd done it anyway, and he'd found some kind of redemption at the end. At least it had seemed like it to her.

"Sabretooth loves his kid," she said. "He's still a bad guy, and I know he wouldn't hesitate to throw us to the crows for Graydon, but he's capable of caring."

"Yeah," said Christopher bitterly. "Just not for us."

But Eva wasn't so sure. Now that she looked back, she saw that Sabretooth had been manipulating them from the beginning, but she wondered if he'd started to care about them despite himself, because it seemed like he'd gone out of his way to be likeable. They were helping him anyway. So he hadn't had any reason to connect with Christopher the way that he had any more than Graydon had had a reason to confide in Eva, except that they wanted to.

She contemplated arguing this with Christopher, but this wasn't the time or the place for it. Not with the Box killing birds left and right and Sabretooth knocking fountains over in his fury. But once they were safely back on the X-Copter and on their way back to the school, she might bring it up, because she could see how much the betrayal hurt him. He'd thought the connection was real. Maybe he'd had dreams of redeeming Sabretooth and bringing him back to the school as another instructor, and now those dreams had died despite Christopher's best efforts. She knew he'd been through some rough stuff, and stress tended to bring all of those old fears to the forefront. It sure had made her reckless, just like in the old days.

So she shelved the topic for now, but she would definitely bring it up later. Maybe they could help each other. Sometimes she felt desperate to prove herself so she could join the ranks of the super heroes where she knew she belonged, and it had made her rash a few times in the past. Really, it had gotten them into this mess in the first place, and she saw that clearly for the first time. If she didn't chill out and quit trying to be the next Captain America, someone was going to get hurt or even die. Christopher helped balance out her eagerness with logic, and she could help him in turn by soothing his pain at Sabretooth's betrayal. For now, she contented herself with squeezing his hand in hers, hoping that it would offer some comfort. Together, they left the fountain courtyard and emerged from a wooded area into the soccer complex.

With so much open space, at least Sabretooth wouldn't be able to sneak up on them, and there weren't many things for him to destroy. Eva scanned the long expanse of green fields but didn't notice anything strange. The goals seemed to be goal-shaped. She didn't see any giant piles of dead animals. Rows of shade trees lined the fields, and all of them seemed to be standing. Even the bathroom building all the way on the other end appeared intact. It didn't look like anything squirted from it, and she was pretty sure it still had all of its walls.

"I'm starting to think we lost him," she said.

"Huh?" Christopher asked.

"Sabretooth. We might have lost him. If he came this way, he would have destroyed one of those goals at the very least, don't you think? Or uprooted one of the trees?" She pointed.

"Oh." He furrowed his brow. "I'm pretty sure I can feel the

Box back there, though. And I think the grass behind the bathrooms is yellowed."

She squinted. The setting sun didn't provide great lighting, and there were two full soccer fields between them and the area he'd indicated. She just wasn't sure.

"You could be right," she said. "Frankly, I trust your Spidey-senses more than I trust my eyes at this point. If you say we should check it out, then we should."

"I think it's a good idea."

They began the long walk across the smooth, damp grass. Neither of them spoke, but it was a companionable silence. As they grew closer to the squat brick bathroom building, Eva could begin to see what Christopher had been talking about. The grass behind the building had turned a sickly yellow which sat in distinct contrast to the well-watered, lush green of the fields. A line of demarcation arced around the building, separating the dying grass from the healthy. But if memory served, that line would only grow as the Box spread its influence. They had to keep that from happening.

It wouldn't have been first on her list of places to hide, but Sabretooth hadn't exactly been rational last time she'd seen him, and the trail of chaos he'd left in his wake suggested that his mind hadn't gotten much clearer since then. But she reminded herself not to underestimate him either. He'd taken them by surprise once, and she didn't intend to allow it again.

She turned to Christopher, a questioning look on her face. He pointed, indicating that she should go around one way while he went the other. He would distract Sabretooth to give her the opportunity to freeze him. She grimaced.

It wasn't her favorite plan, but she couldn't come up with another on short notice, and they didn't have the time to sit here and debate. Every moment they wasted would increase the chance that Sabretooth would sniff them out, if he hadn't done so already. She nodded and began to creep in the direction he'd indicated.

Christopher waited, allowing her the opportunity to get a nice head start. At the corner, she paused, looking back. He gave her a thumbs-up and a confident smile, which she returned. At least she tried to look confident. Mostly, she felt like throwing up. That would have been ironic, considering what he'd been doing most of the day.

The open entryway to the men's room loomed before her, its shadows deeper than they had any right to be. She stayed right up against the building, not daring to leave the safety of its walls, but what if Sabretooth waited for her right inside the entrance? She wouldn't be able to see him until she was right on top of him, and then it would be too late. He could squeeze the breath out of her and she wouldn't be able to do a thing about it. Her heart began to hammer so loud that she was sure that if he was anywhere nearby, he had to be able to hear it. His senses were so attuned anyway. Her heartbeat probably sounded like a stampeding rhino to him.

If he tried to kill her, she'd bubble them both. Hopefully, Christopher would realize something was wrong, and he'd be there when the bubble popped. Together, they'd handle it. At least she wouldn't have to face Sabretooth alone, because for all of her earlier confidence, now that she was here, she felt like prey.

She screwed up every ounce of courage she possessed and stepped out into the men's room entryway, looking inside.

Empty.

Relief gripped her with such intensity that she almost laughed aloud. She had to clap her mouth shut before the noise escaped her, letting only a huff of breath out of her nose. Moving as quietly as possible, which probably wasn't quiet enough, she hurried to the opposite wall and flattened herself against it. The dead zone seemed to be centered on the far wall. If she turned one more corner, she should come face-to-face with Sabretooth. She would get to the corner and wait for Christopher to distract him, then pop out and freeze him before he could hurt her friend.

She edged closer, barely daring to breathe. It seemed like every movement she made was hugely loud in the otherwise silent late afternoon. Gravel ground beneath her feet with every footstep despite her best efforts to place her weight with care. Her breath sounded enormous to her ears, and the more she tried to quiet it, the more starved for air she felt. Her nose itched, and she felt the sudden, desperate urge to sneeze, but that would make noise too. She wiggled it, knowing that the problem was all in her head, but it didn't make it any better.

"I know you're there," said Sabretooth, his voice just around the corner.

CHAPTER 30

Eva froze against the brick wall, her throat gone dry with fear. Of course Sabretooth had heard them coming. Only an idiot would try to sneak up on a mutant with enhanced senses, so maybe she was an idiot. But even though she felt silly, she would have done it again. At least this way, she knew she'd tried to do the right thing, no matter what it cost her.

Sabretooth's voice sounded unusually quiet and close to breaking. He must have worn himself out with screaming and crying and tearing metal and rock into pieces with his bare hands. Eva still didn't move. Even if he was exhausted, he would be a formidable opponent. She had to stick to the plan. Besides, maybe it would do Christopher some good to get things off his chest. If Sabretooth was spent, he might actually listen for once.

"I figured you would," Christopher said. "We came for the Box."

"Well, you can't have it." Sabretooth's voice regained a little of his usual verve.

Marvel: Xavier's Institute

"Oh my god." Christopher's voice registered horror. "What happened to you?"

There was no answer.

"Eva, come out here," Christopher called.

Eva paused. For a moment, she wasn't sure what to do, but he wouldn't throw out the plan like that unless he had a good reason. Cautiously, she peeked around the corner, just in case Sabretooth had grabbed him around the throat and somehow forced him to call to her. But all she saw was Christopher, standing there with a look of dismay as he looked down at a huddled figure on the ground underneath the water fountains. When he saw her, he gestured for her to come out.

"I don't think we're in any danger from him," he said. "From the Box, maybe, but not from him. Not any more."

At first, she thought he was talking crazy, until she got a better look at the thing on the ground. It was Sabretooth, or it had been once. The previously enormous figure had been stripped of its vitality and now was a shadow of its former self. In just the short time since they'd last seen him, the Box had sucked the life from him. Much of the thick, golden hair had fallen out, leaving only patchy spots. The claws and teeth remained but had gone brittle and yellow with apparent age. His eyes had taken on the same rheumy tint, and they seemed to struggle to focus in his sunken face. His clothes hung on him, and even the leather of his trench coat now seemed dry and brittle. It looked like he might turn to dust at any moment and blow away.

She covered her mouth with her hand, tears springing to her eyes. She'd been afraid of him moments before, but now she pitied him. But Christopher was implacable despite his obvious horror.

"Where's the Box?" he asked.

"Don't know what you're talking about," said Sabretooth.

"Come on, man," said Christopher. "It's killing you. Quit being so stubborn and hand it over."

"I'll heal." Sabretooth's voice was raspy and dry. "It's nothing personal, kid. I need it to save my son. That's all. It's just business."

To Eva's shock, Christopher kicked him. Not hard, but in Sabretooth's condition, any contact would hurt. Sabretooth grunted.

"Yeah, well, that's business too, then. Is that how we do things now? Maybe I should follow in your footsteps and do business like you. Is that what you want?" demanded Christopher.

"No," said Eva. "Don't."

"Don't go down that road, Chris," said Sabretooth, closing his eyes. "You won't be able to get back out."

"Who are you to give me advice?" Christopher demanded. "You don't give a damn about me. You set us up. Everything you said to me was a lie. I told you about my dad, man. I told you stuff I never told anyone, because I thought you'd understand. It's one of the stupidest things I've ever done, because why would Sabretooth care about anything? He's a cold-blooded killer. Of course he cares about nothing."

Sabretooth sighed. It rattled in his chest.

"You're right, kid. I'm a cold-blooded killer. But that doesn't mean I don't care. Nothing's black and white like people like Summers would lead you to believe. Good guys like him can do evil things. He's done them too; just ask him. And people like me? Like I said before, sometimes we can do the right thing for the right people."

"Yeah, like Graydon," said Christopher, kicking at the gravel. "But he's gone now, and you probably think that's my fault. I was trying to save him, but apparently that doesn't matter to you."

"Graydon's died four times now. I keep finding him, or finding ways to bring him back, and then I fall short, over and over again. I'm a little salty about it." Sabretooth tried to give one of his old casual shrugs but didn't have the energy for it. "So sue me."

"He was telling me a little about it," said Eva. "Graydon, I mean."

Sabretooth perked up. "What did he say?"

"Just that he didn't remember much between his lives. I think he was starting to realize that his old resentments against mutants didn't quite hold. All this time, he thought you didn't want him because he was human, but you'd gone all out to save him repeatedly, so that couldn't be true. He wanted some time to figure out how he really felt about you."

Sabretooth fell silent for a long moment. When he spoke again, his voice was quiet. "Thank you," he said. "Maybe I failed, but at least I accomplished that much. Graydon's mine. I couldn't rest until he knew that." Then he closed his eyes.

She nudged him with her foot. "You don't get to give up and die now. You've done too much harm for that. You've got to make it right."

"You don't get it, missy. There's no redemption for a man like me. We don't run at each other in slow motion across a field full of daisies. I don't join the X-Men, and nobody sings 'Kumbaya.' There isn't enough time to balance the scales, even if I cared to, and I don't."

"I'm not talking about balancing all the scales. I'm talking about just this one. Graydon cared about us, whether he wanted to or not. So did you. We were a team. We took down a freaking dinosaur together! And you owe us for that. We helped your kid, Sabretooth. Give us the Box."

She spoke with passion and heat, her face flaming with the force of her emotions. Her words rang out in the quiet of the park. After it was over, Sabretooth clapped, a slow and somehow mocking sound. Her head fell. She'd failed. After everything that had happened, she'd finally had her chance to make her mark, and she'd failed.

"The Box is in the alcove behind the water fountain," said Sabretooth. "It's stronger now. It sucked me dry."

"And you still tried to hide it from us. What are you, nuts?" asked Christopher.

"I don't share well. Never have." Sabretooth coughed, a dry hack that shook his increasingly weak body. "Maybe you can contact Dormammu again. Convince him to turn the thing off. Offer me as a trade. I'll go. It's the least I can do."

Eva knew the offer to be self-serving. Sabretooth would strike a deal with Dormammu for Graydon's life. But still, they couldn't afford to turn their backs on any offer of help at this point. Over the past few minutes, as they'd stood and talked, the yellow circle of grass had widened, and the yellow had begun to deepen to a dull brown. The blight would only grow worse. Somehow, she still felt OK, though, and Christopher seemed fine. She glanced at him out of the corner of her eyes, suddenly suspicious. Had he been protecting her from the Box all this time? She wouldn't have put it past him. He had that kind of instinct.

He noticed her giving him the side-eye and returned a concerned look, gesturing for her to step away together to plan their next steps.

"I'm not sure we should trust him," he whispered.

She didn't bother lowering her voice. After all, with his enhanced hearing, Sabretooth might still hear them. There was no sense in pretending that walking a few yards away would change anything.

"Of course not, but what other choice do we have? This thing has been leaking magic all day, and it only seems to be getting worse. It only took a few minutes to drain him. We can't take it back to the school like this, and we certainly can't leave it anywhere. I could try and immobilize it for a while, and we could take it back to Illyana if you want, but it'll take a lot of bubbles to get us back to the school, and I don't think Sabretooth will make it."

"If we send him to Dormammu and he survives it, he'll stab us in the back, the first chance he gets."

"He might think about it. But then he'll remember this. Everything he does, I'm going to keep a record of. And the next time his son comes back, I'm going to tell him everything. In detail." Eva turned to look at where Sabretooth still sat, slumped against the wall of the building. "You hear that? Graydon made his wishes clear. You know what he wanted, and you know that he felt betrayed by you and the rest of his family. By mutants in general. You have a chance to prove that he was wrong about you, and that even though you're a bad dude, you really do love him. If you stab us in the back and betray us to Dormammu, he'll know he was right about you all along."

She meant every word. She knew she would have to plan carefully to make sure she could deliver on her promise. Sabretooth had been at this game for a long time. He'd been a mercenary for hire for decades, and he'd double- and triple-crossed people who had been trained to look for that kind of thing. He would know how to catch people unawares. He'd try to make it so she couldn't deliver. But over the course of the afternoon, she'd come to believe that Graydon Creed had deserved a chance, and he didn't deserve whatever Dormammu intended for him. It couldn't be good. She shuddered just thinking of it.

"I get it, missy," said Sabretooth. His voice barely made it to them. The light breeze threatened to carry it away. "Point made."

"Are we really going to negotiate with Dormammu?" she asked Christopher, shuddering. "Setting aside the part where he terrifies me, he's a dangerous psychopath who wants to take over the world. Illyana's words, not mine. I'm not sure he's really the negotiating type."

"Actually, I'm hoping we can avoid that part. I want to try something…"

As Christopher explained his plan, Eva listened with equal parts nervousness and hope. It just might work. Then again, it might kill him outright, but she couldn't come up with a better plan. It rankled. Frankly, this whole being an X-Man thing wasn't half as fun as she'd hoped it would be. Not in the slightest.

CHAPTER 31

Christopher stared at the Box of Planes. It struck him how such a small thing could be so powerful. It wasn't any bigger than a box of tissues, but it could raise the dead and reunite father and son. It had the power to change destinies. Sabretooth had certainly been irrevocably changed by his interactions with the artifact, and not just physically. He knew he and Eva would never be the same, either.

She stood at his shoulder, and when he glanced at her, she gave him a reassuring nod. He could rely on her. His plan might be dangerous, but it sidestepped all of the direct contact with Dormammu, and they'd agreed that this would be wise. Even Sabretooth had grudgingly given in when he'd realized what Christopher intended. Maybe he thought that mastery of the Box would mean that Christopher could bring back Graydon on his own. Or maybe he just realized that it would be better to live to fight another day. After all, Sabretooth was a survivor at his core.

They'd moved the Box out to the middle of one of the soccer fields. Here, if it went haywire, it would only kill the grass. Sabretooth's condition had deteriorated to such an extent that his teeth rattled in their sockets, and he barely had the energy to speak. They didn't want to risk hurting him further. If the Box's power waned, his healing factor would kick in and he'd recover, so Eva would keep an eye on both of them just to be safe, but they thought that he would want to stay near the Box anyway. He wouldn't want to leave it while there still remained a chance that it could be used to bring Graydon back. Besides, Eva's threat still hung between them. His only option to avoid triggering it would be to murder them both and take the Box for himself. It wasn't completely out of the question.

Christopher closed his eyes and reached toward the Box with his powers, feeling the familiar queasy sensation build in his belly. He ignored it as best as he could, unraveling the threads of life magic as they wafted from the artifact, searching for their source. They had to come from somewhere. Once again, he heard that faint chanting, the deep and dissonant voices reciting unintelligible words. He followed it. The sound had to mean something. He'd heard it too many times for it to be a coincidence. If he could only figure out what it was saying, or have a conversation with the people who were chanting, he hoped that he could deactivate the Box at its source without having to interact with Dormammu at all.

It was difficult going. The energy of the Box had no organization or purpose like a body did. He could look at a body and instantly see it as a whole being with balance and purpose. Bodies had patterns. Injuries and weaknesses stood out to him, their dullness drawing his attention in contrast to the bright illumination of the rest of the being. But navigating the Box felt more like trying to make his way through a foggy swamp at midnight. He might have been going in circles for all he knew. Sometimes he thought the chanting grew closer, but then he realized that nothing had changed. He remained surrounded by eddies of energy and distant sound, but nothing more.

He would have to try something else. He'd resisted the attempts of the Box to pull him in, but perhaps some connection would be needed to communicate with the artifact. This would be dangerous, but hopefully Eva would pull him free if he showed any signs of distress. He could always try again if it seemed like he'd made progress.

He reached out and merged his power with the Box. It reacted instantly, seizing onto him as the distant chanting grew in intensity. He instinctively withdrew in panic as it grasped at him, but forced himself to relax. This was exactly what he wanted to happen. He needed the Box to pull him inside just far enough. Eva would bring him back when the time came.

So he made himself pliant and allowed himself to drift where the Box wanted to take him. As it drew him deeper in, he felt the vast emptiness inside, and he truly began to understand for the first time what the Box represented. He sensed millions of doors, each leading to different planes in the multiverse. Most of them had been permanently sealed by some force he didn't understand. They felt ancient, crafted by some technology from beyond time and certainly beyond his understanding. But a small handful of doors still worked. One of them led to Limbo, and from it leaked that familiar magic that twisted life into unlife and made the dead awaken. The door had been cracked open.

He could hear the chanting much more clearly now, and he finally recognized the voice. Dormammu. The chant pulled life energy in through the door, where it was somehow twisted nearly beyond recognition, only to leak back out to corrupt the world and raise the dead.

Perhaps if he closed the door, the flow of magic would be cut off. If left unchecked, would it turn the entire planet into a barren wasteland full of walking dead? He didn't want to find out. The only way to stop it was to close the door. Reluctantly, he put his hand on the knob.

The door flared into bright light, and Christopher felt the energy from his body as it was sucked into the door, fueling it. Ever so slowly, it began to open.

"There you are!" said Dormammu. "I've been waiting for you! Open the door and let me out."

"Let me go, Dormammu," replied Christopher.

But Dormammu just started chanting again. Christopher tried to take his hand off the knob, but he could barely move. He felt like he was being sucked dry, just like Sabretooth had been. But he didn't know how to stop it.

"Christopher!" Eva cried, her voice sounding further away than ever. "What's happening?"

But he couldn't answer. It felt like all the vitality was being pulled from his bones like dust into a vacuum cleaner. He wouldn't last long. If Eva didn't pull him out soon, he'd die. He tried to call for help, but he couldn't form the words. He didn't have the strength for it.

Then, to his immense shock, Eva was there in the etherworld of the Box of Planes, tumbling past him, and it was all he could do to grab her hand moments before she toppled through the hungry maw of the open door. She clutched at him with desperate panic as the door tried to suck them both in.

"What are you doing here?" he gasped.

"The Box opened all the way up again, and it sucked me in," she said, tears streaming down her face. She ducked her head, trying to hide from the vortex that pulled at them, but there was nowhere to go. "We're going to die in here, aren't we?"

"Can you freeze it?"

Her face twisted in concentration, and the air around the door flickered a few times, but no bubble materialized. Finally, she shook her head.

"I can't. It's just too strong. I'm so sorry."

Christopher tried to detach himself from the door, hoping that without his power to fuel it, the flow would slow down enough so they could disengage and leave. But it held him in an iron grip that he simply couldn't shake. The situation seemed hopeless. Dormammu waited for them on the other side, eager to exit the open door. He would gloat. He would torment them. They'd probably die, and no one would ever realize what had happened to them. Would their bodies remain on the soccer field, or would they be sucked into the depths of the Box? Christopher wasn't sure.

Then Sabretooth came flying at them too. He slammed into Eva, knocking the air out of her. If he'd been his usual robust self, he might have crushed her to death, but his figure was still frail and thin. He scrabbled at her, snagging the hem of her coat, and barely managed to hold on. The three of them hung there as the wind continued to buffet them, trying to knock them loose and devour them whole.

"Fancy meeting you here," said Christopher, overcome by a wave of dark humor.

"How can you laugh at a time like this?" Eva asked once she'd caught her breath.

"What else am I supposed to do? There's no way to stop this door from opening. I can't close it. We're all going to die."

The reality of the situation hit him fully for the first time. He would never grow old. Never finish his training and put on an X-Men uniform for the first time. He'd never fall in love. There were so many things he'd left unfinished.

He wouldn't get a chance to visit his pop's grave and tell him that he forgave him. That hurt most of all. But he could do one thing that was almost as good.

"Hey, Sabretooth?" he said. "I forgive you. I'm still mad as hell at you, and I'm not stupid enough to trust you in the same way again, but I get it. You just wanted to save your kid. It wasn't personal. And even if our conversations didn't mean anything to you, they did to me. I think I can finally let all that stuff with my own pops go." He chuckled, although the wind whipped the noise away. "Heck, maybe I got so mad at you that I didn't have enough room to be mad at him any more. But either way, it feels good, so thanks. I think you're right. I won't try to make you into a good guy, but you can still do the right thing once in a while, for the right people."

Sabretooth grunted. "Mostly, that person is me. I don't intend to die here, kid. Think. How do we close this door?"

"I just said I can't close it. I have no idea how. The magic is too strong."

"Take a look," Eva urged. "There has to be something we can do."

Christopher didn't think it would do any good, but he figured he might as well try. He focused on the door, trying to see if he could disrupt the flow of magic that held it open and weakened them at the same time. Now that he was closer, he could see how Dormammu's chanting pushed at the door. The only way to close it would be to stop Dormammu from chanting.

"I think if we disrupt the chant, the door will close," he said.

"So one of us has to go in there?" Eva asked hesitantly.

Christopher closed his eyes.

"Yes," he said. "And they probably won't come out again. They'll be stuck in Limbo, just like we were before."

"Graydon might be in there," Eva said suddenly. "In Limbo."

Sabretooth considered this. "He's probably in Hell."

"Maybe. But you don't know that for sure. He keeps getting brought back. Maybe they're keeping him in Limbo in between resurrections. You could look for him there. Dormammu wouldn't be able to keep you locked up forever," she said.

"You just want me to volunteer," he accused.

"Yes, I do," she admitted, sounding calmer than she had any right to. But her eyes welled with tears. Christopher let his head hang. He wanted to offer some comfort but under the circumstances he had nothing to give.

Sabretooth chuffed. He seemed to find all of this naked emotion amusing, but she suspected that like her, he was hiding his true feelings under a layer of bluster.

"Fine." He nodded. "It's been nice working with you. I know you probably don't believe me, but I mean it. When you get back, you tell Summers that if he doesn't put you on his team, he's a moron. He's still one anyway, but you've got my endorsement. You got me?"

"Yeah. Sure," said Christopher, his voice choked with emotion.

Tears sprang to his eyes. Sabretooth didn't seem to notice, or if he did, he didn't give Christopher a hard time about it.

"You know," Sabretooth said with wonder in his voice, "even an old cat can learn new tricks sometimes. Isn't that something?"

He let go of Eva's coat.

The magic grabbed him with immediate force, sucking him through the open door. Christopher watched as Dormammu's face brightened with anticipation, only to have Sabretooth fly right at his face, claws bared. Dormammu screamed, the chant forgotten in his pain.

As soon as he stopped chanting, the pressure on the door eased. Christopher pushed at it, and it moved, but it was so heavy, and he'd gotten so weak. He didn't think he could close it on his own.

"Help me! We need to close the door!" Christopher exclaimed.

Eva didn't stop to question him. She put her shoulder to the door and lent her strength to his. Together, they began to shove the heavy door shut.

"No!" Dormammu shouted.

"Do it!" Sabretooth growled.

The door latched, cutting off the flow of life force so quickly that Christopher felt it all the way down to his marrow. The churning in his belly eased. The queasy aura that had surrounded the Box ever since that first moment that Christopher had seen it vanished in an instant as if it had never existed.

Sabretooth was gone.

The Box released them. Christopher fell to the ground of the soccer field, stunned and crying. Eva sprawled on the ground next to him. They wrapped their arms around each other and wept for Sabretooth and all that he could have been, if only he'd tried.

The powerful artifact rolled onto the ground only a few feet away, smoking as if from some great heat. Slowly, the sigils on the sides dimmed until they faded completely from view.

CHAPTER 32

Eva washed her face and took a moment to examine her reflection in the blurry bathroom mirror of the soccer complex bathroom. She felt like a completely different person than the one who had left the school that afternoon. That person had been determined to prove that she didn't need anyone. But she'd seen firsthand what that kind of independence did to a person. Sabretooth didn't trust anyone, and look where it had gotten him. He'd nearly died alone. He would have, if not for Christopher's determination to be a part of a team whether Sabretooth liked it or not.

A wave of worry overcame her. She couldn't hear Christopher, and she knew that he'd taken Sabretooth's loss hard. It didn't matter that maybe he would make a deal with Dormammu and come back. It didn't even matter that he'd betrayed them. The emotions remained the same. At first, Eva had wanted to shake some sense into Christopher, because how could he care so much about someone who had done them so wrong? But then she realized that she felt much the same way about Graydon. He hadn't been the best person she'd ever met, but they'd connected. She felt a pang of loss every time she thought of him.

She rushed out of the bathroom to check on Christopher, worried because she couldn't hear him. But she found him standing quietly, looking out across the soccer fields under the darkening sky. A light mist rose over them, giving them a spectral feel that was somehow fitting.

"You ready to go?" Christopher asked. "I think we missed dinner, but hopefully they saved us some."

He didn't sob or wail, but he wasn't his usual cheery self either. Instead, his quiet voice held a world of hurt. She slipped her hand into his and squeezed it. After a moment, he squeezed back.

"Yeah," she said. "I'm jonesing for some sandwiches. I'll take your pickles, if you don't want them."

That won a faint smile out of him, and they crossed the misty field in companionable silence. It took them a moment to orient themselves, since they had spent so many hours crisscrossing the enormous park, but eventually they found some signage that pointed them in the right direction. They found themselves walking through a large military memorial, with an array of glossy plaques displaying the names of soldiers who had fallen in the line of duty.

Eva continued on, eager to finally get back into the sky, but Christopher pulled his hand free from hers to take a closer look at the display. She paused, trying to contain her impatience. A few more minutes wouldn't hurt, and maybe he needed the time to process what had happened. It still didn't feel real to her either. It seemed like Sabretooth would come leaping out of the trees at any moment, because something so much larger than life couldn't be diminished so easily. She'd seen it with her own eyes, but she couldn't believe it herself.

"You know, I do a crappy job of picking my heroes," said Christopher. "My pops was a mess, and I worshipped the ground he walked on. I knew Sabretooth was bad news going in, but I still latched onto him. Neither of them would ever be on a plaque like this. My pops got discharged from the military. It broke him." Christopher hung his head for a moment. "Sometimes I'm worried that I'll be the same. If I join the X-Men, I won't be able to hack it either."

"If our first mission was any indication, you've got it together," Eva said. Christopher huffed. "No, I'm serious. I'm just the opposite, you know. All my life, I've idolized the big heroes. I wanted to be a Captain America or a Cyclops. I wanted to be a star. That's part of the reason I dragged you out here, and I'm sorry for it. I didn't realize what I was doing at the time." She sighed. "But you made me realize that being a part of a team is better. I think you gave Graydon some chance at redemption, you know? And I honestly believe that you made Sabretooth care, even just a little. Maybe it's not the big, splashy triumph I always imagined. There won't be a parade. We'll never be on one of these plaques." She ran her finger down the list of names. "We'll probably get kitchen duty for about a million years. But if I could do it again, I would. I think I learned more about being an X-Man from you than I did from all our instructors put together."

He flushed, looking down at his feet. "Yeah, well, don't tell Emma. She's a little crazy."

Eva laughed. "I won't if you don't."

He began to walk away from the display but stopped abruptly after only a few steps. "Hey, Eva?"

"Yeah?"

"You deserve the parade, you know. You're the bravest person I've ever met." His face twisted up into the first genuine smile she'd seen him wear since Sabretooth had made his sacrifice. "I might have to quit following my dad's lead on that and start following yours."

"Oh. Well…"

Her cheeks flushed, and she kicked at the ground with the broken toe of her boot. Normally, she accepted compliments with a grin and perhaps a sarcastic comment, but she couldn't do that this time. It felt too special to laugh off. Better than a ticker tape parade any day.

After a moment, the awkwardness passed, and they resumed their walk toward the X-Copter. When they reached the shore, they found a few scattered boats out in the harbor, daring the choppy water and overcast skies. But although the rain had let up again, the cold wind off the lake had kept most potential onlookers at bay.

"Please tell me you still have the remote," said Eva, not unkindly.

Christopher produced it from his pocket with a flourish. Then he fumbled it, dropping it onto the ground at his feet.

"Whoops."

As he retrieved it, a robotic voice from further down the docks interrupted them. It felt all too familiar. Exhaustingly so. Out of all of the things that had changed that day, Christopher realized that this one was the most profound. Fear still overtook him when danger threatened, but now, he also felt incredibly tired at the same time. Perhaps that's what the older X-Men meant when they talked about being jaded, although it seemed like he really ought to be too young for that.

<<UNIDENTIFIED MUTANTS. YOU ARE IN POSSESSION OF AN ILLEGAL ARTIFACT OF UNKNOWN ORIGIN. SURRENDER THE ARTIFACT IMMEDIATELY OR RISK DETAINMENT.>>

A pair of Sentinels stood up from their hiding place behind some boxes at the end of the dock, where they must have been waiting for some time. One of them had a long piece of seaweed wrapped around its metal forehead, and both of them were splotched with seagull droppings.

Christopher and Eva exchanged a look, and he clutched the Box a little tighter. The artifact might be inert now – based on everything that Christopher could sense, anyway – but he didn't like the idea of giving access to all of those doors to the multiverse to just anybody. Let alone a bunch of jerk robots who hated mutants. What if they found some way to use it to exterminate people like him? No way.

"Who's asking?" asked Eva.

<<THE QUESTION DOES NOT COMPUTE. RESTATE.>>

"Who wants the Box?" Christopher asked. He sidled toward the end of the dock, where a rack full of mysterious boat tools awaited the return of the sailors. "On whose authority are you taking it?"

<<ON THE AUTHORITY OF THE OFFICE OF NATIONAL EMERGENCY, ANY ARTIFACT OF POTENTIALLY DANGEROUS MUTANT ORIGIN MAY BE SUMMARILY CONFISCATED PER ARTICLE 6342.B OF THE OFFICE CHARTER. SURRENDER THE ARTIFACT OR BE TERMINATED.>>

Christopher and Eva exchanged alarmed glances. That had escalated fast. They'd gone from hey-can-I-have-that to or-else-I'll-kill-you in just a couple of sentences.

"Sure," Eva said, clearly buying time. She looked at Christopher, trying to wordlessly communicate a game plan. He flicked his eyes toward the rack. She responded with the smallest of nods. "We've got it right here. Come get it."

She took the Box from Christopher, conveniently leaving his hands free, and stood waiting for the Sentinels to approach. They took a moment to scan the artifact, a red laser emitting from the visor of the left-hand robot to fully map the exterior of the Box. Once the scan had been completed, the Sentinel completed some internal process, pausing as if waiting for some feedback or response.

Finally, it said, <<AFFIRMATIVE. REMAIN MOTIONLESS. ANY MOVEMENT WILL BE CONSIDERED AN ACT OF AGGRESSION.>>

"Sure thing," said Christopher.

They waited calmly as the robots approached. At least that's what Christopher hoped it looked like. His heart clopped along at a fever pitch, and his hands shook with adrenaline. He couldn't believe they were doing this. It was one thing to take on some Sentinels with Sabretooth at their side. He could heal any damage so long as no one died, and with the mercenary ripping their enemies' arms off for fun, the odds tended to be stacked heavily on their side. Sure, he'd been scared witless when the dinosaur came at them, but it had never occurred to him that they couldn't beat it. It felt like Sabretooth was invincible, and the rest of them had proven not to be slouches either.

But now, they were about to fight Sentinels without any help at all. No instructors. No Sabretooth. Nothing but each other. Eva and Graydon had already done it, so he knew they could too. But still, part of him wanted desperately to hop off the ride before it crashed. He knew it was just nerves, but that didn't make them less potent, especially when the nerves were caused by two giant killer robots that closed in on them with rapid efficiency.

One Sentinel moved in on Eva to take the Box while the second one held back near the edge of the dock. Perfect. Christopher couldn't have set it up better if he'd tried. As the Sentinel reached for the Box, he coughed with theatrical force, lurching forward. The automatons tracked the movement but otherwise didn't react, so the ruse had worked. He grabbed onto the weapon he'd been eyeing, a long and sturdy pole with a wicked-looking hook fastened to one end. Christopher knew little about boats and had no idea what it would be used for, but it looked to him like a boat jousting tool.

He used it like a jouster would too, planting the sturdy pole onto the Sentinel and using its body to shield both him and Eva as he shoved it backwards with one firm push. It toppled into the second Sentinel, overbalancing it and knocking it into the water. The visor of the remaining Sentinel flared red as it sighted some weapon on them that would probably burn their faces off, if Christopher had any guess. But before it could fire, Eva froze it in place with a bubble, breaking off the end of his boat jouster in the process.

He looked at the useless end of his tool sadly and tossed it aside. He didn't need it anyway, but he'd liked it. The jouster would have been nice to hold onto just in case any other Sentinels showed up.

"That worked great," said Eva, holding her hand out for a high five.

He slipped her some skin.

"Let's get into the chopper before more of those things show up." His brow furrowed. "Too many people want this Box, and I'd like to be out of the way before they all show up to fight over it."

"I can't argue with you there. Call the X-Copter, and let's get the heck out of here."

Christopher patted his pockets. The remote was nowhere to be found. He hadn't picked it back up after he'd dropped it. The killer robots had distracted him. After a quick, panicked search, Eva found it. She picked it up, dusted the sand off, and took firm ownership of it.

"It's mine now," she said primly. "And that's that."

This time, he didn't argue with her.

CHAPTER 33

Eva collapsed back into her seat on the X-Copter with intense relief. Sand and dirt sprayed everywhere, spattering the immaculate control panel. If it stopped working, she would probably cry. But when Christopher began flipping switches, everything lit up exactly the way it should have.

He worked with a practiced hand, without even consulting his notes. It was like he'd been doing this for a million years. Like he'd never even been a student.

A student. Eva jerked out of her blissful haze just as Christopher flicked the switch to turn the comms system back on.

"No, don't!" she blurted, but it was too late.

About two milliseconds after the comms came back on, Cyclops's voice came blasting through the speakers at full volume. The engine wasn't running, so the noise nearly took Eva's eardrums out.

"Where have you been?" Cyclops demanded. "Tell me you're OK before I ground you permanently."

"We're fine," said Christopher. "We're sorry we worried you."

"Sorry. Sorry?! We couldn't even track the X-Copter. Illyana has been in a magic circle all afternoon, trying to get a read on you. Jean was searching for your mental signatures. I've got Hijack working on that decommissioned jet, trying to get it working well enough to come and hunt for you, and all you've got to say is, 'Sorry'? I just… I… You…" His voice dissolved into angry sputters.

"We'll tell you all about it when we get back," said Eva, weary.

"Oh, will you?" Cyclops responded, all icy anger now.

"Yes." Eva sat straight up in her chair. She understood his concern, but she'd had enough of being treated like a kid. "We need to fly home. And you won't ground us, because we're not children. We're X-Men. I understand that we're in training, and I'm more than willing to treat my instructors with respect, but I expect the same in return, Scott. You've been jerking us around like we're toddlers ever since we got here. You keep lecturing us about how this is a war, and we need to be ready to step up, and now that we did, you're upset because we didn't get a hall pass first. But I am not going to ask for your permission to be an X-Man. I sure as heck could use your guidance, though, because…" Her voice hitched on a sudden sob. "Today was really hard."

Christopher reached out and squeezed her shoulder. "She's right. I think you'll be proud of us when you hear everything, but we still have a lot to learn."

"Like what?" Cyclops asked, quietly.

"Like how do you deal with the loss of a team member?" asked Eva. She was crying again. She wiped the tears away with exasperation, but they kept falling anyway.

There was a long silence from the other end. Finally, the comms crackled to life, and Cyclops said, "I think you're right. That's a topic best addressed in person. I'll see you when you get back."

"Be there soon," said Christopher. "Over and out."

The flight back was uneventful. No police helicopters intercepted them and demanded that they land immediately and prepare to be arrested. No government craft surrounded them and tried to force them out of the air. They flew back home and landed without incident as darkness began to coat the sky. Eva thought she was getting pretty good on the stick. Christopher complimented her, but maybe he was just being kind. It was hard to tell at this point.

The debrief with Cyclops and Magik took a couple of hours, lasting deep into the night, and they each wolfed down three sandwiches during the course of it. They held nothing back, not even the bits that made them look like spoiled brats. Christopher talked up the parts that made Eva look good, and Eva found herself doing the same for him. It felt good to do that, although they both struggled to keep their eyes open by the end.

Magik took charge of the Box. She didn't like Dormammu's connection to it, and she liked his ability to control Graydon through its doors even less. She asked Christopher to work with her to study it further, and he agreed readily. Then he suggested that perhaps Eva could be on standby to freeze everything in place in the event of an emergency.

"It just seems like a good idea," Christopher elaborated.

"Buying a little extra time in case something goes wrong isn't a bad thing, right?"

Illyana nodded, smiling faintly. "If you think it is wise, we can certainly make those arrangements. But if you will excuse me, I am eager to begin my evaluation."

She took the Box of Planes with her, frowning at it in concentration, and nearly walked into a wall on her way out.

In her wake, Eva thought they were going to get yelled at big time, but Cyclops didn't so much as raise his voice. Instead, he sat back in his chair, and he said, "I've been thinking about what you said, and you're right. I still firmly believe that we're facing a war, and we don't have much time to prepare. But you're in a tough spot. On one hand, I'm telling you to hurry up and go, and on the other, I'm overprotective. I've let my problems blind me to the stress that I'm putting on you." He touched a hand to the shield that covered his eyes. "Ironic, isn't it? I guess my sight has gotten messed up in more ways than one." He sighed. "I'll try to do better, though."

"Thanks," said Eva.

She stood up, hoping to get out before he changed his mind.

"Rules are rules, though, and I'm going to put you on cafeteria duty for going off on a mission without reporting first," Cyclops interrupted them with a faint smile. "I'm glad you made the choices you did in retrospect, but I don't want Fabio and David getting it into their head that they should go on a taco run."

Eva, who had been marshalling her breath for an argument, found that she couldn't argue with this logic.

"OK, yeah. I get that," she said instead.

"Emma will meet you there tomorrow morning to tell you what to do. Magneto is away from the school for the moment, and I think it would do you both some good to keep busy. I know I need busy work when I come off a mission. Otherwise I end up brooding." Christopher winced, and Cyclops, who was watching them closely, picked up on it. "Is there a problem?"

"Emma has been acting a little strange," he admitted. "There was that whole stabbing thing."

"Ah, yes. She's a bit unconventional, I admit. Years in the Hellfire Club and all that." Cyclops shook his head. "I think she wants you to call her out. Emma's big on independence, and she wants you to think for yourselves rather than blindly parroting what we tell you. She's a big part of the reason I was able to talk to you calmly now that you're back, because she helped me see that a little independence is a good thing given the circumstances, so long as it's tempered with some healthy respect and quality teamwork. I think Emma is deliberately acting out because she wants you to question her. She wants you to realize that you have the freedom to question any of us. I think once you do, she'll lay off a little."

Christopher let out a breath of relief. "I'll do it the minute we get to the cafeteria then, because she seriously freaked me out."

"I'll let you get on with it then. Oh, and Eva? You never get over losing a teammate. I lost Jean years ago, and my heart still aches like it was yesterday. If either of you want to talk about it, you know where to find me. I can empathize.

Even if the person you're mourning is Sabretooth, and he probably called me some awful names."

Cyclops smiled sadly at them. He looked so lonely behind that desk, surrounded by empty walls and sterile space. Eva wondered how he managed it, sitting there hour after hour with only his memories to keep him company. But maybe he wanted it that way. She could begin to understand that now.

"Thanks," she said. Christopher echoed it. Cyclops shooed them away, but as they reached the door to his office, he said one last thing to them.

"Excellent work, X-Men. Glad to have you on the team."

ACKNOWLEDGMENTS

Writing this book was a dream come true.

I owe a debt of immense, world-shattering gratitude to all the folks at Aconyte Books for making this one of the best publishing experiences I've ever had. An extra soupcon of gratitude goes out to Charlotte Llewelyn-Wells, who is not only an excellent and supportive editor, but also a fabulous person to boot. Also, she has a very cute puppy.

Every member of the Marvel team who touched this book made it better, and I'm not surprised by how good they are, but I sure am grateful for it. Special thanks go to Caitlin O'Conneli, who is so blindingly smart that I suspect she might secretly be a mutant. That is a compliment.

Thank you to Stan Lee for making me feel truly cool (by association) for the first time in my entire life.

A few fine people read bits and pieces of this book and provided expertise that I lacked. I owe tons of eternal squealy gratitude to Emily Cooperider, Ali Cross, Jen Fick, and Evelyn Preston. Naturally, all errors are to be blamed on me. I will in turn blame them on any handy super villains.

A tip of the hat goes to the fine folks at Black Cat Comics for being my go-to research buddies. Support your local comic store, and make sure to visit Black Cat if you're ever in Salt Lake City.

Last but certainly not least, thanks to my family for putting up with the constant runs to Black Cat, the repeated requests to "please read this; it's short this time," and a lot of late/slightly scorched dinners.

ABOUT THE AUTHOR

CARRIE HARRIS is a geek of all trades and proud of it. She's an experienced author of tie-in fiction, former tabletop game executive and published game designer who lives in Utah.

carrieharrisbooks.com
twitter.com/carrharr

MARVEL

In a realm beyond Earth, mighty heroes do battle with monsters of myth and undertake quests to restore peace and honor to the legendary halls of Asgard and the Ten Realms.

The young Heimdall must undertake a mighty quest to save Odin – and all of Asgard – in the time before he became guardian of the Rainbow Bridge.

The God of War must explore a terrifying realm of eternal fire to reclaim his glory, in this epic fantasy novel of one of Odin's greatest heroes.